Animus

by
Craig Thompson

Published by Thompson Publishers

Thompson Publishers
https://thompsonpublishers.com

Animus
Copyright© 2022 by Craig Thompson

Requests for information should be addressed to:
Thompson Publishers, PO Box 2605, Cleveland TN 37320-2605

ISBN: 978-1-64407-014-7 [print]
ISBN: 978-1-64407-015-4 [ebook]

This is a work of fiction. Any resemblance to persons past or present is purely coincidental.

Cover design Craig Thompson© 2022. Saint Denis cover photo Craig Thompson© 2011.

Printed in the USA.
First printing.

Contents

"Nothing is covered up which will not be revealed; neither hidden which will not be made known. Therefore, whatever you have spoken in the dark will be heard in the light; and what you have whispered in the ear in a closet will be proclaimed from the rooftops."

–Jesus of Nazareth (Luke 12:2-3)

"The best security system is community."
—Serious

Prologue

Sonian Forest, Belgium
June, eight years prior

Daniel Robertson peered through the binoculars at the expansive estate nestled among the forest of oak and fir trees. To say he was apprehensive would have been an understatement. He was terrified.

It wasn't just the sight, although that was enough to evoke a sense of dread. The buildings on the estate were all black rock. The spires and turrets stood like silent sentinels watching outward to ward off uninvited guests. Or maybe they were watching inward to keep their secrets safe from discovery. Even from this distance, the lenses revealed gnarled bushes surrounding the walls, the tips of their branches grasping at the stonework like long talons.

The day itself was waning into evening. The shadows were growing longer with every passing minute, distorting the landscape into pockets of pitch-black mingled with gray. There was enough of a clearing around the outer wall of the estate before the forest began to make an undiscovered approach untenable and escape improbable. But if he was correct in what he believed to be true, he would not have to breach the walls at all to confirm his suspicions or, if luck was on his side, to make a difference.

As he lowered the binoculars, he looked around. Nestled on a rocky outcropping with just a small break in the trees, he took comfort that he was just as well hidden from view as were the deeds of those within the walls. He checked his backpack for the fifth time against his checklist on his phone. Everything was there. He wished he had a gun of any kind, but this was Europe, after all. He wasn't part of some official governing agency, nor was he part of some network of criminals that could provide firearms at a moment's notice. He was simply Daniel Robertson, a middle-aged businessman who had cashed in his year's vacation early to follow up on what was either the wildest of goose chases or was going to be a night he would never forget. And he was alone.

There were supposed to be others here tonight with him. He sighed as he thought about the discussions they had and plans they made. But reality had set in. Some of the others backed out because of real-life commitments: they could not take off the time from work or had family matters to attend to. The fact that they had a family at all was reason enough for others to bow out. If this were a big mistake and they were caught, they might be charged with trespassing and pay a fine. If it were real, their families might never know what had happened to them.

In the end, their group of eight had dwindled to Daniel and one other, and the other had sent a last-minute message stating that he could not make it. Because that person was also in Europe, he did offer to provide any support possible, including an anonymous phone to use for an Internet connection in the event that Daniel wanted to livestream his activities. With a miniature camera attached to his chest, Daniel intended to do just that. It would prove to be an invaluable decision.

He turned on the phone and made sure it was connected to the Internet. Then he turned on the camera and checked that it was connected to the phone's hotspot. He opened up an app and logged into the group's private chat room and saw that there were two others logged in. After hitting the livestream video button, he held the camera up to his face and started talking.

"Hello. It's me, Daniel Robertson. I'm on location looking down from the hillside from a wee spot on a nice ledge." He swiveled the camera so that it pointed toward the estate and continued. "I'm actually pretty nervous and kind of excited all at the same time. As you can see, there's nothing much happening at the moment. It's beginning to get darker here. If our research is right, I won't see much more until nightfall anyways."

He turned the camera back around to his face and shoulders and looked into it. He was wearing a black shirt. "If you would make sure this all gets recorded, I would be delighted." Then he paused as his thoughts whirled within him. "When it gets dark, you may not see much, but I'll try to keep a running commentary going. I'm not really sure what'll happen, and I don't know whether I hope it ends up being a waste of time or whether I want it to be true. I guess we'll all find out in a little while. Cheers for now!"

2

With that, he turned the camera off. He now only had to wait until sunset, just an hour from now. It was the summer solstice, the longest day of the year. Would the gates open as predicted?

§ § §

In five different locations around the globe, other members of the group made their way to their computers and sat down to await Daniel's livestream. If they couldn't be there in person, the least they could do would be to watch along with him and give him moral support. Tokyo, Bretzfeld in Germany, Evry in the suburbs of Paris, New York, and last but not least, Oneonta, Alabama. Four men and one woman were waiting in their private chat room for Daniel's broadcast to pick up again. Two had been there for his test. The rest had logged in during the past few minutes. It was almost 10 p.m. local time for Daniel.

§ § §

Down in the inner courtyard area of the castle, a light flared. Daniel put the binoculars to his eyes and centered them in that area. He could just make out what appeared to be a torch being lowered slowly. Then another torch flared as it was lit by the first. Daniel paused long enough to get everything turned on and the livestream running again. After giving the livestream a randomly chosen name, he pressed the record button. He received brief confirmations via chat that the stream was working. Then he began his commentary.

"Hello again. For the record, it's me, Daniel Robertson from Inverness. I'm on the edge of the Sonian Forest looking down on the grounds of the Black Castle, as we've come to call it. Everything has been quiet until just a couple of minutes ago. One torch suddenly appeared down in the courtyard area. Then another. Now it looks like they're making a big circle as they light each other's torches. There's definitely something happening.

"I wish you could see better, but I'll keep the camera pointed that general direction. Okay. Right now it looks like they have all the torches lit. I'd estimate that they're in a circle about the size of a two-lane roundabout. That's about twenty meters for you Yanks.

"There's someone in the center of the circle talking. I can't make out if it's a man or a woman. They're wearing a white robe. Looks like they're the only one doing so. Now they're pointing to the south side. The circle is parting just a wee bit.

"Uh-oh…There are some people leading some other people into the circle. They're definitely smaller than the rest. They have to be children or teenagers based on their size. They look like their hands are bound in back of them. They're not clothed as fully as the rest of the people. I can't really tell what they're wearing.

"They've got them all lined up now. I'm counting three, six, seven—there are thirteen of them total if I'm counting just right. The leader is speaking to them. There are two people walking behind them and releasing their arms. The leader is walking up and down the line. He's pointing toward the gate. The group of younger ones is being led toward the gate now. The gate is opening! It's opening! Oh, man, it's happening!"

Daniel watched and described as they opened up both gates. They led the children out onto the drive while pointing all around toward the distant woods. The leader addressed them as if he were giving them directions or instructions of some kind. Then a thought occurred to Daniel.

"Hold on a minute. I just had an idea. I'll look through the binoculars with one eye and hold up the camera to the other eye.

"It's hard to see as the sun has gone down, and there's not much light left. There! He's released them. Most of them have started running just any direction they can. Two of them are still standing there like they don't know what to do.

"Now the leader has just pulled something out of his robe. It's hard to see from here, but it looks like a big knife, a dagger. He's approaching both of the ones that are left. They're running now. Both of them are running away. One of them is headed straight this direction.

"Back in the courtyard, the torches are all moving up and down in unison. It looks like they're doing some type of chant. Here comes another figure; this one is dressed in a black or dark-colored robe with some type of headdress. The people are bowing down to this figure.

4

Now this bloke is reaching out his hands like a priest or a rabbi as if he's blessing them.

"They're all getting up and forming groups of two or three and are marching toward the gate. I can't believe it's really happening! There are one...five...eight...eleven...thirteen groups with torches. All of them are beginning to leave and head out in different directions."

Those listening and watching saw the binoculars and camera pan from the castle across the field and to the edge of the forest. In the dim light, it was just possible to catch a glimpse of movement at the edge of the field right before the trees. The binoculars stayed on that spot for a few seconds.

"I know what I've got to do. That wee child is headed straight this way. If what we've talked about is true, then I've got to do my best to save at least one child if possible. Here, I'm just going to put the camera back on my chest harness and make my way down as quickly as I can."

There was a disorienting shuffle as the camera was moved back to its place. During that interlude, several members of the group sent chat messages urgently imploring Daniel to call the police or to not get involved any more than he already was. Daniel glanced at the messages and then answered them all as quickly as he could while he spoke.

"You all have been like a second family to me. But I can't just sit here and wonder if I could have done more. It would gnaw at my conscience for the rest of my life. Hopefully the phone keeps working when I get down there in the forest." He paused. "I hear dogs."

§ § §

The next twenty minutes of the live stream were mostly dark with little to learn as Daniel navigated the hillside. Eventually, he found the outer perimeter fencing. A path about two meters wide had been cleared through the trees and branches, enough to install a chain link fence three meters high with concertina wire coiled at the top. Daniel had no intentions of attempting to climb over it.

He dropped his backpack to the ground and shone a tiny penlight as he removed a short-but-stout pair of wire cutters. From the perspective of the live stream, it looked like a first-person shooter action game. For Daniel, the adrenaline certainly matched. He clipped a section large enough to crawl through, peeled back the fencing like a flimsy door, and entered the estate.

The following fifteen minutes were mostly dark with an occasional comment from Daniel as he worked his way deeper into the woods. All of a sudden, the listeners could hear a sharp but distant cry. Daniel's lowered voice came through. "I just heard what sounds like a child's voice. I'm headed that direction now."

Three minutes later, the camera began to pick up the glare of two torches. As Daniel crept closer, the viewers could see a clear image of two adults, likely men from their figures and size, each holding their torches aloft. Their faces were shielded by the hoods of their robes. Huddled on the ground between them was a young girl of maybe twelve to fourteen years. Clothed only in undergarments, her body shivered in the night chill—or maybe from terror. Her blonde hair was cut shoulder-length. Daniel had apparently stopped at the edge of some bushes, which concealed his presence: either that or the men were too focused on the girl to notice anything else. One of them was speaking in accented English.

"…what the others have done, our part in the hunt is over. We've found our quarry. Now all that remains is to finish it. Since this is your first summer hunt, it's your responsibility, your privilege, to do that job."

Here the other began replying but in American-accented English. "Man, I've been looking forward to this ever since the invitation came. I just want to have a bit of fun with her first before that happens. It's not every day that I get this kind of chance to break loose. We're a bit more repressed than you all are in Europe."

He knelt down near the girl and continued. "She's really quite beautiful for her age. Where do they get such fine specimens?"

"From all over. This one came from Spain, I believe. Part of the child protective services network we have there. The bureaucracy would say she fell through the cracks. Judging from her appearance, she cost a minimum of three thousand euros."

"Well, we can't let all that good money go to waste, now can we?" said the second man. He reached out to touch the girl's face, but she flinched and jerked away from him. "There, there. Don't you like to have fun?" Turning to the first man, he asked, "Can she even speak English?"

"She probably understands a few words. But she also can read your face and understand your eyes a lot more clearly than your words. But the rules are quite clear: this is not a pleasure hunt, and the quarry is to be dealt with one way only. You know the terms. You agreed to them in writing."

"What a waste," said the second man as he looked at the form on the ground one more time. "Will you hold her for me?" He began reaching into his robe while the first man planted the end of his torch into the soil with a sharp jab. After the first man had walked behind the girl, he suddenly reached down and seized both her arms and yanked them behind her while simultaneously pushing his right knee into her back. The girl gave a startled cry of pain.

The second man reached into his robe and withdrew a cup of some sort and set it down on the ground. Then he slowly pulled out what looked like a long-bladed knife which appeared to be made of some type of jagged stone. The top of the handle was a large round knot set with some type of gem or jewel which glinted red in the torch light. Once the dagger was out, the girl's eyes grew wide with fright. She began to shriek in a terrible cry that cut through the night.

"Remind me how long this is to continue," said the second man.

"Let the adrenaline build as high as you can get it," said the first. "That's what makes it potent."

The second man nodded. He raked the tip of the knife along one of the girl's legs and pressed the point into the arch of her foot. The skin wasn't broken, but the girl cried out in pain even more. She was going to reach a breaking point soon. He continued with the other leg and then her arms.

The girl tried to twist her body away from him. She whimpered and tried to pull free as the blade came to her face and raked under her chin, but the powerful grip of the man behind her held her firmly in place. Finally, the second man's demeanor seemed to change as if someone else had taken charge. He turned the blade point downward and raised it above his head gripping it with both hands.

"HALT!"

The voice came out of nowhere, but the effect was electric. The first man loosened his grip on the girl and jerked his head toward the sound. The second man lowered the knife to his chest and turned his whole body around.

"Who are you?" he asked in a guttural voice.

At that point, the camera began moving closer to the scene. In locations around the world, Daniel's team gasped in disbelief or uttered exclamations. One person began to pray aloud, "Oh, Lord have mercy and help him!"

"I'm one of the wardens here, and you, sir, are breaking the rules of the hunt," Daniel replied firmly.

The second man gave a strange laugh. "I don't know you," he said. Something about the way he said it gave Daniel chills down his spine. Across the globe, one of the team members prayed again, "God, give him a chance. Help him!"

Immediately, the second man went visibly rigid and shivered from top to bottom as if shaking off something. Then he let go of the knife with his left hand and pulled back his hood.

Daniel had to force himself not to gasp. This man was a tech tycoon whose face would be recognized by almost anyone. But something in Daniel gave him the nerve to point to the first man and said, "Now, you next."

The first man turned his hooded face and looked at the second man and then back at Daniel. Then he let go of the girl with one of his hands and pulled back his hood. Again, Daniel had to force himself not to show any sign of emotion. The face belonged to a European politician who was constantly gracing the front pages of the newspapers.

"What exactly did we do wrong?" he asked in his accented English.

8

"It will be explained to you in detail once you arrive back at the castle. For now, I am to take charge of your quarry. You are to return immediately."

"I don't understand," began the first man. "The rules were simple and quite clear."

"And you failed to thoroughly follow them to the letter," said Daniel. "I don't have to remind you what the consequences of disobedience are." The first man stiffened visibly. That seemed to work. "Now, on your bike. Off you go."

The first man stood up and turned to leave. The second man continued standing where he was. Daniel started to speak to him, but when he looked at the man's face, he could see a maelstrom of fury in his visage. The man appeared ready to explode. To be truthful, Daniel wasn't sure why the man with the knife had gone silent to begin with, but it was working to his advantage. He didn't know how long it would last.

"Okay. Well now, I'm going to take your quarry and fulfill my duties. You can look after your friend."

He knelt down and looked at the young girl's face. She might not be sure exactly what was happening, but when Daniel offered her a hand, she took it. He pulled her to her feet and began walking away from the scene. The video feed grew darker as he entered the forest again, but dark as it was, what could be seen of the video feed and what was heard from the sound of his breathing indicated that Daniel was moving at a good clip. As they went along, Daniel began talking.

"Can you speak English?"

"Sí. A little."

"Good. I don't know how long we have. Those men may come after us. Or other men may come after us. We have to make it back to the fence. The fence is somewhere that direction. I have to get you out of here. Do you understand?"

"Sí."

"There is a hole in the fence. I cut a hole. Once we find the fence,

9

we look for the hole and then ..." Daniel stopped mid-sentence as an unearthly scream tore the silence of the night. Another hunting party had carried out their orders.

§ § §

Back at the fire, the first man had been trying to get the second one to move with no success. He seemed not just transfixed but actually affixed to the earth. When the cry reached their ears, he blinked his eyes as if coming out of a trance. Turning his head, he asked, "Where are they?"

§ § §

Twenty minutes later, Daniel and the girl had arrived at the fence. Which way should he go? Left, or right? In the dark, even with sparing use of the flashlight, he could recognize nothing.

"When in doubt, go left," he said and turned that direction.

During their flight, Daniel had spoken to the girl in simple language about who he was and why he was there. He had also told her that if it came down to it, he was going to fight to get her out alive. They had heard at least four more cries from different directions.

Now he stopped and took out a pen and a piece of paper. The video stream showed a beam of light shining downward, but the camera on his chest never quite made it to the angle of his leg where he was writing. That was extremely fortunate.

"This is an address and a phone number. If you can somehow find a way to go here, you will be safe. If you need help getting there, call this number and tell them that 'Daniel Robertson said you would help me.' Do you understand me? Tell them that I told you that they would help you."

"I understand," came the reply. "You are not coming with me?"

There was an audible sigh. "No. Listen. Do you hear them? They've turned the dogs loose."

The girl looked up at him and asked, "You cannot cut hole here?"

Daniel looked at her and then smacked his forehead with his hand. "I don't know why I didn't think of this earlier," he said as he pulled out the wire cutters once more. He began snipping wires as quickly and efficiently as he could while trying to determine just how far away the dogs were. Once he had a hole big enough, he spoke to the girl again.

"You have to go now. I will keep them from following you as long as I can." There was a pause, and then he asked her, "What is your name, child?"

"Marin," came her reply. "That is the only name I know."

Daniel helped her crawl through the broken fence. Then, after retrieving a couple of items from the backpack with the flashlight, he handed her the light and shoved the backpack through after her. "Take this," he said. "It has money in it, enough to help you buy clothes and a ticket."

Marin looked at him through the chain link fence. His face was lined with worry. There was an intense look in his eyes.

"Thank you, Daniel," she said.

Daniel nodded. "Go, Marin. Go. Don't stop. Don't look back. Don't use the light unless you have to." Then he turned and headed back the way they had come.

About four minutes later, he met the advance of the hounds. There were three of them. They began to howl as they circled around him. Daniel had read enough about them to know that if he stayed calm and mostly still, they were not likely to attack him. They were trained to keep their quarry at bay until the hunters arrived. Daniel figured he had less than five minutes before they showed up.

"Here. Come here," he called as he held out his hands. The hounds caught the scent of bacon and came toward him. Daniel made sure that each of the hounds got one of the prescription-strength, large-animal sedatives wrapped inside the meat. The three hounds gulped down their treats. Two of them got a second portion. Daniel didn't know how long it would take before they were out of commission, but he was buying as much time as he could for Marin.

Since the dogs were content to hold him, he left the pepper spray in his pocket unused. He might have need of it shortly.

The flicker of lights and then the sound of boots on leaves and branches announced the arrival of his pursuers. Two men in khakis and black shirts were leading the way while the two men with the white robes were close behind. They encircled Daniel.

"Where is the girl?" asked the politician.

Daniel looked at him and said, "She's gone. Long gone. I helped her to escape."

"No one escapes," said the man. "If you don't tell us, the dogs will find her soon enough."

Daniel said nothing, but he looked out of the corner of his eyes at the hounds. They seemed just a bit more subdued in their demeanor.

"Who are you?" asked the man. "And how did you find out about this place?"

"I won't tell you," said Daniel as he jutted out his chin defiantly. "I won't tell you anything."

The first man was about to speak when the second man, the software genius, walked rapidly toward Daniel. In his hand, he held the dagger. "Hold him," he said to the two other men. The guttural voice was back. As the two men each grabbed an arm, one of them kicked him in the back of the legs. Daniel instantly dropped to the ground on his knees.

The robed man now drew the dagger above his head with both hands. Daniel looked up at the man's face. The eyes seemed black as a coal bin. Maybe it was just the darkness. With a roar, the man shouted, "I demand blood!"

§ § §

Shortly afterward, the camera was ripped from Daniel's body by a hand and turned off. The video stopped. Then the phone was located and shut off. The livestream ended. Five people sat shell-shocked in front of their screens. The lady was weeping. More than one of the men

12

wiped their eyes. Daniel was gone.

Four of the people clicked the "archive" button on their client. The video was saved to the hard drive of their computers. The fifth person was dry heaving. He hit the delete button on the livestream as quickly as he could and killed any chance of saving his own copy of the video.

In the aftermath, it became apparent that very powerful people with some highly skilled employees had discovered what Daniel had been doing with those two pieces of equipment. Within two hours, the server hosting the chat room was hacked into. Any and all logs indicating who had been connected to that server were copied.

Inside of two more hours, the man in Bretzfeld watched in amazement as his screen turned blue with a fatal error. No attempts to recover it were successful, though he spent the rest of the night trying. The entire hard disk had been encrypted. Almost simultaneously, the same thing was happening to the laptop of the man in New York. Both of these had continued to chat with the man in Evry, France and the man in Tokyo. When these two realized that they were no longer receiving chat responses from the men in New York and Germany, they knew they had to react quickly.

The user in Evry shut down his system entirely. He sat in his room looking around wildly as if the walls themselves were closing in upon him. In a panic, he fled his apartment and began roaming the streets. He pulled his phone from his pocket to check messages and then realized how foolish it was to have it with him. He flung it from him as hard as he could and watched as it made a small splash in the Seine, a mere distraction on the surface which could neither stop the river or the flood of what was coming his way.

He barhopped until early in the morning. He drank too much and may have spoken to some of the other patrons about a weird castle in Belgium and how his friend had just lost his life there. Interesting conversation, if one is paying attention and is not focused on more immediate pursuits of inebriation and social conquests.

After twenty-four hours, he had nowhere else to go. He returned to his flat and listened cautiously at the door. Nothing seemed amiss.

Upon entering, he was greeted by the sight of a wrecked apartment and two sets of strong hands which seized him.

His obituary noted that he had apparently interrupted a robbery that went very badly. Foul play was definitely the prime cause of death. Some odds and ends were taken, among which was his personal computer.

§ § §

In Tokyo, the man there had actually thought through a contingency plan of sorts. Although not fully fleshed out, he felt that it would be prudent to begin walking through the steps he had prepared. He took the time to copy the video file of Daniel's livestream onto three separate USB drives. These he placed in protective mailers with a brief note that the recipient was to simply hold the drive in a secure location until it could be determined whether or not the sender was dead or missing.

He noted that he would follow up by mail once per year at the least with proof of life. If one year went by without any contact, the recipient was to make copies of the drive and send them anonymously to local law enforcement as well as local media. One copy was addressed to a lawyer, another to a friend from university, and the last copy to a distant relative who would honor a family bond but would not likely be contacted by anyone searching for him.

He then went online and made three separate purchases for ferry trips leaving the island using his credit card but under three different names. After that, he spent the next few hours packing essentials and tidying his affairs. By midday, he was ready to leave. Looking around at his apartment one last time, he shut off the light, locked the door, and slipped into the wind.

§ § §

In Breztfeld, when Marta's husband told her that his computer had suffered a crash and that he was going to take a break from his online research, she secretly rejoiced. Jagë, as she liked to call him, had gone through a transformation of sorts once he began researching online. While he was still attentive to her needs as a wife, there was a faraway look in his eye that had not been there before and had never left since.

At first, she questioned whether he had met someone else online. But the few times Jagë had tried to talk with her about his research, she was confused and a bit frightened. He may as well have been speaking Russian to her. After the third time, Marta let him know that how he spent his time was really his business as long as it did not interfere with their marriage, but that she had no stomach for conspiracy theories that sounded more like horror stories.

For the next few days after the computer crash, he spent more time talking with her. They even had a very nice evening out together in which he seemed to dote on her with affection, the first time in many months. But he seemed edgy, nervous. When she tried to get him to confide in her, he quickly said that she would not believe him if he did and that it would be best if she didn't know.

They went to bed that night and never woke up. Apparently, a gas valve in their home proved to be faulty and released a copious amount of deadly fumes into the air. Perhaps it was a phone call to a mobile or maybe it was an appliance that created the spark which resulted in an explosion which leveled the house and broke windows for several blocks. The investigation into the tragedy resulted in a recommendation for even greater oversight by the EU into production controls of gas valves.

§ § §

The man in New York had realized that his blue screen of death was no accident. He also felt trapped. If someone was able to track him so quickly and crash his computer, they surely knew who he was and where to find him. Yes, it was crowded New York where many people go to hide, but he had a job to work at and an ex-wife and children to support. Running away did not really enter his mind because of that.

The New York branch of the shadowy organization was not known for their finesse. But what they lacked in originality, they made up for in directness. According to witnesses, a pack of gangbangers accosted a lone man on a street after work three evenings later. No, they told police, they weren't sure what the man did, if anything, to provoke them. It was over in less than a minute, and then the gang scattered in different directions. What with masks and all, there were no good descriptions other than skin color and approximate height.

15

§ § §

In Oneonta, after getting a hurried chat message about what was going on, a young lady decided that it was time to go back to her stomping grounds and visit family for a spell. She left her computer in her apartment after making backup copies of the video as well as all of the other items she considered important. She left a key with a neighbor and asked him to check in on things every couple of days.

Less than a week later, he reported that someone had broken in and stolen a few large ticket items, with her computer being among them. The police had little to no leads. After receiving the news, she decided that life in the country sounded like a good idea—at least for a while.

§ § §

The video itself had a storied existence. All traces of it were removed from the chat server where it had been linked. The company hosting the livestream app software had its worst intrusion in its history. Any vestiges of the video's data on hard disks or even in RAM were scoured clean. It had been uploaded to a couple of anonymous message boards as well as a file-sharing site. Its existence there was short-lived, too.

Who all downloaded the file? Who possessed copies of it? All known extant copies had been stolen or obliterated. Three of the five persons known to have watched the livestream were dead. The other two were being sought as thoroughly as possible.

Thus, the video became the stuff of Internet conspiracy legend. It was known by the random name Daniel had created on a whim: DangleDrop. People chatted about it. It was available on the dark web, or it wasn't. Anyone who watched the DangleDrop video was rumored to go insane from what they witnessed. The FBI was suppressing it like they did the politician's son's laptop. The police who had seen it had broken down in tears.

These and many other theories abounded. Yet no one seemed to ever be able to locate a copy. In time, DangleDrop became just another story that made those who talked about it seem even more unhinged to their friends and coworkers.

Daniel Robertson never returned to his accounting job. The investigation into his disappearance quickly turned cold at the hotel where he was found to have stayed in Belgium. The police surmised that he may have encountered a wild animal on a hike or fallen off a cliff. As significant as his death should have been, he was just one more missing person report to be filed away. He left behind an aging mother, a stepsister and her husband, and a rust-colored cat.

As for Marin, she was never located by the very interested parties who were searching for her. The dogs succumbed to the tranquilizers, two of them permanently, and were of no use. By the time fresh hounds were brought to the area and set upon the trail, the scent stopped at a highway just a few miles from the estate. For a young girl, she was resourceful. Chances are she would end up on the street as a hooker or an addict because of her experiences. She might be alive and in an asylum. But who would believe her? As days turned to months and then years, these results seemed more likely than not.

And so the festivities continued, albeit with a bit more security than before. New members were initiated. Older members showed up occasionally or moved onto greener pastures. Life rewarded those who played the game to win.

Chapter 1

Philadelphia, Pennsylvania
Present Day

Sarah Lewis was perturbed. Her brother Billy was not eating again. He had not eaten in three days, as a matter of fact, and she knew it. Despite her making pork chops and mashed potatoes the first day she had noticed it and chicken fried steak the next, he had not touched his food. Now he had gone without breakfast and lunch.

She knew what he was doing. He was fasting. It irked her that she could not tempt him enough with her best cooking to want to eat, but she had to respect his willpower. She had seen him overindulge on both of those dishes more than once.

Well, if he wouldn't eat, maybe she could at least get him to drink some coffee. As she filled the kettle and began to measure out the coffee, she hummed "Amazing Grace" to herself the way their Momma used to sing it, with a bit of minor key thrown in. It made it more of a haunting melody until the final verse when she would break into full major and belt out the words. It had sent goosebumps up her thin little arms every time she heard her Momma sing it. That woman had faith.

She absentmindedly put away some of the dishes as she thought about her own journey. Her father had been a small business owner back in the forties and fifties, but when the fight against segregation started to take on more momentum, he had begun to spend more time trying to help his community. Although he was never as famous as Dr. King, he made an impact doing what he believed was right. She was just a little girl, but she remembered her father's fiery passion and the calmness she saw in his face. And his aftershave. Funny how things like that stick in a child's mind.

Daddy died way too early from a bad heart, and the strain of looking after four children had taken its toll on her Momma. Sarah never married due to her commitment to take care of her mother. Two siblings they had lost to the streets. Billy was all the family she had left.

He had always been such a serious little boy in spite of being the lastborn. When he was about five years of age, someone nicknamed him "Preacher," and it had stuck. Nobody, including Billy, seemed to doubt that he would grow up to be a minister. It was when he was about fifteen that he had had a profound spiritual experience at the Ebenezer Full Gospel church they attended which seemed to tap into a fathomless reservoir of joy. She remembered the change in his character, even his eyes.

After that, people began to speak more about how happy he always was. Eventually, that name supplanted "Preacher," and the Reverend Happy Lewis became a force to be reckoned with in the small towns surrounding theirs and then in Philadelphia where he said God had called him to work. He became the director of the Old Gospel Mission and devoted his energy to helping the down and out, the addicted and the overwhelmed.

Sarah had remained in their childhood home in Shamokin. Apart from serving in her church and some community involvement, her life had revolved around her flowers and seasonal garden: the former was the love of her mother and the latter something her father had taught her as a practical way to feed hungry mouths. She had resolved to grow old gracefully and just live out her life until the trouble with Billy—Happy—happened. His name had been smeared and his service to the community in the Philadelphia area had been cut short. With no other source of income, he had moved back to Shamokin and started rebuilding his life. Through it all, Happy never lost his joy, not once, but his faith had certainly been tested.

After Mister Ingram with the newspaper called to apologize and ask Happy's forgiveness for the lies he had written, things had actually begun to change. Then, months later, when Mister Ingram had called them to Philly and told them how they were now the new proprietors of a state-of-the-art building where the Old Gospel Mission had once stood, everything came full circle. She hadn't really wanted to leave their home, but sometimes God lays out a path for you that is too clear to ignore. She wasn't going to be separated from Happy again if she could help it.

Sarah shook her head and focused her eyes on the kettle. It was boiling and just starting to whistle. She switched off the stove eye as she switched to a major key and began belting out the last verse of "Amazing Grace" just like Momma used to.

When she was done, from behind her she heard Happy's voice saying, "You trying to bring a tear to my eye, Sarah?"

"Hmph. I'm not sure the last time I seen you cry."

Truth was, Happy had cried plenty, but never for himself. He had shed tears at the bedside of multiple dying AIDS patients. He had cried when a former addict had a relapse and lost her baby. He cried when he sat beside the bed of a young girl whom he had found literally in the gutter dying of an overdose. And he had cried tears of joy when she awoke whole and free three days later.

"You're not going to try to tempt me to eat again with one of your fancy recipes are you? You almost got me with the gravy on that steak yesterday."

Sarah chuckled to herself. "No. Just coffee."

"You know I'm just drinking water like our Lord did."

"That's what coffee is," Sarah said with a crisp tone. "Water with just a little flavor added, that's all. I reckon you could sit and share a cup with your sister, couldn't you?" She turned to face him with the pot held up in her hand.

Happy smiled. "All right, you win. I'll enjoy some flavored water with you. I'll get the mugs and join you on the roof."

A few minutes later, they were seated at a small iron garden table among the many plants which were arranged in neat rows on the roof of the building. This was Sarah's refuge. If she couldn't be in Shamokin, some of Shamokin would have to come to Philly.

They sat in silence for a while, listening to the sounds of the city down below as life echoed up to their ears. Sarah heard the familiar buzzing of the bees as they worked the flowers. It never ceased to amaze her that somewhere in the vast forest of concrete and steel, they had found a place to call home. Finally, Happy spoke.

"I've been praying and listening extra hard these past few days because I think the Lord may be speaking to me, to us really, about making a change in our focus here."

"You mean feeding the poor and clothing the homeless and listening to people's sad stories isn't enough to keep you busy?"

"Plenty busy. Just maybe not the business we need to be involved in right at this moment in time. Sarah, you remember more than I do the fight Daddy was involved in. Tell me again what he used to say about why he did it."

Sarah eyed him for a moment before answering. "He said that among all the good things he could be doing, fighting injustice was what he knew he should be doing."

"What did he say about his neighbors and pastors and other people in the community?"

"You're going somewhere with this, I know. Why don't you just tell me what you want to say?"

Happy was silent until she answered his question.

"He said that plenty of people could see there was a problem but that nobody wanted to be the first to step up and act. He used to quote that Scripture from Isaiah that God was looking for someone to make up the broken hedge and ..."

"Stand in the gap," Happy finished. "That's what we've got to do, Sarah. We've got to stand in the gap for some people who don't have anyone else to do it."

It was Sarah's turn for silence. Her brother had that faraway, sober look in his eyes.

"It seems like everything I read lately says something about human trafficking. Women and children, sometimes even grown men, are being sold like cattle and moved around the country or around the world. Seems like the last government administration put more attention on

21

that than in the past, and more and more people are being arrested. That's a good thing. But I keep hearing a voice in my heart asking, "What about the victims? What happens to them? Then I look around at this big old building the Lord done blessed us with, and I think to myself, 'Why can't we do something here?'"

Happy sighed a deep sigh. "This morning, I just opened the Bible up asking God for some direction. I still do that from time to time because He still speaks to me that way. The verse my eyes fell on was Proverbs chapter 24, verses eleven and twelve. It says we're supposed to rescue those who are perishing, those being led to the slaughter. If we say it's none of our business and pretend we don't see it, God will repay us for ignoring their cries."

Sarah looked at his face. Life had been tough as children and plenty challenging growing up, but his face still had the simple look of someone who believed in something more than evil. She loved her brother. "Why don't you tell me what you have in mind," she suggested.

Happy drew his gaze back in and looked at Sarah with a smile. "I was hoping you'd ask. Here's what I've been thinking."

Chapter 2

Happy and Sarah talked for the better part of three hours. This required a refill on the coffee and, at their age, at least two toilet breaks. But after Happy shared his vision, together they hammered out the details of what it could look like.

What Happy envisioned was a facility where women and children who had been victims of human trafficking could find a safe haven where they could receive counseling and rebuild their lives. There could be job training for those who needed it. There would be daily routines to help bring a sense of order. Most of all, he wanted a place that could feel like a home, but not just any home. He wanted it to have the sense of God's presence and protection.

Sarah had asked whether or not he intended to allow boys and girls in the same facility if they were able to even take children. "It could cause problems if we allow both."

"I realize that," said Happy. "But what if they're family? We can't let the state split them up like they do so often."

They decided that some decisions would just have to wait until they reached that point. The first step would be to approach the people involved in the fight against trafficking in order to offer their help. They would also need to find sources for funding. Then there was the question of staffing. As Sarah put it, "You and I are too old to be trying to make all this happen just by ourselves."

In the end, they took the first step by offering their help. If it were truly God's direction, He would open the doors and send them the right first person to help. They would follow His lead from there.

Chapter 3

Sand Mountain, Alabama

Janine Akers wiped the sweat from her brow and looked in satisfaction at the row of tomato plants she had just weeded. If there was one thing Sand Mountain was particularly good for, it was making fine produce. She looked at her hands. They were stained brown from the dirt and green from the suckers she had pulled off the bottoms of the tomato plants. She loved the pungent smell but hated how the oils made her skin itch.

Before going inside to wash up, she looked once more at the garden. It was coming along well. The first blossoms were appearing on several of the crops. Before too long, she could fry some green tomatoes, make BLTs, and can plenty for soup in the winter.

Inside, she turned on the tap of the three-bowl stainless steel sink before she reached for the bar of soap and scrub brush. She didn't mind getting her hands dirty, but she was still a lady. When Buddy got home from work, she wanted her nails and fingers to look nice for him. And she didn't want to smell like dirt.

She put on an apron and began to prepare supper. A cool breeze filtered in through the kitchen windows which looked out over the back part of the property. It was the time of year when it was hot enough that most people on the mountain would be running the air conditioner, but Janine liked fresh air. She began cutting some onions and putting them into a cast-iron skillet. After mixing in some beef and spices, she covered the top and set the temperature on low. They would have fajitas with a tossed salad tonight.

Because it was Friday, she knew Buddy would want his one beer for the week. When they had first met, Buddy indulged in a whole lot more alcohol than that. It was part of the subculture of the special forces unit he had been in, drinking and swearing. Janine had made it clear that if their relationship were going to go any further than a casual acquaintance, those two habits would have to go. To his credit, Buddy had given up the drinking cold turkey. The swearing had taken much longer. Janine had had to show some patience as he dealt with the association between anger and swearing, bravado and swearing, happiness and swearing. Well, it was a deeply engrained habit that had taken some time, to say the least.

He also began attending Faith Friendship Baptist Church with her. She wasn't sure he had ever made his own commitment to the faith, and he certainly had not yet been water baptized, but Buddy was a good man. He promised at the altar not only to love and cherish her but to always protect her. That meant more than words could ever express.

The weekly beer was her one concession. Buddy had gotten into the Bible just enough to read about Jesus turning water into wine, and he made his argument to her that if the Savior she served would do that, it couldn't be all bad. Janine had smiled and patted him on the cheek and told him that he could have one beer of his choice per week. If that alone had gotten him to read the Bible, that was progress for Buddy.

She had asked her pastor, Derek Blanton, about it sometime later to find out if she had done the right thing. He had responded by asking her why unsaved people always made it a point to invite at least two Baptists on a fishing trip. Puzzled, Janine said she didn't know. Pastor Derek had told her that it was because if you invite one Baptist, he'll drink all the beer himself, but if you invite two, they'll never touch the stuff. They had both laughed, Janine said she got the message, and they had let it go at that.

The sound of Buddy's F-350 pulling the trailer behind it across the long gravel driveway alerted her to his presence. Janine looked in the mirror and pushed a wisp of auburn hair behind her right ear. Her blue eyes stared back at her. She would be due for another henna treatment soon to keep the hair color vibrant. She hung up the apron and went to greet Buddy at the front door with a warm hug and a tender kiss.

"How was work today?" she asked.

Buddy grunted as he sat down on the bench outside the front door and took off his work boots. Janine liked having those big boots right there by the door. They were a statement of sorts that anybody trying to break into that house might ought to think twice about it.

"It was about the same except for old man Silas' piglets. Two of 'em got loose, and I almost run 'em over with the tractor. We had a time rounding up those things and catching 'em. Pete brought his two Shepherds over, and they got 'em corralled pretty quickly after that. Man, them dogs are smart." He took a deep breath and exhaled. "I'm thinking about getting one or two for here. Bet they'd keep the deer out of the corn."

Janine laughed at his story. "That's pretty funny. I can imagine you running after baby pigs." She turned to enter the house and said over her shoulder, "Well, wash up. The food's hot. Fajitas and salad tonight."

Buddy obeyed the instructions and showed up two minutes later with water droplets on his mustache from where he had washed his face along with his hands. Janine took a napkin and dabbed it dry.

"You missed a spot," she said.

"That's just slobber from where you kissed me," he retorted.

Over supper she told him about her day and reported on the progress of the garden. She also showed him a new cheese slicer she had gotten online. Buddy looked at it approvingly. Janine was very easy to look at, but what had attracted him most to her was the vibrancy of her personality. She embraced life. As she put it, she "wanted to get all the juice out of the bottom of the pot" as far as living was concerned.

That was what had directed him into the special forces years ago. If he were going to serve, and it was never a doubt that he wanted to do that, he wanted to give it his all. Finding a woman who could keep a house, plant a garden, love him and cook real Southern food—all with passion—was more than he could have dreamed. If she wanted a new cheese slicer, she could have it. If she wanted a well dug by hand, he would dig it for her. Janine was his woman.

After they met, Janine hadn't pressed him for details about his time in the military, and that allowed him to keep the memories and secrets compartmentalized. He didn't want to lie to her, but there were some things he was sworn to uphold. The nature and locations of his missions were definitely part of that.

He didn't mind going to church with her either. It mattered a whole lot to her, and the people there for the most part seemed genuine in their religion. What struck Buddy was how they treated one another. He had seen enough of the bad side of humanity to know when people were being deceptive or downright mean, but most of the folks at the church seemed to have a genuine kindness about them. And Pastor Derek preached sermons that were interesting and usually not too long.

After supper, Janine suggested they take a walk around the property to get some fresh air and to check up on things. She was the one who had found the farm they had purchased right after getting married. Twenty-five acres of pastureland suitable for grazing or hay production with a nice rancher farmhouse, outbuildings, and privacy was how it had been advertised. The first part he was sure had appealed to Janine, and the latter part had appealed to Buddy.

Along with the purchase had come a couple of tractors and various attachments. Buddy didn't realize he was purchasing an occupation along with the farm, but he had learned to mow the orchard grass and, with the help of a couple of old-timers in the church, had developed a small business of cutting and baling hay for people in the surrounding counties. It was seasonal work, provided some extra money, and allowed him plenty of time for solitude on his tractor.

As they walked around the property, Janine slipped her arm through his. He liked the way she reached up with her hand and stroked his bicep. Occasionally they talked as they walked the property. Mostly they walked in silence. Janine was always looking for a groundhog hole to fill or a fence that needed repair. Buddy couldn't help from thinking of sightlines and which copse of trees would make the best cover in a firefight.

When they were through with their walking and were going back inside, Janine told him that she had made pineapple cheesecake for dessert. She brought it into the living room where he was reading a magazine in his recliner. Buddy took a bite and closed his eyes. "This is absolutely perfect," he said.

Janine smiled and took her piece of cheesecake and glass of milk to the couch. She curled her feet under her and leaned back against the plush leather cushion. Her denim shorts weren't the cutoffs so many of the younger girls wore (and too many of the not-so-young women), but she knew buddy liked seeing her athletic legs. She reached for her Bible and began reading her evening devotions.

Later that night, as she lay curled up next to Buddy's strong frame, she relaxed as much as she could. Life was about as good as she could hope it to be. She thought about her tomato plants and remembered that she needed to fertilize the strawberries. As sleep began to take her, in the deep corners of her mind, she wondered if they would ever find her or if they were even still looking for her. Maybe a German Shepherd wouldn't be a bad idea.

Chapter 4

Two weeks later, after quite a bit of online searching and telephone calls, Janine met Buddy at the door after work. Instead of telling him what was for supper, she told him to follow her out to the barn. "I've got something I want to show you."

Buddy expected to see maybe a table of fresh vegetables or a new hoe. When he turned the corner behind her, she was smiling at him and standing beside a full-grown, solid black German Shepherd. Buddy started to say something but couldn't. He stared at the dog with his mouth open and then stared at Janine and then stared at the dog again.

"Well, what do you think?" asked Janine.

"It's a dog," said Buddy.

Janine laughed. "You're sharp as a tack," she said. "Do you like him?"

Buddy walked toward the dog and knelt down. "What's his name?"

"Midnight," she said. "He's AKC registered, full-blooded. And he's a good boy." The last part she said to the dog as she grabbed his jowls in her hands and half-shook, half-petted him.

"Where did you get him?"

"After you mentioned maybe getting a Shepherd, I got to looking around. I read up a little bit on German Shepherds and realized there was a lot I didn't know. There's a lot of puppy mills just making litters to sell for a profit. I wasn't sure what to really look for, so I prayed about it.

"Then I found an ad that had just been posted online from a lady who served as a caregiver for an old fellow over in Rising Fawn. He always kept Shepherds. He used to breed 'em for a living and loved the dogs. He just passed, and his kids had no use for the dog. So she posted that she was looking for a good home for him.

"I was the first one to call her. She didn't even charge a rehoming fee like most people do. Mainly, she just wanted to make sure that Midnight really went to a good home. I told her I had a husband whose cornbread didn't rise all the way to the top who liked to chase baby pigs, and that won her over."

Buddy chuckled. "Midnight. I like that name." He looked the dog over with an approving eye. "You are a good boy. How old is he?"

"He's just turned two years old last month. He's trained and everything. The man knew what he was doing with dogs. She said he had a dog years ago that would not only fetch his newspaper every day, but it'd also bring him the remote when he sat down near the TV, and it would growl anytime Hillary Clinton was on the news."

Buddy laughed out loud. "Sounds like a smart dog." He had been stroking Midnight's fur and letting the dog sniff and lick his hand to get his scent. "How about you, Midnight? Are you that smart?"

"The lady told me that the past few weeks as the man got sicker, Midnight never left his side except to eat or do his business. Right before he died, the man told her that Midnight was as good a dog as any he had ever had, maybe even his best. He said he could see it in Midnight's eyes."

Buddy scratched the dog under the chin and lifted it up so that he could look at the dog's face. He looked into Midnight's eyes. For a brief moment, Buddy had the feeling that the dog was looking back into his soul. Something clicked between them, and he knew that Midnight was going to be far more than a dog to chase the deer out of the garden.

He stood up and looked at Janine. "Thanks," he said. "I like him."

Janine looked up at him and said, "I just knew you would. He has something special about him, like he has his own secrets." She got quiet and then added, "Or knows how to keep 'em, at least."

Buddy waited, but she said nothing else. Turning back to the Shepherd, which was comfortably nestled in the hay, he said, "Come on, Midnight. Let's go." He turned and began walking to the house. The Shepherd immediately sprang to his feet and walked right beside

Buddy. Janine folded her arms and leaned against the barn doorpost as she watched them walking together. Midnight's stride looked every bit as confident and determined as his new master's.

"Thank you, Lord," she said quietly. "You helped me find the right one."

Chapter 5

Flight 193 Honduras to Philadelphia

Dedra Hutchens was tired but still on her feet. The plane's departure had been delayed due to an engine maintenance issue that had kept them on the tarmac for two hours. But the flight from Tegucigalpa, Honduras to Philadelphia, which was a staple route in her job as a flight attendant, had left eventually with a cabin full of hot and slightly uncomfortable tourists, businessmen, and the usual assortment of travelers.

Then there was 36A. Dedra had noticed the girl in that seat by the window on her first pass through as she had offered complimentary snacks and drinks while they waited on the tarmac. She was brown-skinned, like many of the travelers on the flight. Nothing was unusual about that.

It was her tall, athletic, and very blond traveling companion that served as a juxtaposition to the girl herself. The man was probably 6' 2" and well built. He was friendly: maybe a bit too friendly. He did all the speaking. The girl's eyes mostly stayed downward when Dedra asked if she would like a soda, juice, or water. The man answered for her and requested a juice.

Dedra had smiled and kept protocol. But a little niggle in the back of her brain made her determined to keep an eye on both of them. She had brought the girl a pack of crayons and a coloring book to keep her occupied during the wait. The girl had uttered a very quiet "Gracias" that had elicited a sharp glance from the man toward her, which Dedra caught out of the corner of her eye.

To try and help confirm her suspicions, Dedra had brought all the children in that section multiple drinks during the wait and after takeoff. She knew, of course, what that much fluid would do. Sure enough, there was a veritable beeline for the toilets. Most of the children except for the very young made their own way back to the toilets, did their business, and meandered back to their seats.

Not 36A. Mister Man accompanied her and walked behind her with a hand on her shoulder. He checked the toilet and stood casually with his hand on the wall, glancing around with a pleasant, almost plastic, expression on his face. A couple of minutes later, the door opened, and the pair made their way back to their seats. Dedra pretended to be busy with an overhead compartment a person needed help with and watched the girl's face. The eyes never left the aisle floor, and the hand never left the shoulder.

After checking the flight manifest, she noted that the man's name was James Monroe III. The girl's named was listed as Felicity Navarro Monroe. Nothing that unusual about the names. Maybe an adoption, maybe a mixed marriage or even a relative. Still, she felt that she needed to do more. After asking to speak with the pilot, she voiced her concerns and shared the details of everything she had seen. The pilot radioed for more details on the backgrounds of the travelers.

Mister Monroe was traveling, according to the records in the flight booking, with his recently adopted daughter. There were no copies of the adoption records, however. He had been allowed to travel under a waiver signed by a federal employee in the Honduran government. That set off a few alarm bells with the pilot, who was a father of three and who always seemed to Dedra to be well informed. Of his own volition, he contacted ground at Philadelphia, explained the situation, and asked for a greeting party to be waiting for Mister Monroe for further questioning.

Dedra also thought of one other step she could take. They had a couple more hours after the obligatory stop-over in Miami. What with the enhanced sanitation protocols, she volunteered to take over the lavatory duties for the remainder of the flight. The low member of the totem pole was pleasantly surprised but quickly agreed. Dedra prepared a note in English and Spanish asking simply, "Do you need help?" and put it in the small cleaning basket along with a pen and some tape.

When she saw the man arise from his seat and begin to walk down the aisle with his hand on the girl's shoulder, Dedra slid the lock closed on one of the two stalls so that it showed as occupied. She then smiled at the

33

man and asked him to wait just a moment while she cleaned the toilet in compliance with the new sanitation rules. She walked inside and briefly shut the door and then taped the note and pen to the back of the folding door. Then she cleaned the seat and sink and opened the door.

"It's clean and ready," she said with a smile.

As before, the man gave a brief glance at the stall and then stood outside. The girl took longer than the previous two minutes. The man began to look a bit nervous. Dedra could seem him tap his foot unconsciously. He knocked once and asked a question in Spanish. After a few seconds more, the toilet flushed, and the door opened shortly. The man glanced around inside the toilet after the girl emerged. For a second, it appeared that he was going to enter himself, but Dedra stepped forward with her basket and said, "Excuse me. Before you use it, I need to clean it first in compliance with the new safety protocols."

The man looked at her flight attendant's smile and said, "No problem. I can wait."

When Dedra entered the lavatory and closed the door, she turned and looked at the wall. Her heart sank. On the paper, the girl had simply put the word "Sí." She took the note and slowly made her way a few minutes later to the front of the plane, where she reported her findings to the pilot. He relayed the new information to ground in Philadelphia. They, in turn, confirmed that two agents from Homeland Security would be waiting for the pair at immigration.

The rest of the flight was uneventful, and Dedra stayed on her post with the lavatory to avoid arousing suspicion. As she watched them deplane, she hoped that it would be the last time that hand would rest on the girl's shoulder.

When James Monroe III used the quick kiosk to speed up his entry back into the US, he presumed that he would breeze through immigration as he had done before by simply handing the printed form for himself and the child. But this time, the DHS official motioned to two other agents who were waiting in the area. As they approached, he said, "Mister Monroe, these agents would like a word with you." The female agent placed herself between James and the girl and put a protective arm

34

around her shoulders while the male agent gestured toward a door off to the side. At that point, James knew something had just gone very wrong.

The ensuing investigation into James Monroe III provided detectives with links to several persons of interest. One of these ties led to a mansion in the greater Philadelphia area where other trafficking victims were located and freed.

Chapter 6

Sand Mountain, Alabama

The next four weeks were a lot like the summer of every other year of their five years of marriage. Janine kept the house and made the garden into a lush paradise for fruits and vegetables. Buddy cut hay, baled it, loaded it, hauled it, and stacked it in their barn and various farmers' barns.

The biggest difference was Midnight. Janine observed that when she was in the garden, Midnight would mostly lie down in one of the rows of cool earth near her. Occasionally, he would get up and make a circuit around the perimeter of the garden. Once or twice, he would widen his perimeter past the barn and outbuildings. When she would break for lunch, Midnight stayed near her while she ate. When she was finished, he would lope off into the fields. Curious, she got Buddy's binoculars and watched him. He followed the fence line until he was out of sight. When she caught sight of him again, he was returning along the opposite fence row. Midnight understood boundaries and was guarding them. He had picked up that much just going on walks with them.

She shared this with Buddy. For his part, after supper when they were not walking together, Buddy would disappear with Midnight for an hour, sometimes two or three. When Janine asked what he was doing out for so long with Midnight, Buddy just said, "I'm training him." He said it with that extra-serious look on his face which she rarely ever saw, and she chose not to press him with any further questions.

It was during one of the hot afternoons on a Tuesday while Janine was canning butterbeans that her cell rang. The Caller ID displayed the name "Pastor Derek." Janine answered with, "Hey, Pastor Derek. How are you today?"

Pastor Derek's rich baritone came over the line. "Hello, Janine. I'm doing just fine, thank you. How's your canning coming along?"

"Busy. The garden is about the best I've ever had. To be honest, some days it about wears me out."

"Well, you have one of the prettiest gardens in the county, and that's saying a lot."

"Thank you, Pastor."

"Listen, Janine. The reason I called is that something…unusual has come up, and I need to talk with you and Buddy."

Janine was a bit perplexed. She had never gotten a call from Pastor Derek like this. "Okay, Pastor. Do you want us to come over to the church this evening?"

"No. I'll come out to your house. How does 7:00 sound?"

"That sounds fine. I'll let Buddy know when he gets in."

After supper, Janine put some coffee on and baked a batch of lemon sugar cookies. While they were in the oven, she took the canned jars of vegetables that had cooled enough and began stacking them in the pantry. Buddy came and helped her.

"Reckon what Derek wants," he said.

"He didn't give me the slightest hint," she said. "Maybe he's looking for volunteers early for the homecoming celebration."

Twenty minutes later, Pastor Derek arrived in his Chevy pickup. He was greeted at the truck by a curious, but reserved, Midnight and at the door by Buddy and Janine. He took a moment to squat down and pet Midnight.

"Come in, Pastor Derek," said Janine warmly. "I've got coffee and cookies. Would you rather sit in the living room or around the table?"

"I think I'd prefer the table, Janine. Thank you. Buddy, good to see you. Hay been keeping you busy?"

"Sure has," answered Buddy. "I've got more to do than I can seem to fit in at the moment, but I try to make it a rule to be home by 5:30, 6:00 at the latest. Janine makes dinner the same time every day. If I want it hot, I gotta be on time."

"I wish more families would observe that rule," said Pastor Derek as Janine poured him a cup of coffee. "No sugar, thanks. Except for what's in these cookies," he said as he reached for two of them and put them on his plate.

They chatted for a few minutes about the church and the community. Pastor Derek was a hands-on leader who was involved not only in the lives of his parishioners but also in the greater society. There was a shortage of help among some of the farmers. Lightning had struck a couple of antenna towers, which was disrupting Internet and phone services for part of the county.

After a while, Pastor Derek said, "Well, I'm sure you're wondering about the purpose of my visit this evening. I'm not exactly sure how to go about this other than to just put it out there on the table. Janine, I think it may be about you."

"Me?" Janine asked. "I don't understand, Pastor."

"This morning, I was over at the church making some copies for the Sunday School classes, and two men dropped by. I didn't say gentlemen, mind you. They asked if I was the pastor, and I told them I was. They said that they was with an insurance company and was looking for a woman by the name of Jenny Powell."

When he spoke that name, Janine bit her lip.

"I told them I couldn't help them, as I didn't know anyone by that name. Then they said Jenny might have changed her name. They gave me this picture."

Pastor Derek pulled a sheet of printer paper from his pocket and unfolded it so that the color image faced Janine and Buddy. Janine stiffened. The face staring back at her was a younger version of herself with blond hair. It had been pulled from a social media post a long time ago.

"Did they say what they wanted with this lady?" she asked.

"They wouldn't go into much detail. They hinted that it might have to do with a case of insurance fraud and that they were trying to clear

Jenny's name. But if you want my opinion, they were lying."

"What makes you say that?" asked Buddy.

"Aw, Buddy, you've been around insurance salesmen and probably a few claims adjustors in your life. Some of them are friendly enough, and a few of them are decent folk. The rest of them leave you feelin' a bit greasy. These guys was all business. They seemed…hard. That's the best word for them, I think. They had a hard edge to them. If you don't mind my saying it, Buddy, they seemed more like you than they did Fred down at Farmer's Mutual."

Buddy nodded in acknowledgment. "What did you tell 'em after they showed you the picture?"

"I studied it, and they was looking at me the whole time. I told them that in my ministry, I've seen plenty of women that were pretty, blonde, and blue-eyed and that here in the South, there's a whole lot of women that could come close to matching that description. I asked them how old the photo was. They said maybe seven or eight years. I told them that in that case, the lady they're looking for could have had about five or six children, been divorced twice, and doubled her weight. I'm not sure what they thought of that, but I asked them if I could keep the picture and show it around. They said I could. I also asked how to contact them if anyone recognized Jenny, and they said to call the number printed on the paper."

They sat in silence for a bit. Janine had wrapped her arms around herself and was holding her elbows. She was chewing her bottom lip and rocking back and forth. Buddy had picked up the paper and was studying it. In the background, the clock above the kitchen sink ticked away the moments.

Pastor Derek took a long sip of coffee and then said, "Janine, do you know anything about this?"

There was a long pause. Then a single tear made its way down her right cheek. Janine wiped it away with the back of her hand. She looked at Buddy and gave him an apologetic smile. Then she turned back to Pastor Derek and said, "I always wondered if they would give up. But it looks like they may have found me."

Chapter 7

Over several refills of coffee, Janine told them her story. For their part, Buddy and Pastor Derek sat in silence and just let her talk.

"There was a group of us that all met in a chat room. Now, before you draw any conclusions, it wasn't one of them kind of chat rooms. It was a chat room for people who had been abused in some way or another growing up. People would come and go all the time, but there was a group that was kind of like the core.

"I was seventeen when I joined the group. People were real honest about their lives and their struggles dealing with the past. That was what drew me to it. It's probably what drew everyone to it. We was all looking for some place where we could just be real and open up about how we felt. You got the feeling listening to other people's stories that you wasn't alone, that there was other people out there that really understood how you felt and was rooting for you.

"Over the next couple of years, a smaller group begun to talk more about what was we doing with our lives to make sure other people didn't have to deal with the mess we was all working through. We would come up with ideas on what we could do to help."

Janine's face creased into a smile. "There were some mighty hair-brained ideas people shared. One person wanted to blow up all the state-run children's homes. He was abused there his whole life. Another person wanted to take out full-page ads in every major newspaper and warn people about some circus that had come through his town as a kid—this was somewhere in Europe—and had invited kids to be part of the show only to find out that the ringmaster was a big pedophile. One lady had been raised by a convent as an orphan. She said that the nuns would sell the girls and boys out to important people in her country. I won't repeat what she said she wanted to do, but it was kind of violent.

"The problem was, we didn't live near each other and didn't really know what we could do to make a difference. Then one day, a guy who was from Japan starts talking about a place he called the Black Castle.

He was all excited and going on and on about it. He said it was an open portal from hell to earth where Satan harvested the energy of humans."

She looked at Pastor Derek apologetically. "I didn't say I believed everything that all the other people did, but you gotta understand where these people was coming from. We had Christians, atheists, New Age, and others in the group as far as religions go. Anyways, we started asking questions about this castle, like how he found out about it and what was so important about it.

"He told us that he had found out about it by listening to two really important people in Japan talking to each other when he was doing some work for one of them. They was talking openly about human sacrifice, offering blood to their god and the power that it gave them in business and over other people.

"After they got done talking, he poked around in the guy's office and found some handwritten notes. He copied them. They had a few names and an address he tracked down to a place in Belgium. He shared with us the little that he knew and asked if we would be willing to pitch in and see if we could find out more. We all agreed to do that and started right away.

"It was like hitting a brick wall, but we kept at it. Eventually, we started to find little bits of information here and there. These people were really secretive about their meetings. They had one at the change of every season. We could never find any formal announcement or anything like that, but we started finding pictures with two people we knew who were on the list with maybe two or three more unknown people. Then, we would search some more until we could identify those people. Then we would find a few more. These people all hung around together. Some of the pictures were like what you'd see in a newspaper. Other ones were party pictures. Some of 'em were just plain creepy. It's hard to describe without showing you, but they would be dressed all weird or be naked and have body paint on." She shook her head as she remembered it.

"We came up with a list of thirty-five or forty people we could identify from photos who seemed to be connected. We didn't really know what to do next, but one guy from over in Scotland said we should just show up on the date of their next party and see if what we suspected was really true. It was a bit on the wild side, but nobody had a better idea. It wasn't like any of us was going to get an invitation ourselves.

"Several people in the group said they would go with him. I didn't. For one, I never had a passport. I also didn't have the money to travel that far. But there was supposed to be about six or seven out of the group that were going. The general idea was that they would sneak up and watch as close as they could get. If anything happened, some of them could call for help while the others did their best to interrupt anything illegal.

"When it came down to the end, though, it was just the guy from Scotland who went. Everybody else bailed out for one reason or another. Several of us did commit to being in the chat room so that he could share what he found with us live. He also had a cell phone and a camera so he could do some video streaming.

Janine stopped talking and just stared off into the distance for a few minutes. The clock ticked on the wall. Through the open screened windows, outside in the distance a pack of coyotes began their evening serenade of yipping and yapping. Janine refocused her eyes on the table and continued.

"Everything we had read about was pretty much dead on. There was a group of people down in this castle all dressed in robes, carrying torches and chanting and making a ruckus. Then they brought out the children. They was all dressed in just their underwear. They turned the children loose and told 'em to run, I guess. That's what they did. Then the adults broke up into huntin' parties and started out after them.

"Our guy from the chat room felt like he had to do something. I don't blame him. He cut a hole in a fence and eventually found two men who had caught a little twelve- or thirteen-year-old girl. He interrupted them right before they was about to kill her with a big knife.

"He was able to convince them he was part of the castle and rescued her. Then he took off into the woods. Eventually, the people figured out what was going on and started looking for them. He got the girl to the fence and let her go, but he said that the others were too close for both of them to make a break for it. He went back to give her a chance to escape. Not too long after, they found him. Then they killed him. We all saw it happen live."

Janine shuddered involuntarily at that point. The tears began to flow freely down both cheeks. Buddy put a big hand on her back and rubbed it in circles. Pastor Derek looked down into his coffee cup. Finally, he asked, "What happened after all of that took place, Janine?"

"Within just a few hours, a couple of people in the chat room just disappeared mid-sentence. One minute they was there, and the next they was gone. We didn't know each other by full names, just screen names. Well, some people had chosen to share their names, but not everyone. One of the men who had shared his name was a guy in Germany. I was looking him up later and read that his house had blown up. Anyways, I got a chat message telling me that it looked like we was the ones being hunted now and that I should probably run for cover.

"I left my apartment down in Oneonta and went to visit my aunt Judy. I checked in with one of my neighbors who was watching my place. He said that about five days after I had left, my apartment was broken into. Not much was stolen, but my computer was one of the things definitely missing. I asked him to make sure. I had left it hoping that whoever was after me would be satisfied and maybe leave me alone if they thought they had gotten what they were looking for." She put her elbows on the table and placed her hands over her face and rubbed it slowly.

"What would they 'a been looking for, Janine?" asked Buddy.

"Copies of the video," she said through her fingers. "The livestream was being streamed to all of our computers, and we could save it if we wanted to when it was done."

"Did you?" asked Buddy.

Janine nodded her head twice.

Buddy exhaled sharply. Janine flinched.

"And you saved a copy when you ran, didn't you?" he asked.

There was a pause. Then Janine nodded twice more behind her hands. "I've had three copies this whole time."

43

Chapter 8

It was after 2 a.m. when Pastor Derek said he needed to leave and get back home to his wife and children. They had moved to the living room, where they had watched the video twice. Janine had disappeared outside briefly and then returned with a USB drive and hooked it to their computer. As Janine already knew, the first part of the video was effectively commentary with snatches of useful images. Once Daniel had put the camera up to a binocular lens, there was a rough improvement. Buddy and Pastor Derek watched along but wisely reserved their comments.

Once the video shifted to the scene in the woods and Buddy and Derek were confronted with the reality of seeing a young girl cornered by two grown men, Buddy's eyes narrowed to slits. Pastor Derek muttered, "Lord help us. What has this world come to?"

Then, when the men exposed their faces to Daniel and the camera, Pastor Derek said, "Why, that's Devon Hannah! He's the guy who started Remgold." It was more of an exclamation than statement of fact. Most people would have recognized his face. "Who is the other man?"

"That's Jacques Decantes," said Janine. "He's a big shot politician in France. Some people thought back then that he was going to be their leader one day."

When they got to the part of the video where Daniel had bid his goodbye to Marin, Janine saw tears in Pastor Derek's eyes. Buddy's face remained expressionless.

On the second viewing, when the video ended shortly after Devon Hannah took Daniel's life, Pastor Derek looked at Janine. She was sitting there just rocking back and forth, her eyes focused somewhere in the past. Her cheery, youthful demeanor was gone. To Derek, it looked as if Janine had aged ten years. As a pastor, he had counseled and prayed with people struggling with diverse personal challenges. Still, most of them were run-of-the-mill issues. It was not every day that he encountered evil at this level of intensity and awfulness.

44

He broke the silence and said, "Janine, honey, I'm going to have to leave and get back to Sherry and the kids. Before I go, I'd like to say a prayer with you, okay?"

Janine nodded slightly.

Pastor Derek looked up and said, "God, I've never seen anything like this. My heart is breaking for the things I've seen, and I know your heart must be breaking, too. You see all of this every day. God, right now we all need your wisdom on what to do and how to handle the problems that Buddy and Janine are facing. Please show us the way. I also pray your divine protection over the Akers and their property. Put your angels here in force. Let them know that you really are watching over them. And please help Janine. She's been carrying a heavy burden for a long time. In Jesus' name I pray. Amen."

When he got up, he made eye contact with Buddy and said, "Can I talk to you for a moment outside?"

Once they were outside, Derek looked straight at Buddy and said, "Buddy, I know all of this has to be a shock to you. But the biggest thing I want you to know is that you aren't alone in this. I know you may still be on the outside looking in when it comes to church and all, but I count you as family just the same. You'll be hearing from me tomorrow after I make a few calls." He stuck out his hand.

Buddy was looking straight back at Pastor Derek. He grabbed his hand in a firm grip. "Thank you, Derek. That means a lot to us. I'm going to go back and check on Janine."

When Buddy walked back in the house, he walked over to Janine and stood in front of her, indicating he was ready to head to bed. Janine's shoulders started shaking. To him, she looked like a little girl frozen in the face of danger. "Hold me, Buddy!" she cried out.

Buddy sat down and wrapped both of his big arms around her. Janine grasped handfuls of his shirt, burrowed her face into his chest, and began to sob uncontrollably. Buddy held her there all night.

Chapter 9

Philadelphia, Pennsylvania

Stefani Anderson was a petite and somewhat-frail-looking girl of eighteen years. A naturally light blonde, she had an uncommon beauty and particularly large eyes. The way they kept darting around the room gave the overall impression that she was haunted by powerful specters. Her hands alternated between brushing her hair out of her face and reaching down to pull her skirt over her knees.

She could have been a model. Indeed, that was the type of ad she had answered three years ago, one that had been plastered over several of the utility poles in her hometown. The posters promised a free photoshoot with a professional photographer, a custom portfolio she could use to promote her talent, and an introduction to an industry executive. Stefani's home life alternated between staying out as late as she could to avoid her mother's many boyfriends and skipping as much school as she could. One night, she decided that things couldn't get any worse than they were and that if she actually could get a break into the modeling business, they could get way better. She even fantasized about making enough money to come back and save her mother from the lifestyle she had spiraled into.

Stefani made contact with the person at the number listed and was encouraged to show up for an appointment. The person assured her that they had a modeling wardrobe and a makeup artist. With that settled, two days later, she skipped school and made her way to the end unit of a strip mall in the older part of town. Entering, she was greeted by a woman, the same one who had answered the phone based on her voice. She introduced herself as Maggie to Stefani. Maggie took a long, appraising look at Stefani and then complimented her on her beauty. She seemed pleased, although her smile seemed more like that of a hawk than an angel.

Maggie showed Stefani to a well-furnished room that had clothes of all styles and sizes. There were floor-to-ceiling mirrors on part of one wall. She helped pick out several outfits that were Stefani's size and let her choose the three she liked best.

"Go ahead and change, dear," Maggie said. "I'll let Matthew know that you'll be ready in thirty minutes. I'll be back in to do your makeup in a moment."

After she left, Stefani looked around the room in wonder. Was it happening? Was this her new beginning?

The photoshoot with Matthew went well. He was very affirming in his words and kept commenting on how beautiful she was. Maggie certainly knew how to do makeup just right. Stefani was asked to do a variety of poses sitting, standing, and leaning against props. When it was over, she was invited to come back in three days to review her portfolio photos.

In that meeting, Stefani was overwhelmed at the sight of her own image on a humongous screen. She looked beautiful. She felt beautiful. Matthew had picked out twenty of the best photos and had copied them to a thumb drive.

"Based on how well you did, there may be a chance for you to meet one of our sponsors. But we need to know more about you. Tell us a little bit about your parents, first."

Stefani turned her gaze back to the screen. "There's not much to tell. My dad and mom split up when I was seven. I haven't seen him since. My mom started drinking after that. She...she takes pills and things now."

Stefani missed the knowing look that passed between the two adults. With this revelation, her course was set. The rest of the questions were mostly generic. They probed a bit more about her relationships with family and then friends at school. Anyone with life experience could see that Stefani was a troubled teen who was in a very vulnerable state. This fact was not missed by Matthew or Maggie. They had found another girl to put into the pipeline.

Now, three years later as she sat in Happy's office, Stefani was having a hard time concentrating. It had been just two days since she had been set free from the prison her life had become. A joint task force investigation between DHS, the U.S. Marshals, and local law enforcement had led to the arrest of a prominent businessman. Stefani was found in a locked building inside the compound—locked from the outside.

There were four girls who were rescued. If the investigators had been a day earlier, they would have freed four more who had been moved by private jet to Palm Beach for a party. If they had come a day later, the nest would have been empty. The mole who normally informed the trafficking syndicate of the progress of investigations had been seriously incapacitated by the latest Chinese flu variant and was out of the loop. Thus, the raid and arrest happened without a hitch.

The other three girls were minors and had been reunited with their parents within forty-eight hours. Because Stefani was an adult, the lead investigator with local law enforcement had asked her if she wanted to be given a trip home or something else. Stefani asked what her options were, and the investigator had informed her that the Gospel Mission in downtown Philadelphia had recently begun offering a new program for girls like her. She pulled out a newly printed brochure and handed it to Stefani to look at.

The brochure was entitled "Tamar's Refuge," an intriguing name that meant little to Stefani. What she did notice was the photo with the two African-American people in it: brother and sister, from the description. The brother's eyes exuded honesty and love. The sister looked more serious but just as honest.

"I'd like to go here," she said.

And that is how she found herself seated in the Gospel Mission on a Wednesday morning, nervously looking around and wondering if she had made the right decision. The door to the office opened, and the man whom she recognized from the brochure walked in with a pleasant smile on his face.

"I'm Billy Lewis," he said. "But everybody just calls me Happy. You must be Stefani."

Stefani gave a timid nod in response.

"Well, Stefani, I want you to know that I'm glad that you chose to come here. The reason I'm glad is that we have this big new building God gave to us, and we've been praying that God would send us the right people to help. And here you done come to us out of the blue."

His dark eyes searched hers for a few moments. Then he continued. "You're going to have to forgive us if we don't seem like a big professional outfit. Truth is, you're our first customer. Well, that's only partly true. You see, I've been a minister of the Gospel of Jesus Christ most of my life. I used to run the original Old Gospel Mission that was located on this site, and I've worked with all kinds of people—the down-and-out, alcohol and drug addictions, prostitutes and suicidal."

When he said the word "prostitutes," Stefani noticeably flinched. Happy sighed. "Stefani, I can see I done upset you, and I ask you to forgive me for that."

Stefani lowered her face and put her fingers to her lips. "No. It's okay. That's what I am, isn't it?"

Happy sighed again. The welcome interview with his first trafficking victim was not going well. "Stefani, would you please look at me just a moment?" He waited until she slightly raised her face and looked at him before continuing. "Stefani, I want you to know that what you have been through—and I'm sure I don't even know the half of it—was not your fault. I want you to listen to me very carefully when I say this: the only true help I can offer you is to point you to Jesus, but He is able to restore your life into something truly beautiful. I know that for a fact because I've seen Him do it over and over again with people throughout my whole life. I know it, Stefani, because He's done it for me, too."

A single tear from her right eye rolled down Stefani's cheek. "I want to believe you," she said. "But I don't know how."

"Then we'll just start right there with you wanting to believe," said Happy. "Faith ain't a feeling, anyhow. Somehow, I think faith is more like the direction you're headed in. And I think you're saying that what you really want is a new direction. Am I right?"

A second tear from the left eye began its parallel track down her skin. "Yes," she said. "I want that more than anything else in my life."

49

"All right then. I'm not sure what all you know about praying, but what I want you to learn is that praying is just talking to God like you would talk to me or any other person. Would you just say what you told me to God directly?"

Stefani hesitated for a few moments. Her mind raced back to the day she had gone for her modeling photoshoot. She had wondered if that was going to be the day that changed her life. How true that was. Now she was faced with another choice, another question. Was she about to get into a worse dilemma? A panic raced over her, and she had to fight the urge to flee from the room, this place, this gently smiling man. Everyone smiled when they wanted something.

Then, another question intruded on her panic. Where would she go? She couldn't go back. There was nothing but fear and pain. She felt a tic spasm her face. Quietly, she spoke. "God...God, I don't even know if you're real. But if you are, I want a new direction."

As she finished the words, a convulsion wracked her body. Too much pain and too many memories flooded her all at once. She began to cry tears of deep, bitter pain. Happy placed a box of tissues on the table beside her and wisely kept a handful for himself as he returned to his chair to let the Savior begin His work of healing a broken life.

Chapter 10

Sand Mountain, Alabama

Things moved quicker than any of them would have expected. Wednesday morning, Pastor Derek made some calls to the other pastors. The visitors to the area had been rather prolific and detailed in their approach. Every pastor in the county had been visited with the exception of three, and Derek had no doubt that they were on the list. In addition, they had hit the convenience stores, hardware store, and food markets. While the pastors had all responded similarly to Derek, he figured that it would only be a matter of time before the men hit pay dirt somewhere.

His next call was to the sheriff, Matt Walton, who attended his church along with two of his deputies. They all met for lunch at a county restaurant where Pastor Derek laid out the situation. With Buddy's permission, he included some of the details of the video he had watched the night before.

"What are you thinking?" asked Matt.

"Well, Buddy seems like the kind of man who can handle some things himself, but it would probably help to make things a bit more legal if you would deputize him and maybe some of the other men in the church or in the area."

"Sounds like a plan," said Matt. He turned to his deputies and said, "Keep an eye out for these guys. If you see them, just call in their whereabouts."

To Derek, he said, "Pastor, I don't want you involved in any of this other than organizing. You got young kids and a flock to attend to."

"Okay, Matt. I don't mind defending my family or neighbors if it comes to it, but I'll submit to your authority on this."

By 2 p.m., Derek informed Buddy that he needed to be at the Sheriff's offices by 4 p.m. When Buddy arrived, the gravel parking lot was packed.

Men were leaning against their pickup trucks and cars talking. A few more vehicles pulled in after Buddy. He spotted Pastor Derek talking to Sheriff Matt. He made eye contact and walked over greeting neighbors as he went.

"Matt. Derek. What's going on?"

"Pastor here called around and told people that you and Janine might be in some trouble. So I'm going to deputize the lot of you and give you some guidelines so that, hopefully, everybody is shooting at the same target."

After calling the crowd of men together, the sheriff said, "You all know generally why you're here. To explain a bit further, there's at least two men, strangers to these parts, that have been posing as insurance company employees asking questions trying to locate Janine. In reality, they're lying scoundrels who're up to no good, maybe even to the point of doing Janine harm if they were to get half a chance. Pastor Derek said they were driving a black SUV with Georgia plates: Fulton County, specifically. It's a good possibility that these men are either ex-law enforcement or ex-military and trained. Because of that, we've got to be real careful like about how we approach them. If they get wind that we know what they're really here for, they could tuck tail and run, or they could fight like a mountain lion after a young calf. Plus, we don't know if they're working with anybody else or if it's just the two of them at the moment."

He looked around at the crowd. Nobody was flinching. "There's only the one county road that passes by the lane that leads down to the Akers' farm, and a body would have to pass by two other farms to get there. In other words, if you're going out that way, you should have a reason. Now, everybody raise your right hand and repeat after me while I deputize you. Then I'm going to tell what I want you to do."

Chapter 11

Fifteen minutes later, the trucks started to head out. Some were headed home to take a nap in anticipation of night shift. The sheriff and each of his paid deputies would oversee small groups of the newly deputized. They would patrol the roads in the general vicinity of the Akers farm. At night, they would park in or around one or more of the outbuildings along the lane and keep watch on the approaches. The problem was, nobody knew how long it would be before the strangers might actually find Buddy and Janine.

In the end, that question was answered at church that night. Buddy wasn't sure that Janine should be going out, but Janine said nothing was going to stop her from worshiping with her church family. As they pulled into the parking lot, Buddy noticed a black SUV parked near the entrance. The windows were tinted, but the late summer sun was streaming through the trees just enough to outline a person in the front passenger seat. That meant someone was probably in the driver seat, too. Somebody in the county had recognized enough of an old photo to point them in the right direction.

"Janine…" he began to say.

"I see 'em, Buddy. I already told you, I'm not gonna let them keep me from worshiping God."

Buddy sighed and parked as near the building as he could. But they still had a walk of fifteen or so steps from the vehicle to the front door. Buddy had no doubt that the men were using binoculars or cameras or something to zoom in on everyone entering the church that evening.

The service went well, given the fact that several of the men in the congregation made it a point to ask Buddy if he had seen the vehicle and that there was a heightened sense of tension in the building. There was singing. Pastor Derek preached a sermon. They had prayer at the end. When they exited the building, the SUV was gone.

As a group of men stood with Buddy just outside the door, one of them asked Buddy what his plans were.

"Well, my first job is to check our truck out." That said, he walked to it and felt around the bumper and under the wheel wells. His hand stopped for a moment and then pulled out a small device. He looked at it and then returned it to its place.

"GPS tracker," he said to Pastor Derek and two of the other men who had joined him. "Looks like we'll be expecting company tonight."

"I'll let Sheriff Matt know what happened," said Derek. "You all be careful driving home."

"We will," said Buddy. He motioned to Janine, who was still by the front door. As they drove off, he could see Pastor Derek on the phone and the other two men pulling out to shadow their vehicle from a safe distance.

When they arrived at the farm, Buddy drove slowly down the gravel driveway past the barn off to the side and up to the house. Nothing seemed amiss. Most importantly, Midnight came out to meet them.

"They ain't been here yet," said Buddy.

Regardless, after they went inside, he did a room-by-room search to make sure nothing was amiss. Then he gave Janine instructions to get a blanket and some pillows and helped her get set up in the pantry. Away from the windows, it provided at least a modicum of security and a time buffer in case someone were to forcibly break into the house. He left a shotgun with a short barrel and a handgun with her.

"Use the shotgun first, and aim for the face. It's loaded with buckshot. Better chance of stopping somebody that way."

"Where are you going?" she asked.

"I'll be outside watching. I'll check in with you again, but it may well be after midnight." He looked down at the guns beside her. "I'll be sure to holler first."

He left her and went to the bedroom, where he pulled on a set of completely black clothing, including a thin balaclava and gloves. He applied some eye black to the exposed part of his face. Then he unlocked a gun cabinet and selected some gear, including a pair of night vision goggles and his favorite AR-15. When he was finished, he turned off the lights in the house. Then he slipped out and locked the back door to the screened-in porch, where he listened and scanned the area at the back of the house with the night vision goggles. Seeing nothing, he opened the screen door and went around the darker side of the house to the firewood shed, which was set off about fifteen yards and gave him a clear view of the approaches to the front and rear of the house.

When he was settled behind a half rick of hickory, he gave a low bird whistle. Less than ten seconds later, Midnight nuzzled up next to him.

"Lie down," he commanded. Midnight lay down and put his muzzle down on his front paws next to Buddy's leg. "Now we wait," he said.

Chapter 12

Around 1 a.m., Buddy felt Midnight's body tense. He raised himself up with his ears erect. Twenty seconds later, Buddy could hear the distant crunch of gravel underneath tires. Someone was coming down the lane off the highway—without lights. The vehicle drove just past the driveway entrance and then backed in about five yards. The rear lights had been masked with tape or plastic so that there was no illumination from brake lights. Buddy put the night vision goggles up to his eyes. It appeared to be the same SUV.

Midnight strained forward, but Buddy said, "No." He looked through the goggles as the doors opened quietly, and two men exited, one on each side. They apparently had comm gear because they branched off from each other. One headed down toward the left and the other to the right. When they were within fifteen or twenty yards from the house, they each stopped. Their separation was going to make things a bit more interesting. Either way, Buddy was determined that they were not going to get into the house.

As chance would have it, the man closest to Buddy seemed to decide that the window Buddy had left open on this end of the house would be the best means of entry. He must have radioed his partner because he joined him in a low run across the front of the yard a few seconds later. They had a hurried communication between them and then approached the house together. One pulled out what appeared to be a handgun while the other pulled out a tool of some other kind. The latter walked to the window screen and began prying it out of the frame.

At that point, Buddy leveled his rifle toward the one with the pistol. He didn't want to shoot toward his own house, but he knew Janine was safe inside the pantry. He leaned down and whispered in Midnight's ear. The Shepherd quietly slid out of the woodshed and disappeared into the darkness to the left. When Buddy looked back at the pair, the screen was about halfway out. He put his finger on the trigger and, in a loud voice, said, "Freeze!"

In an instant, several things happened. First, the man removing the screen dropped his hold on the screen and spun around. His right hand was going down by his side. The second man with the pistol lifted it in Buddy's general direction and fired off two rapid shots. The gun must have been silenced because the loudest sound was the bullets splitting into the stack of hickory. Without being fazed, Buddy squeezed the trigger three times in rapid succession with the rifle centered on the man's core.

By this time, the first man had removed his own pistol from his holster and was extending his arm. He had heard the shots and heard his companion grunt and then cry out from the impact. Before he could pull his own trigger, a black mass from his right launched itself as Midnight seized the man's wrist in his mouth and bit down with all his might. The dog's momentum carried the man to the ground, and he began thrashing and trying to protect himself while simultaneously trying to kick out at Midnight.

Buddy dashed over and first glanced to see if the second man was moving. He was not. As Buddy turned back to the first man, he saw him reach down with his left arm toward his ankle.

"Drop it!" he shouted. But the man had already pulled out a knife and was readying his arm to swing toward Midnight's side.

In an instant, Buddy fired two more shots at the man's torso. He stiffened in pain. Then the knife dropped from his hand.

"Release," said Buddy. Midnight dropped the man's wrist and then sat next to the man. Buddy took the night vision goggles off and flicked a flashlight on. Both men were motionless, but he wasn't taking any chances. He knelt down by the first man and checked his pulse. Nothing. Then he checked the second man, whom he had hit first. No pulse there either.

"Guard," he said to Midnight. Then he walked to the back porch, unlocked the door, and stepped in.

"Janine!" he called. "You can come out now."

There was a rustle, and then the pantry light came on. Janine came walking around the corner with the shotgun gripped in both hands.

"Buddy, are you all right?" she asked.

"Yes. I'm fine. But our visitors aren't."

"Did you kill them?" she asked as her eyes widened.

"Yes." He paused. "I had to. One shot at me. The other tried to, but Midnight got him. Then he tried to kill Midnight."

Janine lowered the shotgun and slumped against the wall. "Do you want me to call the Sheriff?"

Buddy looked up and nodded toward the front of the house. "Sheriff's out there right now, I reckon. I've got to get something out of my closet, and then I'll be heading out there. You stay inside until we get this sorted out, okay?"

Janine nodded. She heard Buddy walk down the hallway to the bedroom and then return again. He flipped the porch light on and walked outside. Janine put some water on to make coffee. Somebody would want a cup before the night was done, she was sure.

Buddy walked up the driveway, where Sheriff Matt and a deputy were beginning to walk toward the house holding flashlights with their guns drawn. Their lights played across his figure and face.

"Everything okay, Buddy?" asked Matt.

"Yes, at least now it is." He pointed to the side of the house, and the party began heading that way.

"Johnny and Clarence were sitting up the road and saw when they came by. They radioed it in. I told them to sit tight while we came out this way. Then they called and said they heard several gunshots. Them boys were itching to come on down, but I made them wait. No telling who they might of shot at in the dark."

Sheriff Matt shone his light along the side of the house. Midnight was still in position eyeing both the bodies, but they weren't moving. "What happened, exactly?" he asked.

"The big one was using something to pry the screen out. The other had a pistol and was keeping watch. I shouted for them to freeze. The small one took two shots at me before I hit him. The other dropped his tool and got his pistol. He was fast. Midnight got him by the arm, but he got a knife out and was going to kill him. I had to act quickly."

"He's a good dog," said Matt. "Good dogs can't be replaced so easily." He sighed. "I hate that it come to this, Buddy. Is Janine all right?"

"I think she's a little shell-shocked, but she'll be fine."

"Well, I'll call Don and have him bring the ice wagon over and pick 'em up. We may be able to ID them and find out a little about who they are and what they were really doing here."

"Before you do that, I need to check them first," said Buddy.

"For what?" asked Matt.

"I have a suspicion they may be wired up." Buddy walked over to the larger of the two men and turned on a handheld device about the size of a cell phone. He ran it down the man's body until he got to the thigh, where it beeped. Then he ran it down his leg and got another beep at the man's right boot. He did the same with the second body and got the same results.

Then he took out a hunting knife and worked on the flesh right above the knee. Sheriff Matt and his men watched with curiosity, as if Buddy were dressing a hog or a deer. He extracted a silver-looking capsule about the size of a large vitamin.

"Tracker," he said holding it up. "They've been in the special forces, or they got them after they became mercs." He did the same thing with the second man's leg and then stood up. "I need to go wash these off. I think I smell coffee. You fellows want to step in for a minute and get a cup?'

Sheriff Matt looked down at the bodies. "They ain't going anywhere. Sure."

The men went into the house by the front door. Janine greeted the visitors and offered them each a cup of coffee and then returned to the kitchen to prepare the cups. Buddy walked to the sink and began washing the capsules. Janine watched as he cleaned the blood off his hands and the devices.

59

"What in tarnation are those, Buddy?"

"Satellite trackers. They each had one in their leg."

"How did you even think about that?"

He looked down at her. "We all had one implanted. If you were in special forces, you got one."

"Do you still have one of those in your leg?" she asked with a look of concern.

"I removed mine when I got out. They don't own me, and they weren't going to be able to keep tracking me."

"Good," she said as she let out a sigh. "Why did you remove them? What are you going to do with them?"

"First, I want you to take a couple of good pictures of them. Then we're going to send their masters on a wild goose chase."

"Why would you do that? If they're tracking them, they'll know they've been here, Buddy. They probably told their leaders what they were doing anyway."

"It might buy us some time."

"Time for what?"

"Time before they send the next crew."

With that, Buddy passed through the living room and headed out the door. He returned several minutes later with the two pairs of boots, which he offered to Sheriff Matt. Matt raised an eye at him.

"I've put the tracker from their legs in the sole along with the other device that's in the boot itself. Do you reckon you can find a way to move these out of the county pretty quickly?"

Matt thought for a moment and then answered. "Yep. We've got a few transients that I might convince to move along if I offered them some money and a really nice pair of boots."

Buddy smiled. "That'll be just fine, Sheriff."

A knock at the door notified them that Don, the county coroner, had arrived. He was a wiry man, nearing retirement. He had seen his share of excitement on the mountain through the years. He accepted Janine's offer of a cup of coffee and sat down on one of the chairs. Addressing Matt, he said, "You said you have a couple of bodies for me to pick up. Do you need me to do a formal workup on them?"

"No," said Matt. "Cause of death is lead poisoning. I mainly want to work on trying to find out their identity. You can note any unusual marks, tattoos, or things like that. Take good photos if you find anything. That's important. They can be cremated when you're done. I don't think anyone will be calling to claim the bodies."

As everyone prepared to leave, Matt said to Buddy, "I'll head on over to the shelter now. There's a couple of the panhandlers who are due for some new scenery. I'll even offer to drive them to the bus stop and get them each a ticket to someplace fun. I'll also have a couple of the boys take the SUV and drive it down the mountain after we give it the once-over for any useful details. If they leave the keys in it at a rest area on the interstate, it will be in Mississippi or Tennessee soon enough. Probably has some kind of GPS tracker in it, too."

Buddy said, "No doubt. Thanks, Sheriff. You know this doesn't end here tonight, right? Whoever sent these two is gonna send more. Probably a lot more."

"Then we'll just have to be ready for them, won't we?" With that, Matt turned and walked out the door.

Buddy walked back to the sink and washed his hands thoroughly with soap and hot water. Then he poured a cup of coffee and sat beside Janine. He put his arm around her and drew her close.

"What have I done, Buddy?" asked Janine.

"Shh," he whispered into her hair. "You ain't done nothin' wrong." As he held his wife and sipped coffee, he wondered just how far these people would be willing to go.

Chapter 13

Philadelphia, Pennsylvania

After almost an hour of crying, then resting, then crying some more, Stefani was done. Happy sat with her quietly in the stillness of the room until she looked up and broke the silence.

"I wasn't expecting all of that," she said.

"Nothing to be sorry for," said Happy. "All of us need a good cry now and again."

"I haven't cried like that since..." her voice trailed off. "Since my Daddy left home."

"Well, Stefani, I think your heart has been looking for a safe place to rest for a long time. That's what we're offering you here. Our hope is that over the coming weeks and months, you will be able to find out more about who you really are and be able to confront some of the fears that you've lived with for a while."

"I really hope so," said Stefani. Her face was a torrid mess of mascara and tear streams. Her nose was red, and her eyes were puffy from all the crying.

"You met my sister Sarah already," said Happy. "She's the one who greeted you and brought you to my office. I want her to show you to your room and get you settled. Then we'll all have a good lunch and talk about some plans for the future."

Happy went to the office door and called for Sarah. After a minute, she came to the doorway and took charge of Stefani. She showed her to a room on the third floor. Up and away from the street, it was furnished with a bed covered by a pink comforter, a plush pillow, and a headboard with a built-in bookshelf. There was a side table big enough for a lamp and small assorted items and a chest of drawers. In one corner, there was a desk and chair. In another corner was a small armchair. The lights gave off a warm glow instead of an institutional, sterile white. There was a scent of lavender in the air which Stefani recognized was coming from a diffuser on the nightstand. A door on one wall led to a bath and shower. Sarah showed Stefani into the room and acquainted her with the towels and washcloths. Stefani noticed that the medicine cabinet was stocked with basic hygienic supplies, and the shower rack had an assortment of shampoo, conditioner, and body wash. There was even a new loofah hanging from one arm.

"You can wash up. Take your time. Lunch won't be for another thirty minutes. After we eat, we'll go shopping and try to find you a few outfits. We can't have you living in the same clothes day after day, can we?"

"No. I guess not," said Stefani. "Thank you."

"You're welcome. Just make yourself at home. One of us will call for you when lunch is ready."

With that, Sarah departed, closing the door behind her. Stefani had a brief moment of panic until she walked to the door and looked. The lock was on the inside. She closed her eyes and let out a deep sigh. She reached down, pushed the button on the handle, and twisted the thumb turn. Then she went into the bathroom and took the longest, most relaxing hot shower she had had in years.

Chapter 14

Over a lunch of grilled cheese and bell pepper sandwiches with a side garden salad, Happy and Sarah took turns talking to one another with an occasional question to Stefani. For her part, Stefani liked how they just included her in their conversation. The questions they asked her were natural. Where was she from originally? A small town just outside of Raleigh, North Carolina. What kind of books did she like to read? Dystopian now, but she used to love to read biographies of people when she was younger. Did she have any siblings? None. They talked with one another about the best places to shop and how to get there.

After lunch, Sarah took Stefani out to a handful of thrift stores in the area.

"It might be a challenge finding you some clothes," she said. "What size are you anyway, child?"

"I'm a 00 petite," said Stefani. "More or less."

Sarah grunted an "Mmm-hmmm" in response. "I'd say less than more, but we can at least start looking."

At the third store, they hit the jackpot. Someone small must have either had a life change or decided to empty a wardrobe. Stefani was able to find ten nice outfits. Sarah pointed out a couple of pairs of older denim jeans.

"Happy said to make sure you got some clothes you can get dirty in," Sarah said.

Matched with a few slightly oversized T-shirts and some tennis shoes, that request was fulfilled, and the trip was deemed to be an overall success by both women. While Sarah did not exactly effuse warmth, Stefani could sense that the woman was doing what she was doing because of genuine concern.

They stopped by a retail store to pick up new undergarments because, as Sarah said, "Ain't nobody got any business buying somebody else's used undergarments," and then headed back. When they arrived, Sarah urged Stefani to take her purchases and pick one to wear for the rest of the day. "The rest we'll put in the wash and get the thrift store smell out of them. Do you know how to use a washer and dryer?"

Stefani did. They started a load washing, and then Stefani went to change—everything. She looked for several seconds at the pile of clothes she had worn to the mission that morning. Without another word, she took them and stuffed them into the wastebasket. She hoped Sarah would understand. She never wanted to see them again.

Chapter 15

Sand Mountain, Alabama

After the initial attack, when Buddy had located and removed the tracking devices from each of the mercs, he had snapped several photos with his phone. Then he inserted them back into the boots. After letting Janine rest a few hours, the next morning, he walked into the bedroom.

Janine was curled up clutching a pillow tightly to her chest. She had always been beautiful to him, but now she looked frail and vulnerable. He brushed her hair back from her face and called her name softly. Her eyes popped open immediately. There was a flash of fear; then her eyes found his face and focused on it. She managed a smile.

"What time is it?" she asked.

"Ten," Buddy said. "I've got breakfast ready for you."

Over plates of eggs and toast, Buddy said, "Do you know how to send a message to the people who are hunting you?"

Janine's eyes searched his face. "What are you getting at, Buddy?"

"Just answer me. Do you know how to get a message to them?"

"Not directly. But there are probably a couple of indirect ways that might work."

"Then I want you to do it."

"What are you wanting to say?"

"I want to make it clear that they lost the first round and tell them to back off."

"You know they won't, Buddy. These people are sick, and they're powerful."

"I also want to give them a warning that if they try again, there will be bigger consequences."

Janine sighed a deep sigh. She mentally relived the journey from abuse victim to support group member to an unwitting participant in an event that had forever altered the landscape of her life. Over the years, she had wavered in her mind as to whether or not she would go back and undo it all if she had the chance. Part of her still wished she had never left her innocence—as abused as it had been—and had never partaken of the tree of the knowledge of just how evil some people were. Still, the fact that such people existed and even seemed to prosper made her glad that she knew. The fact that she possessed such knowledge was a threat to those people, and this gave her a measure of strength.

"Okay," she said. She looked at Buddy again. He looked so somber. She realized she hadn't seen him smile since their lives had been interrupted by news of people searching for her. Now that she thought about it, she hadn't smiled much either. "Buddy?"

He looked at her expectantly.

"Buddy, I love you so much!"

His face softened just a bit.

"And you know what else?"

"What?"

"You need a bath!"

That brought a smile to his face. Janine emitted another deep sigh and smiled just a little herself. Maybe, just maybe, they would get through this together.

With the tension broken, she cleaned up the breakfast dishes while Buddy went to shower. She brought her laptop into the dining room. Sitting at the table, she opened up a document and went through a series of steps she had followed religiously years ago. Some of the steps had changed, but the gist was the same. Try your best to mask your identity.

She wasn't sure that it mattered. These people knew where she lived now. But given that there was more than one group of evil people and that some of the people in the groups worked for the governments and law enforcement agencies around the world, it wouldn't hurt to hide her identity as much as possible.

Over the next two hours, she visited numerous public websites and used the contact forms to send messages to the people whom their group had identified as being part of the "Black Castle group." Well, she was probably sending them to a low-level assistant. But maybe some of the messages would get through. And if just one did, she was sure it would reverberate. It wasn't like she had the personal cell numbers of these people.

Each message was the same. There were two images. She included a photo of the trackers that had been embedded in the legs of the attackers and a photo of the two pairs of boots sitting side by side. The text in the message read:

```
Chateau Sauvageon
Walk away
DangleDrop
```

It was straight and to the point. At least one assistant would probably consider it strange enough to bring it to the attention of one of the principals. Janine included a link to a public Internet forum known for its free-wheeling atmosphere where she had posted the exact same message at the beginning. Any replies would be posted there.

She shut down all the connections and closed the laptop. Someone would send a message back. Of that, she was sure. Right now, it was time for lunch.

Chapter 16

Cyberspace

On a computer located somewhere in the world, a pinging sound alerted the owner that an important matter needed to be reviewed. After clicking on the alert, one of several message boards that were consistently researched opened up to a post with the word "DangleDrop" in it.

After studying the two images intently for several minutes and doing a cursory search on Chateau Sauvageon, the user began typing a message:

```
After years of waiting, it looks like we may
have something solid on DangleDrop.  All hands
on deck!
```

The user hit the send button. While waiting for the others, the analysis of the boots might prove to be interesting. And what were those capsules? This looked very promising indeed.

Chapter 17

Philadelphia, Pennsylvania

"Put your left index finger on the F key and your right index finger on the J key," Happy said to Stefani. He waited while she did that. "Now line up the other three fingers on each hand so that they rest on the other keys. Your thumbs will just kind fit right on the space bar."

He and Sarah had been in agreement that anything practical they could teach to the trafficking victims God placed in their care would be of value as they tried to establish their lives. Typing was something Happy knew. Cooking was something Sarah knew. This was Stefani's first lesson.

"There's a bump on those keys. I can feel it," Stefani said.

"That's right. That didn't used to be on the old manual typewriters or even the early computer keyboards. Somebody got the bright idea of adding those. That way you could feel what was the right key even in the dark. Now we're gonna do your first lesson in typing the same way I learned it years ago. We're gonna go back and forth on these keys until you know them by heart and by muscle memory. When I say the letter, you type it. Make sure the right one shows up on the screen. F, J, F, J, F, J, F, J, F, F, J, J, F, F, J, J."

On and on Happy recited while Stefani struck the keys. He watched the screen with her and nodded his approval. "Good. Now I'm going to put a piece of paper over here, and you read it and type the letters as you read them yourself."

Over and over, Stefani typed with both oral and written dictation until about twenty minutes had passed. Happy said, "All right. We'll give your fingers a break before we add in another couple of letters. Do you have any questions?"

"Yes," said Stefani. "Why do we start with these letters? Why not..."

she paused as she looked at the keyboard, "Why not 3, or the letter L, or something else?"

"That's a good question. The answer is, in order to succeed in learning to type, you have to have a starting point and a reference point. The most commonly used letters are spread out so that not just one finger hits them all the time. But as your fingers fly around the keyboard, and trust me, they will learn to go faster in no time, your hands have to have that reference point to know where they are at all times. Otherwise, you'd be typing gibberish. My teacher used to call it the resting place for the fingers."

He paused and looked at Stefani. She looked back at him, waiting on him to continue.

"It's like real life, Stefani. If we don't have a reference point or a resting place, our lives just bustle about with no way to know that what we are doing is making any sense."

"And you would say that God is your reference point," Stefani said.

"I'd say that a person can have several. One of them is certainly God. If we find our meaning and our reason for existing in Him, it makes everything else fall into line. But I'd also say that knowing that another person or group of people really love you can serve as a reference point. We can find a powerful lot of strength if we know that we're loved, not just by God but by real flesh and blood people here on Earth."

Stefani pondered that. "I can't say that I've ever felt that since my parents split up. I used to think my Daddy loved me, but I don't know why he left me." She paused for a few seconds and then said, "I do feel safe here with you and Sarah, though. I don't know why you are taking me in and helping me. And sometimes I still question your motives. I hope that doesn't offend you. But you both have been nicer to me than anyone I've met in a long time without asking anything in return. Maybe this place can be my place of rest." She smiled a hopeful smile up at him.

Happy smiled back. "We hope it is too. Now, let's see if you can learn D and G as good as you did the first two letters. On your left hand, your middle finger rests on D..." he said as the next lesson began.

Chapter 18

Sand Mountain, Alabama

Punji stick traps were used to great effect in the Vietnam war. Usually, a pit two feet deep or more is dug in the ground. Then, bamboo or other sharpened material is placed deep into the earth so that it will hold firm. The top of the pit is covered with a loose frame of branches, and the frame is covered with leaves or other natural, local material to disguise the mouth of the pit. In the larger varieties of pits, a large animal could be caught and perhaps killed. With the smaller version, a human's weight would drive the foot and lower leg onto the spikes, thereby impaling the extremity. The pain would be unbearable. The psychological damage inflicted on an army or a team is also severe. If the punji sticks were covered with urine and feces, it would hasten serious infection which could result in the loss of the limb or even death if not treated immediately.

As he placed the thick oak board studded with number 80D nails in the bottom of the hole, Buddy made sure that the ground was flat and level. The nails had been sharpened on his bench grinder to fine points. They were spaced unevenly but about an average of three inches apart. Only a child's foot—and a lucky one at that—would be able to miss hitting at least one. An adult would probably catch two or more. He had coated each of the spikes with a mixture of rat poison and petroleum jelly.

Buddy had reckoned on another night visit from the next team. And he was pretty certain that there probably would be at least four and as many as eight members. While he could hold his own in a fair fight, he wanted to create a little havoc for his uninvited guests. He spent the next few days preparing a suitable reception for them.

After checking the property from multiple angles, he determined that the most likely entry points would be from a patch of woods that bordered the fence near the back side of the house, a path that led away from the barn in the front along a very mild swell, or a direct approach from the road and driveway. Most likely, they would use a combination of at least two of those. Everything else was just too open and flat. Living on top of a mountain did have its advantages.

The woods were thick enough that getting through them in the dark would be a challenge, even with night vision equipment. There was one game trail through the trees, and Buddy was sure any mercenary worth his salt would find it quickly enough. It was here that he placed three traps. One was in the middle of the path, and two were at the egress point as the path left the woods. He also placed a couple of WiFi-enabled game cameras at different angles up in the trees.

The path leaving the barn was a different matter. Out in the open with only a slight hill to block a bit of the view to the house (or from the house, if you were an attacker), a hole in the ground would be difficult to blend in with the surroundings unless the grass were high, and Buddy was not going to give them the advantage of using grass as a cover. After mowing the grass for hay, he went down to the local co-op and bought a few rolls of high-tensile barbed wire. With a load strength of over 1,000 pounds, it's designed to be pulled taut: very taut, in fact.

After installing a few sets of wooden posts as H braces along the slope, Buddy had the makings of what appeared to be some simple cross fencing one would expect to see dotting the landscape of rural Alabama. His was a bit different in that one end of each strand of wire was locked down to an H brace by wrapping around the post entirely and then twisting it seven times around itself. The other end was formed into a similar loop, which was pulled extremely tight with a come-along tool and then attached to a simple latch with a quick-release pin.

Each of the four strands of barbed wire was rigged in alternating fashion: one end was attached firmly to an H brace with the quick release on the other end. Then, all the quick-release pins on the latches were connected to a strong steel filament that was placed ankle-high about three feet away from the fence on the same side as the barn and house. It was a simple tripwire system used the world over, but it was nearly invisible during the day unless you were looking for it. At night, using no lights, it would be virtually undetectable. For the most part, it looked just like a standard four-strand barbed wire fence designed to keep in cattle. Two more game cameras mounted on the H braces completed the assembly.

At Sheriff Matt's recommendation, Buddy met with Dale Ray and Elam. As Sheriff Matt put it, "Those two boys are the best hunters in the county, maybe the state. They could walk up and tag a buck, and he'd never know it. People around here say that Dale Ray killed a ten-pointer with just his bandana."

Dale Ray showed up on an '80s model Harley Davidson. He was a lean man of average height sporting a thick blond horseshoe mustache, a do-rag, and a reserved demeanor. He dismounted and nodded at Buddy. He leaned against it in silence until the next vehicle turned the corner into the driveway.

Elam arrived in a dusty red pickup that had more dents and scratches than Buddy thought he had ever seen. Once he hopped out, Buddy could see that he was red-haired, hyper, and surprisingly pudgy. He had a toothpick in his mouth that seemed to be in constant motion.

"You got a varmint problem?" asked Elam in a nasal twang as his boots crunched on the gravel. He stuck out his hand and gripped Buddy's in a very firm handshake. Elam sauntered over and joined them.

"Something like that. What do you know so far?"

"Word is that a couple of fellers was out to hurt Miss Janine. Seems it didn't turn out too good for 'em."

"That's right," said Buddy. "And you know why I'm asking for your help, then?"

"Well, if someone sent 'em, and they didn't get the job done, there's bound to be more where they came from."

Buddy nodded. "That about sums it up." In all his travels around the world with the military, it seemed that the locals always had a clear understanding of the situations at hand. Common sense often counted for more than a barrel of classroom training.

"I figure we have as little as two or three more days before they get here. Maybe more, but I doubt it. Then they'll either make an all-out assault or spend a couple of days reconnoitering the area." Buddy told them about the surprises he had installed around the property. "I've also kept the dog in the house during the day just in case they're doing any satellite reconnaissance. The less they see, the better. I'll have you fellows come in so that Midnight can get your scent. I don't want any cases of mistaken identity in the dark."

After making acquaintance with Janine and Midnight, Buddy walked them around the property. Elam eyed the barbed wire approvingly after Buddy pointed out the tripwire.

"Remind me not to get on your bad side, Buddy," he said as he spit out the chewed-up toothpick and replaced it with another from a small spice jar in his pocket.

"What do you fellows think?" asked Buddy.

"I think you picked the right places," said Elam. "Dale Ray?"

Dale Ray gave a slight nod in response.

"Where do you boys want to hole up?"

"I think I'll be happy right up in your barn loft. It has sight lines up here and down past the house. If I know Dale Ray, he'll probably want to wander around a bit. He played free safety back in high school."

"I've got radios if you want 'em, and you can come to the house any time you need to use the restroom or want to get some food or drink."

"I think we'll be okay for two or three days," said Elam. "I've got plenty of bottles to drink from and pee in, and I brought some Tupperware if I need it. Dale Ray has the good ol' outdoors."

"You can park your truck and bike in the barn, and I'll let you take it from here. I've got a bit more preparation to do myself."

"One more thing, Buddy." said Elam. "What's the rules of engagement?"

"These people tried to kill my wife—and my dog," said Buddy.

"All I needed to hear," said Elam. They both looked at Dale Ray. His mustache moved only slightly as he set his mouth in a grim line. Buddy noticed for the first time that his left bicep had a tattoo of the grim reaper with three vertical slashes below it. He wondered if it was a running total and, if it were, how many more lines would be added before it was all over.

Chapter 19

Back at the Sheriff's office, Matt was reading through the coroner's report. As expected, there was little in the way of identification on the two attackers with the exception of a single tattoo of what looked like a delivery truck with the word "pizza" on its side. The tattoo was located on each man's left buttock. Matt read the description and clicked on the accompanying images attached to the report. While he had an idea what they might mean, he logged into the Justice Department's NGI, or Next Generation Identification system, and uploaded them.

After a relatively brief search, several matches came back. The use of the word "pizza" was a known pedophile symbol. The fact that it was located on a delivery vehicle was an indication that the person was involved in the actual distribution or trafficking of children. Matt surmised that for someone to have such a tattoo indicated that they were likely part of a larger organization. At the least, they were committed enough to their decadent path to have it stamped into their skin.

Matt's face twitched. He had dealt with all kinds of criminals, most of them homegrown and many of them idiots who had gotten hooked on meth or opioids. But he hated pedophiles. In the instances where he had dealt with abusive parents, he had been firm in his dealings with them. On more than one occasion, after having frank talks with the parents and helping them to see the error of their ways, he had arranged for a child or siblings to move in with grandparents or close relatives. Many of them genuinely regretted the harm they were inflicting on their offspring. But people who intentionally sought out children to prey on them were in a class all by themselves. Matt considered them the lowest form of humanity—that is, if there was any humanity left in them at all.

The tattoos seemed to confirm, at least partially, what he had heard from Pastor Derek about the video. He texted Buddy, Dale Ray, Elam, and his core deputies: "It's important to take one of them alive if you can." If someone were bringing a war to his county, he wanted to know who he was dealing with.

Chapter 20

Philadelphia, Pennsylvania

After a week away from her captors, Stefani was beginning to think that she might really be free. While she had not left the Mission building alone, she had made a couple of shopping trips with Sarah. Upon their return, as Stefani was handing Sarah items to place into the refrigerator, she asked, "Sarah, did you always want to do something like this?"

Sarah looked at her with a cocked head as she placed some mushrooms and lettuce in the vegetable drawer. "I can't rightly say that I ever thought about doing this."

Stefani was confused, and her face registered it. "Then why are you here?"

"I could say that Happy is the reason, and that would be partly true. He's the one that roped me into leaving my house and coming to live here in the city with him. But really, I'd have to say the good Lord ultimately had His hand in it."

"What is it you wanted to do in life, then?"

That made Sarah pause. The refrigerator began beeping at her. She motioned for Stefani to hand her more fresh vegetables. "I never had any big plans for life. Some people have big plans and big callings to go out and change the world. Me? I just wanted to live life as it came, I reckon. Planting a garden, having some pretty flowers. Those are the things I wanted." She paused and then added, "And sing in the choir like Mama did." She sighed. "That woman sure could sing."

"I think you sing beautifully," said Sarah. "Sometimes, when I listen to you sing, it makes me sad. Sometimes it makes me feel hope. Sometimes when you sing, I get goosebumps down my back."

Sarah chuckled. "Well, maybe I inherited Mama's gift. Her singing used to affect me the same way."

"Didn't you ever want a family?" Sarah asked.

"Sure, I did. But life doesn't always turn out the way you expect. Lots of girls in my neighborhood got married. I had a few boys want to court me, but none of them were the kind that I wanted to spend my life with. Good men exist, but they're in high demand, especially in our community."

"I can't really think of any good men that I've known—except for Happy. Why isn't he married, Sarah?"

"He is married, at least in a way. He's sold out completely to the Lord. When we was growing up, there was a number of girls tried to turn his head with their charms. It just never seemed to faze him. He treated them all the same way he treats me: like sisters."

"Is he attracted to...anyone else?"

Sarah caught the inflection in Stefani's voice and shot her a cross glance. "Absolutely not!" she snapped. "Just because a man doesn't have an interest in marrying a woman doesn't mean he has to be one of them Sodomites!"

"I'm sorry," Stefani said quickly. "I didn't mean to offend you."

Sarah's tone lost its edge. "That's okay, child. You don't know no better. In the Bible, there were plenty of men who served God without being married. Jeremiah the prophet, John the Baptist, even Jesus. Happy's just like one of them."

They finished putting the food away. Then Sarah asked Stefani, "What about you? What did you want to be when you were a little girl?"

"Everyone always told me how pretty I was and that I needed to be a model. But when I think back, I just wanted to be married to someone who would love me and be a mom. I had a friend in school whose mom was really nice. She probably was the best mom I knew growing up. But I don't even know how to be like her."

Sarah studied Stefani for a few moments. Then she said, "Well, it looks like I've got my work cut out for me. Come on. Let's get you comfortable in a kitchen and teach you how to cook."

Chapter 21

Standing side by side in front of the counter, Sarah was instructing Stefani in what to do.

"Break apart that bulb of garlic into the tiny cloves. Pull as much of that papery stuff off as you can. Now reach over to that drawer and pull out the small knife. Yes, that one. Cut the rough end off the cloves of garlic. Now pull the rest of that skin off. You can use the knife to help skin it. That's just fine right there. Have you ever eaten a clove of garlic by itself?"

Stefani shook her head no.

"Well, part of making good food is understanding what it is you're mixing together. Cut you a thin slice of one of those cloves about the size of your fingernail. Now put it on your tongue and just suck on it for a few seconds. That'll give you the big taste in a mild way."

Sarah waited while Stefani did that. Then she said, "Now I want you to bite down on that garlic with your molars. Grind it up, but don't swallow it. Just let the pieces sit in your mouth and let your saliva mix with it."

Stefani did as she was told. Sarah watched as her face went from impassive to somewhat curious to concerned all in a matter of seconds. Then Stefani's eyes began to water.

"Burns, don't it?" said Sarah.

"I think I need some water!" Stefani gasped.

"Not yet you don't. It burns, but it ain't gonna hurt you none. I want you to get the full experience of what garlic tastes like. Let it sit there a little bit longer. Let it move around your mouth and all over your taste buds."

Stefani's eye begged for relief, but she kept at it. After another thirty seconds or so, she said, "It's not as hot as it was. It actually has a really good taste!"

"Now for the kicker," Sarah said. "Go ahead and swallow it."

Sarah's eyes blinked, and she opened her mouth wide. "Wow! That burns going down, too!"

"It does. What I want you to realize is that some spices and herbs not only add flavor, but they add to the experience of how you feel when you taste them. Too much, and they can overpower the food. Of course, some people like it that way. But if you know what a particular spice does by itself, you're better off when it comes to knowing what it will do for ground beef or pork, for instance."

After a few swallows of milk, Sarah had Stefani tried a few other herbs and spices. With each one, she first let Stefani try it with no introduction. After Stefani described what she was tasting and feeling, Sarah gave her commentary on what that particular spice was good for.

"And now you're going to put these into that frying pan over there and make the fajitas for our dinner with Mr. Ingram tonight."

"What? I can't cook! I don't know what to do!" Stefani protested.

"Which is why I'm going to tell you exactly what to do. But you're going to be the one to do it. I learned to cook the same way. Mama would pull a chair over to the counter and tell me how to make all kinds of dishes. I listened to her until I remembered the steps. And when I got older, I started changing her recipes to suit my taste or started making my own new dishes."

Stefani gave a smile of relief. "I think I could do that."

With that, they began working on the preparation for the evening meal. As the two women were working at the counter, Happy walked by the kitchen and quietly peered in. As he watched Sarah taking charge and instructing Stefani, his mind raced back to his childhood in a flash of déjà vu. Sarah was his mother, bustling about the kitchen. Ignoring the skin color, Stefani was little Sarah all over again: green as a spring bough but eager to learn, watching Mama with admiration at how skilled she was.

He backed slowly away from the entrance to avoid disturbing them. He smiled and said in a low voice, "You were right again, Lord. You were right again."

Chapter 22

Introductions already having been made beforehand, after the dinner of a salad, spicy fajitas, boiled corn on the cob, and mashed potatoes, they finished with a dessert of blueberry cobbler. Alex Ingram put his spoon down on the empty dessert plate and said, "Sarah, I have to hand it to you. You really know how to cook. The meal was simply wonderful as always."

"I can't take credit for this meal," Sarah said. She looked over at Stefani. "There's your cook right there. You can thank her."

Stefani blushed bright red as Alex and Happy both effused praise on her. But the look of happiness and delight on her face was as evident as the coloring in her cheeks.

"I...I really didn't do it by myself. Sarah told me everything to do," she stammered.

"Now don't you start," Sarah said. "It was your hands that done all the work, wasn't it?"

"Yes," Stefani said meekly, again with some degree of satisfaction in her expression.

"Ain't no shame for any cook using somebody else's recipe," said Happy. "But putting it together requires some skill."

"I don't care who did what. If I ate like that every day of the week, I'd be a lot healthier at this point in my life," said Alex. "That's one of the downsides of being a bachelor." He shot a glance at Happy and added, "Without a big sister to cook for me."

Happy laughed. "I do have it made in that department, Alex. I surely do."

The ladies began clearing the table. Sarah said, "Happy, you and Alex can take care of the coffee, and then we can all go up on the roof. I'd like Stefani and me to join you this time."

"That'll be fine," said Happy. "Come on, Alex. You can get a tray and cups while I make a pot."

After the dishes were put in the washer and the coffee was prepared, they moved to the roof, where they sat around the cast iron patio table. Surrounded by Sarah's plants, the atmosphere was almost rural, with the exception of the sounds of the city echoing up from the streets below. After drinks had been poured and cream and honey added as desired, Happy looked across at Alex and asked, "What would you like to discuss this evening, Alex?"

Since Happy's return to Philadelphia, he and Alex had been meeting on a weekly basis as much as Alex's schedule allowed in order for Happy to mentor him and serve as a guide as Alex sought out answers in the Scripture. Although they were near enough in age to be brothers, Alex acknowledged that Happy was many years beyond him in things of an eternal nature. He referred to Happy as his guru when they were together because he knew it tweaked Happy's humility. With everyone else, he was content to refer to Happy as "the best man I've ever known."

Alex brooded over his cup for a few moments and then said, "This past year has really opened up a lot of old wounds for me and quite a few cans of worms. Just dealing with all of the repercussions of everything I helped to uncover and publish has put me face to face with more evil than I ever wanted to admit existed." He sighed a deep sigh. "I have had enough good experiences now with God to believe that He truly is good, but I just don't understand why evil of this magnitude is allowed to exist. Maybe that's more than you want to talk about tonight or even have time to discuss, but that's what has been bothering me so much."

"Mmmhh," Happy grunted. "Big question. I think the way people usually ask it is, 'If God is good, why does He allow evil to exist or allow bad things to happen?'"

"I didn't want to put it that way," Alex said. "But I guess they're the same question after all."

"There's a lot of Scriptures I could point you to, and we may get to them," Happy said. "But I want you to look at the big picture with me for a minute. Just stay with me for a bit, okay?"

Alex nodded.

Happy nodded with his hand toward the sky. "Up there in what we call heaven, some long time ago, God decided that He wanted to have a family. He already existed as Father, Son, and Holy Spirit. But as a perfect Father who loved His Son, He wanted a whole family just like the Son. The only way to have that was to create. God's a big God, and He does big things. So He created a whole universe and made a perfect spot to sustain life.

"He put all kinds of minerals, resources, and everything that His family would need to use, experiment, develop, and have in order to grow in their knowledge and character. Then He planted a garden, a perfect place." Looking at Sarah, he said, "It sure must have been beautiful if God was the master gardener. Then He created a man first and then a woman as a suitable helper, or companion, for the man."

Sarah glanced at Stefani. She was holding her cup but wasn't drinking. The look on her face indicated that she was absorbed in what Happy was saying.

"He loved this man and woman so very much. And He wanted them to love Him in return. Remember, that's why He created them: to have that big family of men and women who would act just as wonderfully as His own Son and love Him back for who He is. But out of all the plants, animals, trees, fruit, vegetables, and everything He put inside the earth, do you know the most important gift He gave to that first couple?"

Happy paused and looked at each of the other three and then continued. "He gave them the gift of choice. Without that gift, there was no meaning or purpose to any of the rest of creation. If God had created them hardwired to only serve Him and never be able to choose otherwise, they might serve Him faithfully and forever, but it couldn't be called love, could it? He could have created them with or without emotion, with or without choice, with or without the kind of mind that allows you to write like you do or the kind of mind that built the great buildings all over the world. By giving them that gift of choice, He gave them the ability to understand Himself, and He gave them the ability to know what love is.

"Unfortunately, that gift is a double-edged sword. If you can say 'yes,' you can also say 'no.' That was the risk that God the Father took. He wanted that family so badly to be able to share love between Himself and His creation that He was willing to suffer the pain of rejection if that first couple decided they didn't want to do things His way.

"You know what happened with Adam and Eve. They made their choice, the choice to disobey and eat of the one tree God had commanded them to leave alone. And because they were the representatives of the entire human race, the fallout from their choice affected everyone born since all the way down to our time and all the way here in Philadelphia."

Alex sipped from his cup and then said, "Okay. I can understand that. But why doesn't God just wipe out the ones who are really evil? They've had plenty of time to make choices, and they have continued to choose what is wrong because they want to. Why doesn't he just say, 'You're done!' and then fry them in hell where they deserve to be?"

"And would you do that if you were God?" asked Happy.

"Yeah, I think so," said Alex. "At least that's how I feel after what I've seen this past year or two."

"And where would you have fit in the scales of justice just a few years ago?"

"Ouch!" said Alex. "That's not fair, Happy."

"Isn't it? If you asked any of the people whose lives you affected with your writing years ago, what would they have said? What if I were the one who was holding those scales and I was thinking just like you?"

"Okay, okay!" Alex said. "This is getting too close to home. You've made your point. I still don't understand why, though."

"The Bible tells us that God is longsuffering and isn't willing for anybody to perish but wants everybody to come to a place of repentance. Alex, I think that the Spirit of God keeps whispering in a person's ear right up to the moment they breathe their last breath. Not everybody hears Him. Most don't. But there still are a handful of really rotten evil people who see the error of their ways and cry out for mercy on their deathbeds. And God loves them just as much as He loves His only Son. Don't you think it makes Him so very happy when that happens?"

Alex was somber in thought. "Yes. I suppose it does. I can't begin to imagine how it must feel for Him when someone who has held out for so long really does turn back and ask Him to forgive them for all they've done wrong." He sighed again and then added, "But what about predestination and foreknowledge? If God knows what is going to happen anyway, why doesn't He just say, 'That person is never going to choose me' or 'I didn't create that person to choose me' and then zap them?"

"What all have you been reading, Alex?" Happy asked. "Seems like you've been latching onto some mixed-up theology books."

"I've picked up a few books by some of the popular authors," said Alex.

"Mmm," Happy responded. "Just remember what I told you at the beginning. God gave everybody the same Bible to read. And He gave every one of His children the same Spirit to teach them. But to answer your question, you've really brought up two different problems. The Bible tells us that God sees and knows the end from the beginning. With that being the truth, we also have to accept the fact that God sees the ways in which the existence of evil people doing evil deeds will cause righteous people to fight harder than ever. That's one thing to consider. The other is that He knows how many of those people will eventually make a choice to serve Him, just like you did later in life. You know, according to statistics, only four percent of people make that decision after the age of thirty. The odds were against you. His foreknowledge gives Him an understanding of how little actions influence big events for somebody on the other side of the tracks.

"Now if you choose to look at things from the hard, Calvinistic approach and say that God determined whether or not a person was going to follow Him or not, first of all, I don't buy that. It runs smack dab against everything I read about God in the Bible. My Bible tells me that God loves everyone, that He sent Jesus to die for everyone, and that He wants everyone to come to repentance. And before you tell me that these book writers have redefined the meaning of the word 'everyone,' I already know that. Once you start changing words around, you can make the Bible or any other book say whatever you want it to.

"But remember what I said earlier. God wanted people who would love Him. If He decides that for you, then it ain't love. I think that anybody who says God makes those choices for you just doesn't understand the very heart and nature of who God is.

"And even if they're right, if somehow God does program people to serve Him against their will and decides who gets to be in the club, then the simple answer to your question of why would be, 'It's none of your business.' Because the strict Calvinistic view of God puts what you think and how you feel completely out of the picture. So if you want to go down that road, you can't ever say, 'That just don't seem fair to me.' Make sense?"

Alex chewed on his lip before answering, "Yes. It does. But it doesn't make it any easier to deal with all of this."

"Anybody, politician or preacher, who promises you an easy time in life has their hand in your pocket looking for your wallet," answered Happy.

There was silence for a few moments. Then Stefani spoke up. "What you just said makes sense to me, at least what I can understand. I do understand that being forced to be intimate with someone because they have power over you isn't love. I hate the people who treated me like that.

"But there have been a lot of times over the past few years that I have cried myself to sleep. I've asked God over and over why He let this happen to me. How do you answer that question for someone like me?"

Happy looked at her steadily for several moments. When he spoke, his voice was low and gentle. "Stefani, what you have been through is pure evil, no argument. Wicked people have preyed on you and abused you." He paused and then added, "But it all started with your own choice."

Stefani stiffened in her seat. Sarah noticed it immediately and said, "I don't think that's very fair to act like this was all her fault." There was fire in her voice.

Happy glanced at his sister. "I didn't say it was. What I said was that this began with her choice. Stefani told us that she answered an ad in the paper promising to help start her on her way to becoming a high-paid model." He glanced over at Sarah and then looked back to Stefani. "At least that's what I thought you said."

"That's right," she said. "But I didn't sign up for all the abuse."

"No. No, you didn't. The Bible says that each person is tempted by the desires inside of them. It doesn't say evil desires either, just 'desires.' You wanted to get out of your life situation with your mother and her boyfriends. That's not a bad desire. You wanted to be able to make money. That's not a bad desire. There may have been some desires in there about wanting to be thought of as beautiful, or maybe you just wanted someone to love you like your father used to love you when you were a little girl."

Stefani's body tremored when he said that. Sarah shot another sharp glance at her brother, who ignored it and continued.

"But it was a combination of those desires that led you to answer that ad. Once you acted and made a choice, you started down a path. It was the wrong one, but it was a choice you made, nevertheless. At that point, a whole bunch of other people who made choices to seek out girls like you acted on your decision. They took advantage of you, and that was their choice. Every one of those men who used you made a choice. God didn't approve of their bad choices any more than He approved of the choice you made to leave your mother and your home and go your own way.

"But if people are going to be given the choice to love Him and be in relationship with Him, they have to have the ability to make those bad choices, too. And when they do make those bad choices, they always hurt someone other than just themselves. If God stopped every evil deed from happening, He would be denying every human being the choice to love Him or hate Him.

"I don't particularly like the way things work, but God didn't ask my permission. And the more I've thought about it through the years, I can't think of any other way that God could have done it and have people who really love Him." He sighed, then added, "But whether we like it or not, that's the world we live in. The evil that people do affects a lot of others, especially if they are high up in positions of power."

He sat contemplating over his cup of coffee. Alex stared off into the distance in thoughtful silence. Stefani was sobbing quietly. Sarah had an angry expression on her face. She reached over and put a hand on Stefani's shoulder.

They sat like that for several minutes, and then Alex stretched and let out a deep breath. "Well, Happy," he said, "I can't say that this is the most enjoyable time of discussion we've had, but it's certainly one of the most insightful. I thank you for your wisdom, as painful as it may have been to hear it. I've got more to think about, but at least I have a framework for sorting through some of my questions—and my emotions."

Happy nodded. Alex stood to leave. "Stefani, Sarah, thank you again for the dinner. It was truly delicious. You ladies have a pleasant rest of your evening."

Each nodded their acceptance of the compliment. Happy stood and said, "I think I'll clean up. You can stay up here as long as you like. Shall I leave the pot? No? All right then. I'll carry it downstairs." With that, Happy made his exit carrying a tray laden with cups, containers, and napkins. He didn't need to look back as he went downstairs. He could feel Sarah's eyes boring a hole in the back of his skull.

Chapter 23

"She cried for two hours! Two solid hours. She could barely get words out. And to make things worse, you took all the napkins, and I had to scramble to find a cloth for her to wipe her eyes and blow her nose!"

Happy winced. Sarah wasn't one to mince words, but ever since she had cornered him in his office, she had been reading him the riot act for twenty minutes with no sign of letting up. Eventually, she took a deep breath and finished with, "How dare you make that young child feel like she was responsible for anything that happened to her!" With finality, she added, "And in case I haven't mentioned it yet, I'm very upset with you."

Happy sat quietly for some time before responding. He wanted to make sure Sarah had made herself heard. He had learned that there was no use responding before all the venom came out during times like this.

"Although I never said she was entirely responsible for what has happened in her life, the truth remains that she is responsible for her own choices that led her down that path. I know that's a hard pill to swallow. But it's the truth. 'All we like sheep have gone astray.' I tried to speak it in love the best I knew how. But at the end of the day, I have to speak the truth. The only way for her to be free is to know the truth. At least that's what the Lord said."

Sarah bristled. "Did you have to do it now? Maybe she wasn't ready to hear the truth about that! Did that occur to you?"

"Yes, it did. But that young girl has seen more evil in a few years than most people see in a lifetime. If she can be exposed to that much evil and still be alive, then she ought to be able to hear the truth and not have it kill her. Did it hurt her? Yeah. It did. Truth hurts more times than I want it to. But it's the only path that brings healing."

Sarah pursed her lips. She knew her brother was right. She had lived enough to see that what he was saying was true, and she had read her own Bible enough to know what it said. She couldn't quote it the way Happy did, but she knew what was in it.

"How is she now?" Happy asked.

"I tucked her in her bed like a child and sat with her and sang to her until she went to sleep. She was clutching one of the pillows like her life depended on it."

"Hmm," Happy grunted. "Most people never do come to the understanding that if the roles were reversed, they could be the person doing the evil deeds themselves. The people that do realize that seem to be stronger in their faith. I think that's one reason Alex is so solid now. He's got questions, but he knows how bad he can be because he's been down at the bottom of the barrel."

"Well, if Stefani wasn't down there before tonight, I think she's there now," said Sarah. "I'm going to bed. I ain't felt this exhausted in a long time." She walked out of the office and closed the door firmly behind her. It had been open when she entered.

Happy knew it was her way of adding a punctuation mark to everything she had just said. He looked up to the ceiling and said, "Well, Lord, things sure are progressing. I ask you to give peace to Stefani as she sleeps tonight. And help Sarah to embrace who you've made her to be." He paused and then added, "And would you look out for Alex? If he's gonna read other books trying to find truth, please help him to find some good ones and steer him clear of the ones that are just going to confuse him." Then he opened up a folder and began sorting through a stack of bills which needed to be paid. "Jehovah Jireh," he hummed to himself. "You will provide for me."

Chapter 24

Sand Mountain, Alabama

The reply had arrived on the message board inside of four hours. It was a series of images. The first was a pentagram with the goat's head embedded inside of it. The second image was of a slender, Caucasian, female right hand holding what appeared to be a stone dagger. It was cropped so that the bottom knob of the implement and only an inch or so coming out of the fist appeared in the image. On the index finger was an ornate metal band with what was apparently a large ruby set into knotwork. The third image was a closely cropped photo of a man's face. The lifeless eyes stared into eternity with a look of pain. The face was unmistakably that of Daniel Robertson.

There was a brief line of text that read:

`We never walk away from unfinished business. Pray to your god all you want. He cannot save you.`

Janine's chest tightened when she saw Daniel's face. It was not part of the original video. Someone had chosen to take that photo as proof or as a trophy. They had kept it close all these years.

She shared the message with Buddy, who took a photo of it with his phone and passed it to Sheriff Matt. The image would be passed along to those deputized with a warning that there would no doubt be more trouble incoming and to be vigilant. Buddy showed it to Elam and Dale Ray.

A few minutes later, Janine's phone rang. It was Pastor Derek. He asked if it would be acceptable for him and some of the church elders to come to their home that evening. Janine told him that it was fine, and they set the time for 6:30 p.m.

A short time later that evening, Pastor Derek arrived with a small convoy of vehicles. After parking along the gravel driveway, he and a group of seven other men were welcomed into the home by Janine.

"Buddy will be in in just a couple of minutes. He had to go check on something out in the pasture," Janine said. She offered them coffee, but Pastor Derek politely declined. The front door opened, and Buddy walked in.

"Hello, Derek," he said.

"Thanks for allowing us to come," Derek said. "I know you all have a lot on your mind, and I don't want to waste any of your time. The reason we came here tonight is to answer the message that you and Janine got back on the Internet this afternoon. All of us realize that this is a threat, but there is a bigger picture that I really believe needs to be addressed. In that message, whoever wrote it is actually taunting you and telling you that God will not help you."

"I know," said Janine. "That made me so angry."

"It should," said Derek. "Throughout the Bible, there have been several occasions where people made it a point to defy God and to taunt or challenge Him directly. Nimrod and the tower of Babel was one. Pharaoh was another. Goliath did the same. Remember? He said, 'I defy the armies of Israel,' and David said that he had defied the armies of the living God. But what came to mind immediately was the story of Hezekiah. Do you remember that one?"

"Not very clearly," said Janine. "And I imagine Buddy wouldn't know what you are talking about. Why don't you just tell us about it?"

"Well, Hezekiah had become king of Judah. During his reign, the king of Assyria had come up against Judah to attack it. He sent one of his field commanders to tell Hezekiah to give up. He even gave his speech in the Hebrew language in order to cause the people listening on the walls of Jerusalem to lose courage. Let me just read you the story, beginning in second Kings chapter 18."

Here, Derek began reading the story and continued through chapter 19. When he was done, he said to Buddy and Janine, "Back here in chapter 18, remember that the field commander had basically said, 'My master has destroyed all these other nations, and who is your God versus any other god? They weren't able to save their countries, and your God is just as impotent as they are.' When Hezekiah prayed and sent messengers to the prophet Isaiah, he acknowledged that the threat was real and that the king of Assyria had been successful in doing what he had claimed.

"But Hezekiah pleaded to God and said, 'Those gods could not save their people because they were just idols, the creation of men's hands.' He acknowledged God as the only true God, and he asked for God's help. You know the rest of the story now. Isaiah the prophet sent back a message from God saying that this seemingly helpless and small nation was laughing in the face of the king of Assyria. He promised that He would defend Jerusalem for His own sake. That's a big thing. God cares about His children, but when He says He is going to do something because of His own honor, you can bank on it with your life. As we read in the story, He did just that."

Janine closed her eyes and breathed deeply. "What do we need to do?"

"We're here to pray with you. But I believe it would be right for you or Buddy to be the ones who pray that prayer. When you're done praying, me and the elders want to go around the property and anoint it with oil. I couldn't shake the feeling that this was important. You are welcome to join us if you like."

Janine reached over and squeezed Buddy's big hand. "Buddy, I ain't gonna pressure you into praying. If you want me to, I will. But I would at least like to know here and now if you really want me to do this rather than just allowing me to."

Buddy gave her a quick glance and then looked at Pastor Derek. "I reckon I'd be a fool not to ask for help when Janine's safety is on the line."

"And yours," said Janine, squeezing his hand tighter.

"Mine, too," he said. "Go ahead and pray."

Janine closed her eyes. Before she opened her mouth, tears were already streaming down her cheeks. She sniffed and began, "God, right now, we're in a mess. You see what we're up against. I never knew what

I was getting into years ago when we witnessed what we saw with those poor children. Those people are just as wicked as Pharaoh throwing the babies into the river. They're just as wicked as them idol worshipers were who sacrificed their children. I don't know how to protect ourselves fully from what they have planned for us. But I believe you can. And I'm begging you to."

She started crying harder, and she leaned over into Buddy's shoulder. Her words came in gasps between sobs. "I love Buddy more than anything, God. I don't want anything to happen to him. Please save us. Please, please save us somehow. And show us the way out of this. Only you can bring an end to it." She began weeping and was unable to continue.

Pastor Derek picked up where she left off and added, "Father God, I believe you want to show Buddy and Janine how much you love them. But I also believe that you want to make a statement that you are just as powerful today as you were during Hezekiah's time. I'm asking you to judge the king of Assyria, whoever that is in Buddy and Janine's story. Judge that king and make him answer for his pride and what he has done already and for what he wishes to do. I ask that in the mighty name of Jesus your Son!"

After several minutes, Janine had stopped crying enough to talk again. She looked over at Buddy. One single tear had streamed down the outer edge of his cheek. It was more than she had ever seen the entire time she had known him. "Pastor Derek, thank you so much for coming. I would like for me and Buddy to come with you and the elders. I think it would be best for Buddy to lead the way around the property."

The group of ten headed out from the house with Midnight among them. Buddy took flashlights in case the prayers waxed long. All told, they were done in less than two hours. The elders poured oil over the corner posts and property markers and prayed for protection over the family and property. Buddy watched quietly. Janine joined in with the prayers.

When they returned to the house, the elders got into their cars and began to depart with promises to keep praying for their safety. Buddy asked Derek if he could speak with him for a moment privately. Janine took the cue and went inside, leaving the two men standing on the gravel in the deepening darkness.

"Derek, I want to thank you for coming. It means a whole lot to Janine."

"You all are family, Buddy," said Derek.

"That story you shared in there tonight. Do you believe that really happened?"

"Just like I read it. One hundred percent."

"Well, I gotta say that it sounds too good to be true. But it would be nice if it was. I'm wondering if you read it because you think that I'm not supposed to be doing anything to protect Janine, because if that's…"

"No, no," interrupted Derek. "That isn't what I meant at all. Buddy, God made you a man. That means you not only want to protect your wife but also you should do that. Be a man."

Buddy looked at Derek in the glow of the light coming from inside the living room. "Okay. I aim to do just that with all the strength I've got."

"Buddy, I know you will. I read that story because sometimes our best isn't enough. Whether you believe in Him or not, I think that God wants to show you that He is involved in this situation, too. I hope—no, my prayer is that it becomes clear to you that He is involved."

"Fair enough." Buddy stuck out his hand and shook Derek's with a firm grip. "We'll all know pretty soon, I imagine."

Chapter 25

Philadelphia, Pennsylvania

As the days turned into weeks, Stefani's life had settled into a routine. In the mornings, Happy taught her typing. The way he put it, it was a skill she could use to make money, and in the computer age, she would likely be able to benefit from it for the rest of her life. After lunch, she studied for her GED.

After studying, Stefani and Sarah spent time talking while they prepared dinners and desserts or planned shopping trips for supplies. In the evenings, she was either on her own or free to join Happy as he conducted services for the down and out who still attended chapel at the mission three nights a week. Wednesday evening dinner and discussion was still reserved for Alex Ingram as often as he could make it.

She was now typing proficiently and working on her speed. It was a comment about this one Wednesday evening that perked Alex's ears.

"You're already up to over fifty words per minute?" he asked.

"Yes," she answered shyly.

"She's holding back," said Happy. "She's hit seventy on occasion on the short speed tests, but on the long assignments I give her, she's a solid fifty. And that's with some numbers and symbols thrown in."

Alex finished chewing a bite of food, wiped his mouth, and then said, "Stefani, I need someone who can type up my notes from various investigative pieces I'm working on. Would you be interested and available to help with projects like that on an ongoing basis?"

Stefani looked at Alex and then over to Happy and then to Sarah. Happy looked back at her and said, "He's not asking me. He's asking you. What do you think about it?"

"I…well, I would be interested. It's just that I don't have my own computer."

"I'll supply you with a laptop," said Alex.

"Where would I work? Would I have to come to your offices?"

"That's up to you. If you prefer to work here, I can send you the transcription files electronically or drop them off. I also have a crazy amount of legal pads full of notes I've made that need to be typed up, collated, and then sorted. I don't know if you are up to that task, but I have to start somewhere." He smiled at her. "Well, what do you say?"

"I'd like to do it. Well, at least try to do it. I think I'd like to start here first. Maybe if things go okay, I could come into the office once I get comfortable with it."

"Sounds good to me," said Alex. "I'll be by first thing tomorrow if that works for you all." He looked at Happy.

"It'll give me something different to teach her in typing, that's for sure. Do you have one of them foot pedals she can use?"

"I'll find one."

Stefani looked confused. "A foot pedal? What for?"

"It's used with electronic transcription files. You use your feet to play, stop, fast forward, and rewind while your hands keep typing. It's easy to learn," said Alex.

They finished their meal, had their usual theological and life discussions over coffee, and then said good night to Alex. The next morning, he arrived at 9:00 with a laptop, a nice headset, and a foot pedal. After assembling everything, he opened a folder on the desktop. It was filled with MP3 audio files.

"This folder is synced with my online storage. Any time I upload files from my phone or from my computer, they'll show up in here. You can click here to sort files by date or by file name."

He then showed her how to open the transcription software, load a file, and then use the foot pedal to navigate through the file. There was

99

another folder on the desktop synced to his online storage where Stefani was to save the files under different folders named for different research and stories. After making sure she and Happy were comfortable with the system, he left.

Keeping the headphones unplugged for the moment, Happy spent that morning's typing lesson talking to Stefani about the differences between typing something already printed versus listening to transcription. "You have to use what you know about grammar to put in the commas and periods. If you don't know all of that, the program will suggest things or try to fix it for you." He looked at her and saw a worried expression. "If you don't get it perfect, they pay people to edit. So don't get too worked up about all that right now. Alex will be happy just to get his notes typed."

"I never really thought about what goes into making a newspaper story," Stefani said.

"Not just newspapers. People all over the place do the same thing to get stuff typed up—doctors, lawyers, just to name a couple. If you learn how to do this well, you could start your own business for other customers."

Stefani's face beamed as the reality of it set in. "My mom told me several times that I wouldn't amount to much. Most of the time she was drunk, but it still hurt. It got in my head. I think that's one reason I wanted to make it in the modeling business so bad." She had a faraway look in her eye, and then she turned her face back to Happy. "This is the first time in a long time that I actually feel like I can do something and maybe succeed at it. It's not modeling and making a ton of money and being famous, but I feel like I can actually do this."

Happy patted her on the shoulder and said, "That's the spirit! God don't make junk." He got up and said, "I'm going to leave you to it. I've got to make a few calls. If you run into any hiccups, you give me a shout. We'll figure it out together."

Stefani plugged in the headphones and put them on. Then she selected a new audio file from the list and loaded it. She poised her fingers over the keyboard and pressed play with the foot pedal. She began typing as Alex's voice came through the headset: "Concerning the investigation into John de la Rouche, things are ongoing, as he seems to have disappeared."

Chapter 26

Some days later, after beginning work on yet another dictation, Stefani pushed the stop button on the audio controller. She couldn't type any more words. Her eyes wouldn't focus through the tears. It was the name she had just heard. Senator Dom Acworth, the ranking senator on one of the most prestigious Senate committees. The senator who was held as a paragon of virtue by his party. The senator who had made her call him "Papa" in her former life whenever he visited one of the mansions she had been held in.

She felt panic rising in her, and her breath came in short gasps. She looked around at the walls of the room where she had been working. Was he here? Were they here? She was sure they were coming for her.

Flinging her headphones off and shoving her chair backward where it fell onto the floor with a loud clatter, she ran away as fast as she could. Sarah was knitting just down the hallway and heard the commotion. She got up from her chair quickly and was headed to the doorway just as Stefani ran past her toward the stairs.

"Stefani! What's the matter?"

Receiving no reply and fearing the worst, she pressed the intercom button and said, "Happy! Stefani's in trouble. She's running down the stairs."

Happy got the message and left a donor sitting in his chair, mouth agape, as he ran out of the office with only the words, "Emergency! Hang on!"

He caught sight of Stefani coming down the stairs and shouted at her, but she paid no attention. Both of her hands hit the door full tilt; then she was outside. Happy was just a few seconds behind her. He glanced in the direction she had gone as he tried to turn on what speed he could muster. She was running down the sidewalk bumping into people, seemingly oblivious to everything around her.

Happy ran after her, calling her name repeatedly. For a split second, he imagined a bird's-eye view of himself on someone's camera phone recording an older black man chasing a white girl and shouting her name. He shook his head and gritted his teeth. If he showed up on the news, it wouldn't be the first time.

He looked ahead and saw Stefani approaching an intersection. The crosswalk indicator was red. Traffic was barreling through. He managed to wheeze a prayer between labored breathing. "Lord, a little help, please. I'm too old for this."

Just as it looked like Stefani would run straight into the onslaught of vehicles, a powerful hand shot out, grabbed her arm, and held tight. Stefani started jerking and pulling and shouting to be let go. Closer now, Happy managed to shout above the noise, "Don't let go! She'll hurt herself!"

The young man who was holding her had grabbed her other arm as well and showed no intention of letting Stefani loose from his grasp. Happy was panting as he approached the man and the crowd of onlookers.

"Who are you, and why are you chasing her?" the man asked in a firm voice.

Happy held up a hand indicating that he needed to catch his breath. After a few moments, he said, "I'm Reverend Happy Lewis from down there at the Old Gospel Mission." He paused to breathe a bit more and then said, "She's staying with us at the moment. Something must have triggered a memory or something. She just ran out without any explanation."

"How do I know you're telling the truth? Maybe I should just call the cops?" the man said as he reached for his phone in his pocket.

"I don't care if you do. Just make sure to ask for Detective Gravely. He knows who I am and what we do. But you could just hold onto her for another couple of minutes. I think she'll calm down enough to tell you what's going on herself."

Addressing Stefani, he caller her name softly a few times until the hunted-animal look left her eyes. It was replaced by bewilderment. She looked at Happy, and her eyes clearly focused on his face.

"Where am I? What am I doing here?" Then, turning to look at the man who was holding onto both her arms, she said, "You're hurting me. Who are you?" A look of fear started to creep back onto her face.

Quickly, Happy said, "Stefani, this man saved your life. You were running straight out into the road. There's not a doubt in my mind you would have been hit and maybe run over."

Stefani's eyes searched the man's face and then returned to settle on Happy. "I heard a name, and it brought back too many memories, I guess."

Happy nodded his head. "I understand. There's a lot to walk through yet, I reckon. But you'll make it. Do you want to go back to the Mission now, or would you rather walk for a bit?"

"A walk would be nice. Thank you." She turned to the man, gave him a sad smile, and said, "You can let go of me now. I'm not going to do anything crazy."

The man loosened his grip, patted her on the shoulder, and said, "Okay. You be careful."

"Thank you again for saving me," said Stefani as they parted ways.

She walked beside Happy as he ambled down one street after another. She wasn't sure where they were going, but Happy knew the streets well. More than once, they stopped to say good morning to a person here and ask how life was going for a person there.

"You sure do know a lot of people," said Stefani. "And they really seem to respect you."

"Lot of folk have been in and out of the Gospel Mission over the years. A number of fine, upstanding business leaders have spent their time in the gutter, truth be known. I just happen to know the Way out."

"There's more to it than that," said Stefani. "You and Sarah, you really care about people. I wish there was more people like you and Sarah."

"Oh, there's lots and lots more people like us. The good Lord has a big old family stretching all around the world."

Happy guided her to an open park bench in a grassy area.

"My knees could use a rest for a spell. I have to say, I ain't used to sprinting like that since I was a young'un."

As they watched the birds poke among the blades of grass for a morsel, Stefani asked Happy, "Do you think I'll ever really be able to put all this behind me?"

"That depends," he said.

"On what?"

"On a number of things. But mostly it depends on you and the choices you make."

"But you said that much of what had happened to me was because of other people's evil choices, didn't you?"

"That I did. That's why I said it does depend on a number of things. But Stefani, nobody but you gets to make the choice of which direction you are actually headed. They can try to turn you around. They can try to sidetrack you or derail you. But they can't make the choice of where you really want to go every day of your life."

"That's actually pretty simple and profound at the same time," said Stefani.

"That's the Gospel," said Happy. "God wants each and every man, woman, boy, and girl to choose the right path. And once they do, He'll move heaven and earth to help them in that decision. But He will not violate their will. God respects our choices more than we do."

"You think that's really how it works?"

"I've got more stories than I have time to tell you right now. I've seen women that have sold their bodies to buy drugs to put into those bodies so they could feel good for a little while. They've been so addicted that the hospitals gave up on them. Wouldn't even admit them anymore because they said, 'There's no hope for you.' I've held their babies that had the DTs because of what their mamas put in their bodies and passed on to them. It's enough to make this grown man cry.

"I had one of them ladies look at me with eyes that was as wild as a lion and shout at me at the top of her lungs, 'Help me, preacher! Help me!' I told her the same thing I've told everyone else since I found the Answer. I told her to call on Jesus and He would save her from herself. She shouted loud as she could, 'Help me, Jesus! Help me, Jesus!' And right then, He did. I watched her face go from fear and torment to peace. Sin had left its mark on her, and she had a twisted, angry, wild look the whole time I had known her. But it was like her face rearranged itself into something that was almost childlike. It was like a big old steel band around her mind had snapped and all the pressure was gone.

He paused as an older couple strolled by arm-in-arm. After they had passed by, Stefani turned back to Happy, who continued.

"And there was a man that had started drinking too much. He had some problems at his business. The more he drank, the worse things got at work, at home, and with everything around him. He lost all of it. He come into the Mission one rainy Sunday morning smelling like a wet dog and a dirty toilet all rolled into one. He sat there while we sang. He sat while I preached. Looked like he wasn't hearing a thing. But when I asked if anybody wanted to make a change for the better, he got up and walked toward me. I'll never forget what he said. He had been looking down the whole time since he came in, but he looked up at me and said, 'Preacher, I'm at the end of my rope. I want to change.'

"I looked back at him and said, 'Well, friend, if you're still holding onto your rope, it means you're still trying it your way. Are you ready to let go and let God catch you in His big arms and try it His way?'

"He nodded and said, 'Yes, I am.' I told him, 'Then tell God that you want Jesus to be your boss from now on and that you believe that He really is alive.' He did that, and then he looked at me and said, 'Now what?' I said, 'Welcome to the family, brother. Let's get you a hot shower, some clean clothes, and a hot meal.' He's one of our city councilmen today.

"I wish all the stories was as good as these, but they ain't. I've sat by the hospital beds of many addicts who heard the same thing from me. More than one of 'em told me, 'Preacher, I just can't let go. I've got to have a fix to make it.' I've watched as the life left their body and they passed into eternity, unprepared to meet their Maker because they were unwilling to change directions."

He sighed, looked down, and shook his head slowly. "I know what I believe is real, that Jesus is the only way, the truth, and the life. But I can't make people believe that. I can only tell them and point the way. It's like watching a big party where some people are dancing to the music and then some people are missing the beat and doing their own thing." He looked over at Stefani. "Everyone dances to a tune. Just make sure it ain't the devil who's playing the fiddle for the one you're dancing to."

"Is it really that easy?" asked Stefani.

"I never said it was easy. But it is that simple. And once you make the choice to head in God's direction with Jesus truly being your Lord and tell Him He's the one who gets to call the shots, then it doesn't matter if it's easy or not. You just know that you're finally headed in the right direction."

"But how do you really know that?" asked Stefani. "How do you know it's true?"

"There's several ways. One is that God puts His Spirit in you. Something really does change inside of you. He also puts His love in your heart. You begin to understand what it means to be truly loved. And then there's the peace that passes all understanding. Even in the middle of the worst trials of my life, God's peace has always been there to comfort me. And as you begin to walk with Him, you develop your own history, your own stories, your own experiences where you know that God came through for you and answered your prayers."

Stefani looked out into the park for several moments. Then she spoke. "I'd like to think about it."

"And you should," said Happy. "This is a lifetime choice, a big change. You should make the decision only if you're really willing to see it through to the end. But I also have to warn you that when the times come that you really sense that God is knocking on your door, you should answer it right then. Some people only get that chance one time, and then it's gone."

"You really think that no matter what these people do, they can't make me go back to that life?"

"I do. I've seen too many people completely set free from their past who have never gone back." He gestured with his hand toward the park. "He said He watches over them birds out there. And I believe that the same God that can save people out of a mess can keep them out of that mess."

Stefani was still staring into the distance. "Happy, what made me run away was that I heard a name on Alex's dictation. I need to talk to you about Senator Dom Acworth."

Chapter 27

After telling Happy part of her story involving Senator Acworth, Happy had encouraged her to consider sharing it with others. There were a few choices to make, in his opinion. She could remain silent, which really wouldn't help anything. She could talk to the police, which might result in an investigation or not, depending on who believed her. Or she could share her story with the public in the hopes that the spotlight might turn upon the Senator.

"You never know what might happen if you tell others," said Happy. "There might be somebody else out there that realizes they're not alone. They might come forward too."

"But I thought it was the police's job to investigate crimes like this," Stefani said.

"It is. And they do, by and large. But they also have to decide whether or not they believe your story, a young girl they don't know, or the word of a famous congressman. On the other hand, the media is a powerful weapon in the fight against corruption—or it can be. We're blessed to know somebody like Alex who's willing to use it the right way."

In the end, Stefani had decided that she would do it. Alex listened to the idea and then pitched it to his editors. They had cautiously agreed under the terms that Stefani's story be vetted as fully as possible. To that end, Alex had a lawyer handle the questioning of Stefani with the understanding that she was actually laying the grounds for a lawsuit and giving her sworn statement. The entire process was recorded on video so that it could be used later if necessary.

At Alex's direction, Stefani also submitted to a polygraph and an array of psychological tests. Each of those indicated that she was telling the truth.

During the questioning, the lawyer allowed her to tell her story as she remembered it. Both Alex and the lawyer asked questions for more details. Alex would later take the material and work it into a printable format.

When it was all complete, Alex first showed Stefani the stories and allowed her to review them for accuracy and details. Then he submitted them to his editors and publisher. The only question that remained was when to print them. That question would answer itself soon enough.

Chapter 28

Sand Mountain, Alabama

It was decided that an eight-man force would be used for the clean-up operation in Alabama. Six would breach the property in two teams of three (designated as Red and Blue). Two would hold back as drivers of two separate vehicles. They would be available in an emergency to assist the teams but were instructed to remain in the vehicles otherwise.

The mission was succinct: if possible, the two targets would be taken alive for extraction and subsequent questioning. If the man provided resistance, he was to be eliminated. The woman was the HVT, or high-value target. Her life was to be preserved at all costs barring extreme circumstances. Injury to her was allowed as long as it was non-life-threatening.

Satellite reconnaissance photos had been used to determine the layout. Topography maps were used to provide suitable locations for entry. A high-grade drone with night vision technology would be used to allow one of the support drivers to both monitor the situation and give guidance to the teams based on real-time observations. All comms would be channeled between all eight members over a proprietary encrypted network that used an overlay of the cellular phone network. This gave them the benefits of a group call while scrambling the transmission for anyone who might be listening to any one number. A separate call on a satellite network was kept open between the two drivers and their director, who was in another location out of the country.

One day after Pastor Derek's visit (which had been observed from afar via binoculars by two of the team members), the assault was launched at 2 a.m. The half-moon shone only occasionally as clouds dotted the sky. The drone had been set aloft and was moving through the air slowly and carefully. The two team leaders walked through a comms check between their own members and each other. The drivers acknowledged comms with the teams and then with the director, who gave the permission to go and turned over leadership to the team leaders.

111

It was at that point, after the go signal was given, that things began to go awry in what appeared to be a cascading series of catastrophic events. First, the server that was used to provide the encryption service to the group call was hit with a denial-of-service attack. Later, it was revealed that the hosting provider had been targeted in what seemed to be a retaliation for hosting material deemed harmful to an Asian nation's policies. Billions of packets from around the globe were directed at all of the IP addresses in the hosting provider's network block and quickly saturated all of their connections to the Internet. In moments, the encrypted comms dropped.

In mid-sentence, the Blue team leader found himself unable to communicate with the two men next to him, much less the Red team or the support drivers. Immediately, the men on his team closed in and formed a tighter group to allow for whispered instructions and hand signals. Red team did the same after realizing that their comms were gone.

The second thing that happened was that the low Earth orbit satellite used by the team for staying in touch with the director of the operation suffered from a glitch which prevented the departing satellite from handing the call off to the next satellite. A direct lightning strike to the Earth station in that region caused a temporary failure in the routing algorithm. One moment, the director and drivers were in touch: the next moment, the call dropped. Inexplicably, all attempts to reestablish the calls failed.

Meanwhile, Buddy was awake and scanning the property through his night vision binoculars from the woodshed. Midnight's ears had perked up a couple of minutes earlier. He knew they were out there. How many, and exactly where, he was trying to determine.

The Blue team leader and his two men were making their path from the pasture. Because their comms were nonfunctional, they were clustered together instead of spread out. The topographical map had indicated there was a bit of a hill from which they could reconnoiter and then proceed down a swell with good sightlines to the house. Using their night vision equipment, they spotted the barbed wire fence. It was apparently built for cattle, as the strands were wide enough for a man to crawl through without too much difficulty.

The Blue team leader motioned for one of his men to go between the strands. He did and began to proceed cautiously forward. His foot reached the tripwire just as the second member was beginning to pass through the barbed wire. As chance would have it, just as the tripwire was pulled taught and the retaining pins were pulled free, the moon began to peek from behind the cloud and gave a silver glint to the barbed wire. An eerie whistling sound broke the stillness of the night as four strands of high-tensile wire streaked like rockets through the air. The team leader instinctively dropped to the ground and was spared. The first member to pass through felt the tripwire and almost stumbled, but his training kicked in. He flung himself backward, thinking of an IED. One of the strands laced his left arm with ragged cuts. The mercenary passing through the fence wasn't so lucky. Three of the strands ripped his thighs, arms, back, and neck with hundreds of sharp teeth. Two of the wires wrapped around him several times in the recoil. He stifled his cries, but he still gave audible grunts as the cuts began to pour out his blood in throbs.

The team leader swore as he examined the situation. No comms to let the Red team know what was going on. One team member down. He asked the first man if he was still able to proceed and received an affirmative. Together, they used their multitools to clip the barbed wire off of their comrade.

"Hang in there," the leader told him. "You're going to make it." But when he got the last wire free and began assessing the cuts, he realized it was in vain. Two arteries had been cut deeply enough that, without a medevac, there was no way that he would make it. The leader made the decision to proceed. "We'll come back for you as soon as we've secured the target," he told the injured man.

"Don't leave me," he begged in a whisper. His voice was already trailing off.

The leader motioned to the other man, who was dripping blood from his left arm, to move forward with him. Side by side, they began their downhill descent. Luck was again with the Blue team leader. He missed the punji sticks by a mere six inches. His team member stepped onto the false cover of tarp and grass and found his right foot falling into a void. The next instant, the sole of his foot and his Achilles tendon met the 80D nails at the bottom of the pit. Unlike the first man, he could not stifle his cry and shouted in pain as the nails drove through his boot and into the flesh and bones of his foot.

"Quiet," hissed the Blue team leader. But when he looked to his left to find out why the other man had broken operational silence, he took in the grim sight in the green glow of his night vision goggles.

"Another booby trap!" He swore again. "Let me help you get out of there," he said.

He lifted the second team member off the nails and lowered him to the ground beside the pit. As he worked to remove the man's foot, he had felt the sticky coating on the surrounding nails. He held his fingers to his nose and sniffed.

"Rat poison," he said through clenched teeth.

"Rat poison?" gasped the other man. "That's going to keep me from clotting. I'll bleed out!"

"I'm going to wrap you up tightly. You stay here. You shouldn't bleed out before I connect with Red team and finish the job."

He took off the man's boot and used his and the other man's field bandages to wrap his foot and ankle as tightly as possible. When he had wrapped it, he said, "Keep watch as best you can. With luck, I'll be back soon with the rest of Red team and get you out of here." Then he began to slowly zigzag down toward the house. Whoever did this was going to pay dearly.

§ § §

Red team chose the woods on the opposite side of the property as their entry point. It took extra time to reach. The goal was to have two approach and attack vectors in the event of opposition or detection. The director had felt that one team of three would be able to succeed in the mission should one of the teams be engaged by enemy fire. As it so happened, the drone was covering their area, and the entire incident unfolding with the Blue team on the upper part of the property was completely missed by the driver monitoring the feed.

They cautiously worked their way through the woods. Overhead, the moonlight filtered through the clouds, causing the woods to go from dark space to patchy shadows in the green hue of the night goggles. As they neared the edge of the trees, they heard a cry of pain from up in the direction of the hillside. The Red leader held up a fist to call a halt. The three knelt down near one another and listened.

"Do you think that was Blue team?" asked one of the men.

"Could be. Could be an enemy."

"Shouldn't we go check? If it's Blue team, they may need help."

"Negative. Our objective is to get inside that house and complete the mission one way or the other."

"I don't like it," said the first man. "It feels like a setup."

"You backing out?" asked the leader. "Then leave now. But you know what that means."

"No. But I don't like it. Just reminds me too much of Kandahar."

"This is Alabama. These idiots don't even know what a toothbrush is. Let's go. Single file."

As his not-so-good luck would have it, the Red team leader began a swift trot out of the woods straight into the first punji trap that Buddy had dug in that section. To make matters worse, instead of his foot going straight down onto the nails, he stumbled down and forward. He felt the agony as six of the nails pierced him in the toes of his boot and drove into his leg from his shin up to just below his knee. For the second time that evening, a cry rent the darkness as he howled and swore.

The other two team members got on each side of him and slowly lifted him out. In his case, it was a very painful process to remove the spikes from his leg. They applied a tourniquet and then bandaged the wounds as best as possible.

"We're getting you out of here," said the man who had spoken first.

"No!" said the leader. "You get to that house and complete the mission. We have a job to do! I'll look after myself."

The other two looked at each other with some apprehension and then turned and headed toward the house. As they left, none of them saw or heard a shadowy figure approach the wounded man from behind.

Up above, the drone had given its operator a clear enough picture of what had happened. Under the rules of engagement, he and the other driver were to provide emergency support. There was no way to drive his vehicle down to that edge of the property, so he decided to continue monitoring the situation. With their comms shot, he had no knowledge that things had gone badly for Blue team. Otherwise, he might have decided to cut their total losses and drive away into the night.

On the ground, the remaining two members of Red team departed from the line they had been following. They rightly assumed that there could be other booby traps ahead. They wrongly assumed that departing from that line would be safer. Halfway to the house, one of the men stopped his companion and pointed ahead. There, nestled up against the stump of a dead tree, was the shadowy outline of a man. They strained their eyes to see details. Then the man who had stopped first pulled out a pair of night vision binoculars and focused on the figure. The head was drooping down. By all appearances, the guard had fallen asleep on his watch.

Using hand signals, the first man motioned to himself and then made a semicircle and then pointed to the figure. Pointing at the other man's gun and then the figure, he made it clear that his teammate was to keep a lookout on the figure and be ready to fire. The second man nodded.

Slowly, the first man stealthily moved low along the ground as he made his way to the stump. Pulling out his KA-BAR knife from its sheath, he came at the figure from the side and to the rear. With one swift motion, he swung the blade into the figure's chest. Perplexity ran through his mind as the blade felt little resistance until it hit the wooden stump. Yanking the knife free, he grabbed what turned out to be an old plastic wig head. Disgusted, he looked back at where he had left his teammate. He was nowhere to be seen.

A normal person would have panicked, but he had seen combat in rough areas. Logic said that the enemy was behind and possibly also in front of him. Now that he knew his cover was blown, there was no point in subtlety. He turned and ran toward the house as swiftly as he could, gun drawn.

§ § §

The drone operator had raised the altitude of the drone so that he could keep both of the Red team members in view. As the new leader had moved forward, he had seen a figure approach the other member from behind. Then the team member had gone down without a struggle. Just as quickly, the figure was gone.

He made a decision. He was to assist in case of an emergency, and this qualified as just that. He broke all the rules and dialed the other driver's number on his cell phone. No encryption. He knew someone would be listening. They were always listening. But this was an emergency. He would be as brief as possible.

"What's up?" the other driver's voice was strained. Not knowing what was happening added to the tension of the mission itself.

"Red trouble. Going in main entrance. Meet me there. Over."

"Roger. Over."

He clicked off the call. He didn't have time to recall the drone. He put it in a circular holding pattern. With luck, it would stay aloft and not be too far out of range from wind drift when this was all over. Then he turned the ignition and gunned the engine.

§ § §

Blue team leader wasn't sure how Red team was doing, but on his way down the hill, he had heard a cry from their side of the property. Most likely, they had run into a few snags themselves. His mind processed the irony of that word passing through his mind as the vision replayed of barbed wire flashing in the moonlight. He had to be careful. Someone was prepared for their arrival. But he had survived more than one tour of duty because he was smart.

Dropping to his knee, he stopped and analyzed the situation. If he were expecting company, where would he be right now? His eyes focused on the barn. It was high enough to command a view of the property. Someone had to be there. Was it the husband? They knew he had special forces training. If so, he would confront him directly. If he could take out the husband in the barn, Red team would be free to deal with the woman.

Likely, the man would have some type of night vision goggles himself and might be focusing on him. There was no way around it. He sprinted toward the barn, zigzagging as he went. There was no gunfire. Maybe the barn was empty. He had to check.

He went to the barn doors and eased one open. Inside, he saw a truck and a motorcycle. Did they belong to the family or to somebody else? No way of knowing. He could hear no movements. If anyone were keeping watch, they would be in the loft.

Slowly, as quietly as possible, he walked up the wooden stairs. He knew absolute silence was impossible. His gun was pointed up as he made his way into the loft. When his head cleared the landing, he peered around. There were several bales of hay in random stacks, which made it impossible to see if the loft was occupied or not. Looking toward the window that faced the property pasture he had come from, he saw nothing. When he turned toward the window that faced the house, he saw it: a couple of chip bags lying on the floor next to bales set up like a recliner. It made sense that whoever was up here would be keeping watch on the house. That meant it likely wasn't the husband. He would be in the house or nearby.

He eased up the rest of the stairs and then decided to circle around the bales from the opposite side. As he turned the corner, he realized that the makeshift seat was empty. There were numerous bottles and wrappers scattered. Someone had been here keeping watch. Where were they now? Just then, the hairs on his neck bristled as he heard a Southern drawl calmly state, "Drop your weapon, and you jess might live."

Pure, unbridled fury coursed through his veins as he thought of his team lying injured on the hill, fallen prey to a couple of tricks. Again, the phrase echoed through his mind: these people were going to pay. He whirled around, ready to shoot whatever he saw moving. What he saw were rapid, brilliant bursts of light from a 100,000-lumen tactical flashlight. The flash of light in his night vision gear overwhelmed his retinas, and his pupils immediately constricted. In the same moment, the goggles' automatic brightness control reacted to the light and shut down the night vision.

Still, his muscle memory enabled him to point at the light source and begin firing rapidly. Booms echoed through the loft as he unloaded his 30-round magazine. Unfortunately for him, the flashlight that blinded him was the kind that could be activated by a remote switch. Elam, standing off to the side and tucked behind a solid wooden beam, squeezed the trigger on his rifle once and watched as the man jolted backwards and then fell to the floor, gun clattering beside him.

"Welcome to 'Bama, baby," said Elam. Then he switched off the light and strode to the window to listen and watch. He was pretty sure they weren't done yet.

§ § §

Buddy had seen the lights in the hay loft, heard the multiple handgun rounds, and then heard the single shot followed by silence. Then the light was extinguished immediately. He was sure that Elam was in control. A few moments after the excitement had died down, Midnight tensed with his head pointed in the direction of the woods. They had heard a cry from that direction earlier, and Buddy was sure someone had found one of his traps there. There seemed to be someone coming from that direction for Midnight to alert. Still, he exercised patience. Elam and Dale Ray had warned him that he was to guard the house only. They would take care of the perimeter. As Elam had put it, "Whoever comes may create a distraction to lure you away from the house so they can get at Janine." In spite of his desire to act, he remained quietly in the woodshed.

§ § §

The remaining Red team member was sprinting toward the house when the action in the barn loft occurred. He wasn't sure who had won or lost that round, but in his mind, it gave him an opportunity. Between him and the house was a small structure or shed about forty or fifty yards away. From there he could assess the situation—if it were empty. There was only one way to be sure, and that was to clear it with a grenade.

He stopped and retrieved one from his pouch. He pulled the pin with his left hand and drew back with his right hand to throw it. At that moment, he felt a steely grip seize his right hand and clench it tightly until his fingers hurt. Simultaneously, his right arm was twisted inward and jerked high up his back. A foot locked in front of his instep, and he was pushed violently to the ground. The hand never lost its grip on his.

"Who the devil do you think you are?" he snarled.

An icy cold voice whispered back, "The fella you never saw." He felt a sharp sensation in his upper back. Pain coursed through his body as a knife entered him. Regardless of the way the movies portray it, he couldn't scream. He gasped and reached back in vain with his left hand, wildly thrashing to try and remove the blade. He could only lie there until the last of the eerie green light from his goggles disappeared from his vision.

When he was sure the man was dead, Dale Ray searched the man's pockets and pouches with his left hand until he found what he was looking for: a roll of tape. It wasn't good old Alabama chrome, but it would do. He tightly wrapped the dead man's right hand around the grenade until he was satisfied that it could not be activated. Then he withdrew his blade and wiped it clean on the man's pants before putting it back in his sheath.

When that was done, he gave the clear call of a whippoorwill. A few seconds later, Midnight was trotting toward him with Buddy standing at the edge of the woodshed, dimly backlit by the security light on the barn in the front yard. Buddy walked toward Dale Ray as Midnight sniffed the motionless visitor.

"Any trouble?" Buddy asked.

Dale Ray shook his head no and then added, "He was about to frag you and Midnight."

Buddy was troubled by the news. "Any others?"

"Two more. One down past the stump. One down by the traps."

"I take it they're no longer a threat."

Dale Ray shook his head again. "Probably more somewheres. I heared a faint whining sound up above us down there. Somebody probably watching what's happening."

That was the most Buddy had heard him speak yet. "Drone."

Dale Ray nodded.

"Well, if they can see us, then we probably should split up. They can't follow us both."

Their discussion was interrupted by the sound of engines roaring as two dark SUVs turned into the driveway and began racing toward the house.

Chapter 29

The driver who had been operating the drone was under no illusion that stealth was going to succeed. On the phone once more with the other driver, he had simply told him, "Straight up. Full force." Then he hung up and concentrated on driving. If the perimeter were guarded, it might mean the house was unguarded. How many people were they up against? He didn't know. If they tried a blitzkrieg tactic, they still might succeed.

Normally, any operational commander would have called off the mission and pulled remaining forces. Live to fight another day. But once you swore an oath to the organization, you were in for life whatever that meant and however death found you. They were sent on this mission to literally do or die. Back in his military days, you knew that if you survived, you would get out of the forces eventually, and he had. Now you were in—period.

As he gunned his engine straight down the gravel driveway with the other driver beginning to fan out from behind him so that they represented two more difficult targets, he took stock of the situation. Nobody visible in the headlights. No Red team or Blue team in their gear. No enemy targets. Still taking the lead, he determined to get as close to the house as he could and then force his way inside. The other driver would either do the same and join him or hang back and give suppressing fire if they encountered opposition.

Up in the hay loft, Elam had heard the vehicles just before they made the turn. With only seconds to react, he pointed his rifle at the driver's side of the windshield of the lead vehicle and pulled the trigger.

The driver's windshield exploded as the bullet entered and whizzed past his head. The spiderweb of cracks made seeing out nearly impossible, but he aimed toward the house, swerving as he continued closing the remaining distance in order to make a clear shot at himself impossible.

The second driver heard the boom and saw the flash of light from the barn window. He slammed on his brakes, threw his door open, and began shooting in that direction with his own rifle. Elam dropped down and back from the window as bullets began tearing into the wood around him.

Approaching the house beyond the woodshed, Buddy had understood in an instant what the play was from the two vehicles. He had no idea how many men were in each. He gave the command, "Midnight, away!" and then watched as the dog began running away from him at an angle. Then he began racing toward the front.

The second SUV had stopped up the driveway after a rifle shot sounded from the barn, and Buddy could hear gunfire coming from that direction. He hoped Elam was safe. The first SUV had continued toward the house in an erratic motion. He didn't know if the driver had been hit or not. His question was answered as the vehicle braked into a slide. The driver door swung open, and a man began running toward the front door with an assault-style rifle in his grip. No one else got out of the vehicle.

Buddy raised his gun and fired, but the man was not distracted by the sound. Unless he was taken out, he was going to get into the house, where Janine had no one to defend her. As the man started to leap onto the porch, from behind him came a black blur, and then the man went down.

Buddy was sprinting now. The sounds were a cacophony. Ahead, he could hear the man on the porch screaming in pain and swearing at the top of his lungs as Midnight was crushing his wrist. The rifle had fallen to the side. Midnight was growling louder than Buddy had ever heard. Up the driveway, the sound of rapid gunfire from the other SUV was punctuated by another boom from a hunting rifle. Then the firing ceased completely.

On the porch, the man was trying to kick and beat at Midnight. The powerful Shepherd let go of the man's arm and went straight for his throat. The man's screams were sheer pain and terror. Midnight was in a frenzy as he shook his muzzle back and forth while deep throaty snarls and rumbles emanated from his chest. The man was flailing his bloody right arm and grabbing at Midnight with his left when Buddy reached the porch. The man's body shivered and convulsed; then he lay still.

"Release!" Buddy said, but Midnight continued to clamp down on the man's throat in his mouth. Buddy had to forcibly remove Midnight. Even then, the dog continued to growl and snarl at the inert figure.

"Everybody okay?" shouted Buddy.

"Good here," said Elam from the doorway of the barn as he flicked on a flashlight. He began walking to the second SUV to survey the damage there.

"Dale Ray!" Buddy shouted again. He turned around to look back toward the woodshed and found himself a yard away from the man. In spite of his training, Buddy jerked backwards. He let out a deep breath. "Don't you ever do that to me again. You about gave me a heart attack."

Dale Ray nodded and then looked at the man on the porch. "Good dog," he commented and then said, "You got a shotgun and some birdshot?"

Buddy looked at him quizzically. "Yeah. What do you need that for?"

"Just one more thing," Dale Ray answered.

"Let me check on Janine first, and then I'll bring it out."

Buddy shouted Janine's name and let her know that everything was okay outside. Then he stepped around the man's body and unlocked the door. He flicked on the porch lights and the living room lights and entered the house. He repeated his message inside. A couple of minutes later, he returned with a shotgun and handed it to Dale Ray, who nodded and then disappeared back into the dark toward the woods.

Chapter 30

Buddy called Sheriff Matt's number and gave him a quick summary. As expected, he was already en route. Janine had already called after the first sound of trouble, as had the neighbors. Ten minutes later, with lights flashing but no sirens, Sheriff Matt arrived with three other cars close behind.

They made their way around the first SUV near the barn, where one car stopped. The other three drove down to the house. Sheriff Matt got out and approached Buddy.

"Everybody safe?" he asked.

"Yes," said Buddy. "At least the ones we want to be," he said looking down at the man on the porch.

Sheriff Matt studied the prone figure and then flicked his eyes at Buddy. "Awful close. How many were there this time?"

"Dale Ray said there was a team of three that came up through the woods. They're all present and accounted for. We heard a noise up on the hillside, so I'm guessing that there was another team of three up there. As far as I know, only one made it down to the barn. He went in after Elam."

"And the idiot never came back out," said Matt.

Buddy nodded. "Then these two SUVs came blazing down the driveway at the end. They only had one driver each and nobody else that we could see. I'm guessing it was two three-man teams with these lying back in support. Oh, and Dale Ray is sure he heard a drone. I don't know if one of these guys was operating it or if there's another person or two unaccounted for."

Matt looked at two of his deputies. "Search the vehicles and see if you can find any radio for operating a drone."

Just at that moment, a shotgun blast punctured the night. The boom reverberated off the buildings and the far hills. Sheriff Matt and his men instinctively reached for their sidearms.

"That's Dale Ray," said Buddy. "He wanted a shotgun with birdshot for some reason."

They continued talking, and Matt placed a call to the coroner to show up "with extra help." A few minutes later, Dale Ray came walking around the corner of the house with a large object in tow.

"That would be the drone, I'm guessing," said Matt as Dale Ray dragged it into the light. He whistled. "That's a government or military-grade, if I'm not mistaken." He looked over and said, "Dale Ray, how in the world did you shoot that thing down in the middle of the night?"

"I kindly tracked the sound for a minute or two to get the pattern," said Dale Ray matter-of-factly. He shrugged.

"I'm inclined to think some of those stories I've heard about you hunting at night are true," said Matt.

Dale Ray's expression remained impassive under his moustache.

"If there are maybe two unaccounted for, then I'm thinking that we ought to settle that question sooner than later," said Matt. "I'll leave two of the men here at the house while the rest of us search the property."

"Might not be a good idea to walk up there with flashlights not knowing who is out there," said Buddy.

"What do you suggest then?"

"I'll go," said Dale Ray. "If'n I can take Midnight with me."

Both men looked at him and then back at each other. They nodded at each other and then turned back to Dale Ray. "Okay," said Buddy. He knelt down to Midnight and pointed at Dale Ray. "Go," he said.

The two of them walked up past the barn and then disappeared from view.

"That's one scary guy," said Buddy.

Matt nodded his head. "Yep. If there's anybody else out there, I hope they don't make the stupid mistake of challenging him."

While they waited for Dale Ray to return, one of the deputies had walked down with the drone controller in his gloved hand. "This is the only one we found in both vehicles. It was in the one here near the house."

Matt nodded. "Good work." To Buddy he said, "I guess the drone was handled locally then."

"They were either autonomous or they were in touch with their bosses remotely. Probably ought to look at their phones in detail. Might find out some more information that way."

While the deputies were searching the vehicles and bodies of the four men in and around the house and barn, Dale Ray came walking into the light with a man draped over his shoulders like a buck. He came near the porch and then placed his load on the ground. The man grunted and groaned as Dale Ray dropped him. His feet and hands were bound tightly with tape. One foot had no boot and was tightly wrapped with bloody gauze. Buddy noticed the left arm of his jacket was ripped. The man's eyes indicated that he was in pain—and that he was afraid.

"Any more?" asked Buddy.

"Just one. He must've got tangled up on some barbed wire and bled out."

"Sheriff, I think we can go collect the other three in the woods now if you can get your men to guard the house and this guy while we're gone for a few minutes."

Matt, Elam and Dale Ray walked alongside Buddy as he slowly drove an ATV. After passing the woodshed, they came upon the prone figure of the last man Dale Ray had encountered. Sheriff Matt whistled when he saw the grenade taped securely in the man's hand.

"I reckon he saved your life," he said to Buddy.

From there, they passed along to the dead tree stump where they saw the wig-head decoy. After that, they found the second man next to his rifle. Then they made it to the edge of the woods where the Red team leader had been left. All three men had suffered a single knife wound to the back.

"Be careful where you step and just follow me," said Buddy. "There's been some major digging around here by some groundhogs, and there are a few more holes that I know of right in this area."

Sheriff Matt shone his flashlight down into the punji trap near the man and said, "Looks like he mighta stepped into one of these here groundhog holes and injured himself. I'd suggest filling these in so Janine don't hurt herself."

"I'm hoping to be able to get rid of all 'em," said Buddy thoughtfully.

"Well, let's get these three up to the barn for Don," said Matt. "He should be here shortly if he hasn't already gotten there by the time we get back. How do you want to haul them?"

"You could strap 'em on like deer," suggested Elam.

"Only if you'd field dress 'em first," said Buddy.

"I can do that," said Elam with an impish grin as he rolled his toothpick back and forth. "But Don might sic the union on me for doing his job."

"I really don't want to have to clean the four-wheeler," said Buddy. He pulled out several coils of rope from the milk crate strapped to the back platform. "I figured we could just pull them up. What do you think?" he asked as he looked at Matt.

"I doubt anybody is coming to claim them," said Matt. "And given what they were here to do, I don't reckon we owe them any particular courtesies."

Twenty-five minutes later, they arrived back at the barn, a few minutes having been spent carefully removing and securing the grenade. The coroner had arrived with two ice wagons. As they pulled in, Buddy kept his eyes on the sole mercenary who had survived. The man's face registered increased apprehension as Buddy drove up into the light dragging the bodies of his fallen comrades. That was the sign Buddy was looking for. The man had been holding out hope that someone had made it out alive who could signal for help or let their leaders know what had happened. Now that hope was extinguished. Buddy knew he could use that to his advantage.

"Good morning, Sheriff, fellows," said Don. His bald head shone in the light. "Buddy, it looks like you're beginning to have a mighty serious pest control problem around here."

"We did. I think we caught 'em all tonight."

"Good, good," said Don. "Same as before, Sheriff?"

"Same as before," answered Matt. "Make sure to note any and all tattoos and markings on them. Take prints and dental in case we can match any of them, although I wouldn't be surprised if their records have been scrubbed like the first two. Oh, and there's one more up on the hill somewhere. Have one of your boys go with Dale Ray to collect him too."

After Don and his workers began processing and loading the corpses, Matt looked at the remaining Blue team member while he spoke to Buddy. "What about him?"

"I was hoping I'd get to ask him some important questions before you took him in," said Buddy.

"Well, the three of you are duly deputized," said Matt. "I think I can trust him to your care. Besides," he said as he squatted down and looked the man in the eyes, "he looks like he's hurt pretty badly. I don't know that he would be able to last the car ride back to the jail."

The man's eyes widened. "Wait! Don't leave me here with them! I demand to be taken into protective custody. I know my rights!"

Matt studied him long and hard and then spoke quietly. His voice was calm and measured. "Mister, I'm the law in this county. And the law says you gave up your rights when you trespassed on this man's property with the intent to do him and his wife bodily harm. You should have thought about that before you came here." With that, he stood up, turned, and walked away. He called over his shoulder, "Buddy, I'm gonna have two men up at the county road on shifts for the next forty-eight hours."

"Thank you, Sheriff," said Buddy as Matt got into his cruiser and drove off. The three men had subconsciously tightened their circle around the man as he lay on the ground.

"You can't get away this!" the man cried in frantic tones.

Elam removed his toothpick from his mouth and pointed it at the man. The impish smile had returned to his face as he spoke. "Fella, did you know that a passel of hogs can devour an entire human body and never leave a trace?"

Chapter 31

Paris, France

Chantille de Bruner held her breath and concentrated deeply. Her hands held a long, slender stainless steel tube with a plunger. Slowly and very carefully, she pushed the plunger with one hand while the other guided the tip of the tube in what seemed to be a random pattern. Out of the tube came a lush violet paste of confectioners' sugar, butter, raw goat milk, coloring, and (for this client) aged Madagascar vanilla.

The petals grew before her eyes as she created the flower which would serve as the focal point of the cake. When she had finished, she straightened her frame and stepped backward before exhaling a deep breath. She surveyed her work. She was, like most artists, her own most exacting critic. What she examined with her eyes was a masterpiece. It was not among her greatest of works, but she knew that this was the door-opener. If the client was pleased, this would not be her last or her most expensive order to fulfill.

Known to her clientele only as Chanti, she stood a petite-but-athletic 167 centimeters. Her frequently changing hair color was currently a deep rouge but had often been midnight raven or even a mix of pink and purple. No one could ever discover who did her magnificent styles. (She did them herself because the privacy kept others from knowing that the spectrum of changes belied very blonde roots.) Her luscious brown eyes were captivating to most of her male clients and the object of envy for many of the female ones.

"Chanti can bake your darkest secrets into a cake!" was how one prominent public figure had exclaimed to her social circle. And that was how her business had gone from making cupcakes for weddings to designing memories for millionaires. She worked alone, averaged one order (of usually one but sometimes several pieces) every week to two weeks, and lived well above average means. One did not walk into a shop and ring a bell for her services. New customers must be referred by an existing one. Only then would Chantille de Bruner consider your order, and she had turned many away.

Her services had been used across the breadth of Europe and, on rare occasion, one or two Asian countries. She had completely eschewed the Arab clientele. She considered them to be pompous in spite of their overly pleasant social graces. Churches were not among her customers, save one church of no particular prominence.

For this church, once per year, she created an exquisite work that was delivered in time to be duly advertised before it was placed into the general fundraising auction. After word had gotten around that the cake up for bid was "very possibly" or "most likely" created by Chanti, the bids exceeded every other item on display.

The previous year's work had been of the head of the Christ with his hands held before him plaintively. From his brow and streaming down his face were great drops of blood. The eyes on the cake seemed to be alive. The pain in his face seemed to reach a private part of everyone who looked at it. The simple script in icing had read, "Man of Sorrows. Acquainted with Grief."

A private donor had purchased it for over €5000 and had immediately donated it to a museum, where it was placed on display for the public to enjoy for four weeks. Photos of it had then been commissioned, with one being given a place of distinction in the museum's religious section. When asked to attest to its origin, Chanti would neither confirm nor deny. She would only say, "If there is a God, I hope that he would enjoy such a cake as that."

As for her other works, she had her doubts as to whether or not the Deity would be pleased. They ranged from the lurid to the macabre. Truly, she baked the darkest secrets into existence and placed them on a platter as a spectacle to her clients and their guests, whether many or few.

Sometimes her clients would request a specific design. More often than not, they would ask Chanti to surprise them. She never failed to exceed their expectations.

New clients had to meet with her in person: no emissary, head butler, or chief of staff. "Chanti only deals with principals," was the word that passed from client to client. The client himself or herself had to agree to meet with Chanti directly. Many found it most unusual that Chanti asked for their right hand. She would hold it, stroke it, close her eyes at times—this could last for up to fifteen minutes. She would ask only a minimal number of questions. Then she would leave and go create cakes from their dreams—or nightmares.

She was called a clairvoyant. Some said she had second sight. Others were sure that she was a full-fledged witch. Whatever her secret, it was hers alone. She shared her heart with no one who could be traced by any of her clients, many of whom had whole security apparatuses devoted to their safety. She made no phone calls that could be tracked to anyone other than her clients or her suppliers. She had no social media accounts, close friends, or lovers (active or jilted).

What she did have was unparalleled skill. She had been privately tutored by one of the best cake designers in France and had studied baking with an organic culinary school in her mid to late teens. That much could be ascertained by attempts to vet her. Beyond that, she would never divulge any details of her family or her background. Some assessments indicated that she could have arisen from one of the Gypsy clans within France or even Romania. Their disdain for government registrations of births was widely known. Initially, this presented some cause for concern, but after creating an especially lovely arrangement for the President of France's wife which pleased her to no end, the referrals came faster than she could fulfill. If she was good enough for the leader of the country, she could be trusted. Thus, Chanti could now pick and choose her customers.

Baron Klaus Maginon was the man for whom this cake was intended. He was extremely wealthy. His family was from old blood. He was powerful. And he was giving a party for a group of friends at one of his chateaux in two days.

Chanti looked at the whole creation once more. The cake was a meter long by a half-meter wide and was at first glance a simple sheet cake with white icing. Across the surface of the field of white lay a single flower with a long green stem and violet petals. Encircling the stem at a slight angle was the figure and body of a slender serpent. It was near in color to the stem but was readily distinguishable once the eye caught it. The body disappeared underneath the base of the flower itself. At the far end of the flower, one could see that the petals were slightly disturbed and that underneath them was the snout of the snake. In the shaded area beneath the petal, one could just discern a glowing set of wicked, slitted eyes.

The cake melded beauty and death together into a subtle display of danger and caution. Chanti placed the silver lid in its position onto the serving tray. When possible, she always asked for the clients to provide the trays or platters themselves to fully match the occasion. This one was a solid silver tray and lid with intricate knotwork.

Chanti would deliver the cake herself. It was another of her nonnegotiable demands. She explained simply that she would trust no courier other than herself to ensure that her creations were handled exactly. She had ridden in limousines, exclusive coaches on trains, and had even flown on chartered or private jets in order to deliver her creations to her clients. They provided the transport or the cost of it, of course.

She placed the entire silver service into her commercial cooler. The Baron would be sending a limousine for her the next morning to take her from Paris across the border into Belgium. She would take the time to fastidiously clean her kitchen, wipe all the counters, and then relax in a bath before calling it an early night.

Chapter 32

At dawn the next morning, Chanti was already seated at a window in her top floor apartment with a steaming cup of strong black tea. This morning, the taste was more bitter due to the anti-anxiety medication she had mixed into the drink. It was a cloudy day, but there was sunlight to be enjoyed. So she sat silently watching the morning transcend the night. First, there were familiar shapes on the skyline and then the sight of landmarks near and far. In the street below, the headlamps on the cars joined the streetlights as they together closed their eyes for their daily rest.

Chanti loved sunlight. She basked in its warmth no matter how hot the day, and she mourned its passing every evening when it set. Most of her life had been spent in darkness, whether physical, spiritual, psychological, or emotional. It had shaped her, scarred her, and stamped its cold, lifeless fear upon her very being.

She had been accepted into several culinary schools to study the art of baking but had chosen the one which had windows in its kitchens and classrooms. When the days were dreary and rainy, most of Paris seemed morose, but Chanti could look out her window and still see some daylight. It brought her comfort, the same primal sense of safety and wellbeing that our ancestors must have experienced in the fields or forests when they lay around even the dying embers of their campfires.

By 8:00 a.m., she was fully dressed and ready for the limo which was to arrive at 9:00 sharp. She took the time to look over her schedule. One week from now, she had a three-tier cake to celebrate the birthday of a duchess. Three weeks out was the gala where she would be preparing a massive cake for the attendees. That would require extra work. She made calls and placed orders for supplies she did not have in stock.

A ring on the buzzer alerted her. She looked at the clock: 9:00 a.m. sharp. She called down and told the visitor that she would be down as soon as she loaded everything into the lift. She placed the silver service tray onto a rolling cart, added a kit with essentials for any minor touchups that might be necessary after the trip, grabbed her bag, and then locked her apartment. On the way down, she placed her shaded glasses on her face and began breathing slowly and rhythmically. "Pass the test, Chanti," she repeated to herself in her mind.

As the doors to the lift opened in the lobby of the apartment building, she found herself looking through her glasses at the chauffeur. He was a complete stranger. That was good. At least the trip would be less stressful.

"Ms. de Bruner?" he inquired in a professional tone.

"Chanti. Please, call me Chanti."

"As you wish, Chanti. My name is Frederic. May I assist you with anything?"

"Frederic, please hold the door open for me. I will manage the cart myself out to the limousine. It folds up, and I will take it with me."

After the cake was placed flat on the floorspace of the limousine in the passenger compartment, the cart was folded up and placed in the boot. Afterward, Frederic saw her into the vehicle, shut the door behind her, and then eased the big car into the street to begin the journey. Chanti closed her eyes behind her glasses and tried to settle her mind.

Three hours later, the limousine arrived at the chateau. The outer gate was brick and wrought iron inset from the road about twenty meters. The driveway itself was an immaculate set of brick pavers which looked ancient but felt as smooth as glass. Chanti supposed the limo absorbed most of the bumpiness. But, then again, the ultra-rich had more than enough money to spend on their driveways. As they passed down the tree-lined avenue, Chanti wondered if anyone who lived here was ever truly happy. Some places felt soulless no matter how beautifully decorated or ornate they were on the outside.

They passed through the trees into a clearing and then approached the main inner gate of the chateau. Once inside, the driver pulled the vehicle to the side of the chateau where the kitchen and service area was located. After turning off the engine, he opened Chanti's door and said,

"Welcome to Chateau Sauvageon, Chanti. This is the ramp which leads straight into the kitchen and food storage areas. We have a cooler inside which meets your specifications."

As Chanti was about to load the cake onto her cart, two men approached the limousine with a large dog on a leash. Chanti recognized it as a Malinois. It looked alert and very intelligent. Chanti gasped and consciously stepped behind the cart.

"Excuse us, Ms. de Bruner, but we are part of the security team. Would you be so kind as to allow us to have our dog perform a quick search of what you are bringing into the chateau? It won't take a moment." Noticing her reaction to the dog, the handler added, "I can assure you he is quite trained and won't touch or damage anything."

Chanti jerked her head at the chauffeur and said, "No one said anything of dogs! I was bitten by a dog when I was a small girl, and I have hated them ever since!" Turning back to the handler, she said icily, "I will not be so kind as to allow a dog's nose anywhere near my cake or my personal belongings." To the chauffeur she added, "If this is how I am to be treated, I will deliver this cake at once—onto the ground!"

Taken aback, the handler was about to stand his ground and demand that she allow the dog to proceed. He had strict orders, and the dog's snout had worked its way around and over the luggage and effects of people more important than a baker, in his opinion. The matter was settled at once when a man's deep baritone voice spoke from a window which had been opened. "See that Chanti is not disturbed in any way. And please show her to the library when she has finished unloading."

In an instant, the two men turned and walked away with the dog heeling. The chauffeur had a new look of respect in his eyes as he approached Chanti. "Please, if I may assist you in any way…"

Chanti's face was pointed to the window. Through her darkened glasses, she had caught sight of the face. She nodded her tilted head courteously. "Thank you," she said. The face in the window acknowledged her response and then disappeared.

After placing the cake onto the counter inside, Chanti shooed the chauffeur outside the kitchen until she could check it in privacy once more before placing it into the cooler. It had suffered nothing from the trip. Satisfied, she opened the doors to the cooler and placed the cake inside on a large, empty shelf. When she exited the kitchen, Frederic showed her to a wide staircase and walked with her. The curved wooden rails were dark with age. After two flights, he walked with her down a hallway and knocked on a door.

"Come in," was the reply.

Frederic opened the door and allowed Chanti to pass before closing the door behind her as he exited the room. Chanti found herself face to face with Klaus Maginon, one of the most powerful men in Europe and possibly the world. He had a strong jawline, slender nose, and a strong forehead with a receding hairline. His skin bore the look of a man who couldn't be bothered with yachts or winter vacations in the tropics.

"Chanti, thank you for coming. Please, have a seat," he motioned to a large leather chair by a fireplace, which was currently empty of flame.

Chanti took the seat and forced herself to smile. "I'm delighted to be able to prepare a cake for you, Monsieur Baron," she said.

"I am very much looking forward to seeing it," he said. "My colleagues tell me that your work is unsurpassed. I must say I found your interview to be most intriguing."

Chanti laughed. "Most of my clients say that until they receive their first order."

"And then what do they say?"

"Some are silent. Some laugh nervously. Some gush on about how much they love what I have created for them. It depends. I am prepared to offer you a private viewing of your cake, or, if you prefer, you can see it for the first time when you show it to your guests."

"What do you recommend?"

"I usually recommend that the host enjoy it for the first time in the company of his guests. The reactions are shared with those who matter to you. But some cannot wait that long or are too afraid of what I may have concocted. It really is your choice."

"Then I shall adhere to your council and wait until tomorrow evening."

"You will do me the honor of letting me know personally how you like it?"

"I will call you as soon as I'm available and tell you everything."

"Thank you, Monsieur Baron. Now I must be on my way. The next three weeks are particularly busy ones, and I must prepare for my other clients."

Baron Maginon rang a silver bell on the table beside him. The door opened immediately, and Frederic stood at attention.

"Frederic, please see that Chanti returns home safely. And show her every courtesy."

After Chanti had departed in the limousine complete with a full meal which had already been packed by one of the chef's assistants, Baron Maginon rang for his security chief.

"Please proceed with the test," he said and then hung up the phone.

A few minutes later, a man arrived in the kitchen area with a long, slender rod shaped much like an oversized toothpick. He carefully lifted the lid on one side just a few centimeters high enough to insert the rod. After he removed it, he swabbed the rod and placed the swab into a handheld device. A green light showed. He made a call back to Baron Maginon, who answered on the first ring.

"It's fine. No traces of poison at all." He paused and listened. "Yes, sir. I'll notify the chef that it will be served as planned."

Chapter 33

Sand Mountain, Alabama

In the end, he had talked. It took some prodding, the cattle kind, along with other sorts of persuasion. But the attacker had told them everything he knew. They were part of a security force that had belonged to Trantwa Holdings before it had dissolved and its owner had disappeared. Now they received their directions and pay from a base in Europe.

Their mission had been to abduct Janine—and Buddy, if he did not present any hindrance. Otherwise, he was to have been neutralized. They were to take Janine to a warehouse in the Atlanta metro area, where she would be questioned by two people in the organization who were trained in interrogation. Yes, it would have included drugs and torture if necessary. They had done it before to American citizens both in and out of the country.

They wanted all computers, cell phones, thumb drives, and anything else that might have contained a copy of a video named DangleDrop that was deemed highly important to the organization. No, he didn't know who was at the top. There was a company by the name of Drieëndertig. He also gave them the name of the operations director who was supposed to have been monitoring the situation until all the comms had failed.

When they were searching him, they discovered that he also bore numerous tattoos including the counterclockwise spiral. Buddy recognized it as the pedophile symbol Sheriff Matt had mentioned to him from the coroner's report and stated as much.

"So, are you a child diddler?" Elam asked him in his nasal twang.

"It's the price of admission," the man answered. "If you want to be in, you gotta pay the price. But once you're in, you're set for life."

"Which, in your case, looks like it's not gonna be that long," said Elam. Turning to Buddy, he said, "I had a cousin that was messed up by a fella like this. Coached his Little League baseball team. It ruined his whole life. He ended up committing suicide when he was about to graduate high school. Left a note telling everything that had happened and who done it. The queer that done it left the state before we could get him. Buddy, if you don't mind, I'd like to settle a score for my cousin."

Buddy looked into Elam's eyes for just a moment. There was a look of malice and determination that he hadn't seen there before. "Go ahead. He would've killed me or you without a second thought. Or Janine." He looked at the man and said, "It's obvious you been in the service. I've only got one more question. Why would you hook up with an organization that hurts families and children instead of something honorable?"

The man's eyes flashed an intense look of hatred at Buddy and Elam and Dale Ray as he hissed his answer. "Power! We serve a power that you don't understand!" With that, his voice changed to a guttural and hollow sound as he began to speak in strange syllables. His head jerked from side to side, and his eyes rolled back in his head. Foam begin to form in a crest around his lips.

The hair on Buddy's arms and on the back of his neck stood up. He looked at Dale Ray and Elam. They seemed to be equally affected. "Get him out of here," he said. He wasn't sure what was happening, but it wasn't natural. He left to go back into the house to check on Janine. The last sight he had of the man was Elam wrapping duct tape around his mouth to silence him before loading him up into the bed of his red pickup.

Chapter 34

Paris, France

Sunday mid-morning, Chanti's phone rang. She looked at the number, took a deep breath, and answered.

"Hello?"

"Chanti, Baron Maginon. How are you this morning?"

"Baron, I am doing well. Yourself?"

"In fine health, thank you. I wanted to tell you that your cake created quite a stir at my party last evening."

Chanti voiced a soft laugh. "I hope, Baron, that it was a good stir."

"Quite. The guests found it intriguing, and for a few of them, they said it was very fitting for the occasion."

"And you, Baron? What were your thoughts?"

"Chanti, I have never witnessed a more artistic and yet so expressive work of culinary art. And you can rest assured that I have been served by the best my whole life."

"That is indeed a high compliment, Baron, and I accept it as such," said Chanti. "Then you found my hidden surprise?"

"I did. There was some question as to why there was icing within the cake. But after cutting a few slices, it was apparent that the cake was home to several more other hidden serpents. Five, to be precise."

"Making the total number six."

"Yes. I don't know how you do it, but your work is on a level which surpasses all others. That is the main reason I called you."

"Oh? And why is that?" She waited for what she suspected would be his answer.

"I must have you bake another cake for a larger gathering that is coming up very shortly."

"Baron, I'm afraid that I am booked for the next several months."

"Chanti, I will triple or quadruple your normal price. Please do not be offended when I say that I cannot take no for an answer here. Please tell me that you will cancel a booking or find a way to fit my needs into your schedule."

"I will consider it if you will tell me a date and how many guests it must serve and any details you wish to share about the meeting or the guests. Be as reserved as you wish."

"The meeting will be held on September twenty-first. You may think of the people attending as a mix of a company's board of directors as well as participants in a festival which I host at one of my estates."

"And how many would I be preparing for?"

"Less than forty in total."

"Very well. As I said, I will consider it and give you an answer in the next three days."

"Thank you, Chanti. I cannot stress to you how important it is to me if you would indeed agree to make something for this occasion."

"Yes, well, I will bear that in mind. Thank you for calling, Baron."

"Thank you, Chanti."

Chanti ended the call, put the phone down, and then pressed her hands against her face with her elbows on the counter. The autumn equinox. It would, of course, be the autumn equinox. She rarely cried, but tears began to moisten her fingers as the cake and its decoration began to form in her mind.

Chapter 35

Sand Mountain, Alabama

"It was one of the craziest things I've ever seen," Buddy said to Pastor Derek and his wife, Sherry. He and Janine were seated in the Blantons' living room. They had finished supper and moved to the more comfortable setting for conversation. The children were playing in another room.

Buddy had shared the rough details of the attack on their family with Derek and Sherry. (Pastor Derek had gotten more details from Sheriff Matt already.) He had just finished with the part about the man they had questioned.

"It sounds like the man was likely possessed by a demon," said Derek. "I've heard of that type of thing before but can't say that I've ever encountered it in quite the same way that you did."

"What about his voice changing and speaking a bunch of gibberish?"

"Again, I've not experienced it, but Pastor Wendy over at the Pentecostal Free Tabernacle has shared some stories with me that have frankly raised the hair on the back of my neck just hearing about them. The Pentecostals believe in being filled with God's Spirit in such a way that He will speak through them in what the Bible calls 'unknown tongues.' If that's the case, then it stands to reason that for everything real, the devil usually has a counterfeit. She has told me that on more than one occasion, they've had people come into their services and start acting the way you described this man—jerking, eyes rolling back, foaming at the mouth, even the gibberish at times. In every case, Sister Wendy and the elders over there cast the devil out of them and saw them completely delivered."

"I ain't never heard of nothing like that," said Janine emphatically.

Derek shrugged. "It's in the Bible. Jesus and his disciples cast demons or devils out of numerous people."

"Well, sure," said Janine. "But I mean in this day and age."

"Think about the video you showed us, Janine. You remember how the man's voice changed in that video, don't you? I believe that what that man experienced was no different than what Buddy saw happen with the man out at your farm. It's not like all the demons died and no longer exist."

"It's awful scary, Pastor. To think that the devil was so close to us like that."

"But what about God?" asked Derek. "You remember what we prayed when me and the elders were there, don't you? Think of what Buddy said the man told him. All of their communications were cut off from the moment they began their attack. If it had happened a few moments sooner, they would have called it off and come back another night. Who knows? They might have had a different outcome on another night. What about the fact that not one of you were hurt in the least? Things could have turned out quite different, especially based on what their plan was for you both. There are a lot of 'what ifs' that could have gone against you, but not one of them did."

He looked at Buddy. "You remember what I said, that I believed that God wanted you to see how involved He is in your situation? Can you see that, even a little bit?"

Buddy looked thoughtfully at Derek. "It could have been a whole lot worse. They could have come from different directions than I thought they would, but I studied long and hard to try to figure out what their plan of attack would be. Or there could have been more of them. I didn't know how many there would be, but two teams seemed most likely to me. The communications thing is what I can't explain. If there's a God up there, that seems to be more His doing than anything else. There's no way I could have accounted for them losing their ability to communicate, and that made a big difference in the end." He looked over at Janine and said, "Maybe there is a God up there."

"The question is," said Janine as she looked at Derek and Sherry, "what does He want us to do now?"

"Honey, may I put a word in?" said Sherry.

"Go right ahead," said Derek.

"I had an old pastor that used to say that life with God is like a big ol' checker game. When it's your move, He won't. And when it's His move, you can't. There may be some moves you still have to make, but I believe deep in my heart that the next big move is not yours to make."

"Why do you say that?" asked Janine.

"Sometimes I see pictures in my mind. When you all were talking, I kept seeing a picture of you and Buddy, both of you, sitting with a calendar in front of you. You were pointing to a date in the future. You kept tapping your finger on that date like it was important, and you were saying 'It's over!' with the biggest smile on your face I've ever seen."

"What date was that?" asked Janine.

"I don't like to speculate, and I don't know if the actual day matters…"

"Honey, trust what you believe God has shown to you," prodded Derek.

Sherry took a deep breath and said, "The date you kept pointing at was September twenty-first."

Chapter 36

After Buddy and Janine returned home that night, Buddy entered the house first and did a room-by-room search. While he checked the house, Janine sat on the porch with Midnight. As she grasped a handful of hair on his jowls and stroked her fingers through his fur, she looked into the dog's eyes and said, "You're a good boy, you know that?"

Midnight looked back at her with his hazel brown eyes as if he understood every word. His mouth was open with his long tongue hanging out as he panted to cool himself in the steamy late summer heat.

"I don't know how much more of this I can take, Midnight," she said as she smoothed the hair on the dog's snout and forehead with her fingers. "I never wanted to be involved in something so evil as all of this. Part of me wishes I'd never seen what happened that night. And part of me is glad I did, that because I saw it, them evil people can't hide no more. But I can't go back, Midnight. There's no way I can go back."

At that moment, Midnight's body tensed, and he emitted a low growl. He leaped off the porch and ran straight toward the edge of the barn, barking as he went.

"Buddy, come quick!" Janine shouted.

A few moments later, Janine heard his heavy boots pounding the floor as he yanked open the door and asked, "What is it? What's going on?"

Janine pointed to the edge of the barn and said, "It's Midnight! He ran that way!"

Buddy already had his pistol in his hand. "Get in the house! And lock the door!" he shouted back as he ran to the barn.

Janine did as she was told, but she couldn't go further than just inside the front door. She wasn't sure Buddy has finished searching the house. For all she knew, someone was waiting in their bedroom. Her nerves were frayed. She tried to pray something coherent but could only repeat, "Jesus, help!" over and over.

After a couple of nerve-wracking minutes, she heard Buddy's voice shout, "Janine, come on out! It's okay!"

She opened the door and peered out. Buddy was standing off the edge of the porch.

"Come on out," he repeated.

Janine walked out and looked down at Buddy's side. Midnight was seated on the ground with a baby possum in his mouth.

"See? It was just an old possum that Midnight was after," he said.

Janine burst into tears.

"Janine, it's just a possum," Buddy protested. "Calm down!"

"Calm down?" she shouted at him with tears streaming down her face. "There's people trying to kill us in our own home! I can't sleep! I can hardly eat! And you tell me to calm down?"

"Janine, it's going to be okay," Buddy said in a firmer tone.

"How do you know that? How do you know they won't keep coming back until they kill you and take me somewhere and do who knows what to me?"

"I don't know that," Buddy said. His tone had an edge to it.

"Then don't tell me to calm down! You don't know whether it's going to be okay or not!"

"You're right. I don't!" Buddy said. After a slight pause, he added, "But none of this would be happening if you hadn't gotten involved with a bunch of strangers in a chat room!"

"So now you're blaming me? This is all my fault?" she said. Her voice was near-hysterical.

"Well, I sure didn't know what I was getting into with all of this. When I left the military behind, I never wanted to have kill someone again. It does something to you! You ain't been the one to have to shoot a man and see the light go out in him."

Janine was sobbing uncontrollably now. "I can't believe you're blaming me for this. You think I wanted this? You think I knew what would happen?"

"You poke a bear, you can't be surprised when it lashes out at you," said Buddy. "You ought to at least thought about that."

"I was just a young kid! I just wanted to help other people who had been abused like I had!" She turned away from him, her shoulders shaking. She pounded her fist against the house.

Midnight looked up at Buddy and emitted a low growl.

"Janine, I'm sorry," said Buddy. "That wasn't fair of me."

"You've said your piece. Now I know how you really feel."

"I said I'm sorry. I'm just under a lot of stress, too, is all."

"How do you think I feel?" Janine asked. "I can't live a normal life anymore. I'm always having to wonder whether someone is out in the barn or out in the woods with a rifle pointed at me."

Buddy said, "As long as I've known you, you've gone on and on about how God will protect you and watch over you. You've prayed. Your pastor has prayed. Well, do you believe in this God of yours or not? Is He real, or is He just something you made up to make you feel good when things are easy?"

Janine collapsed to her knees and then sank down on the corner of the porch against the wall of the house. Tears, sobs, and wails all intermingled in the glow of the night lighting to render the effect of a wounded animal. Midnight left the possum and came over to her prone form. He nuzzled her and lay down beside her.

Janine reached up with one hand and grabbed a handful of fur tightly. "Midnight, at least I know you love me," she said softly.

Buddy threw up his hands and then walked up to the porch and knelt beside Janine. He reached a hand over and laid it on her shoulder. She flinched. Buddy withdrew his hand, got up quietly, and walked inside.

Janine knew she shouldn't have flinched. But she couldn't believe

Buddy would just up and leave her there all alone. Something clicked in her mind, and she made a decision. She would stay here all night then, outside her own home—like a stranger—while her tough husband slept inside in comfort. Here she would make her bed on a hard porch with a dog.

These thoughts and a hundred different scenarios of the future ran through her head for several minutes. Then she heard the sound of bootless footsteps coming out the doorway. It had never been closed, she realized. Buddy settled his big frame down near her head. She smelled coffee. Then he put a blanket over her.

"I thought if you was gonna camp out, you might at least want something hot to drink," he said.

"You idiot," she said, looking up at him with her wet and dirty face. "You ruined my pity party!" She sat up and took the coffee mug from him.

Buddy didn't say anything. Janine sipped her coffee. Eventually, she leaned her head against his shoulder with her eyes closed as she kept petting Midnight. In the distance, a chorus of frogs was performing its nightly serenade in a neighbor's pond. Further still was the occasional yelp of a coyote. A lone cricket that had been quieted while the drama unfolded now resumed its surprisingly loud chirping somewhere just off the porch. All of these sounds intruded on Buddy's consciousness.

Then, out of the corner of his eye, he saw a slight movement. The baby possum had decided that the danger was past and had resurrected. It began its slow waddle out of the pool of light as it headed back to wherever home and safety were.

After it disappeared into the dark, Buddy looked up into the night sky at the brilliant array of stars overhead. He thought about the attacks, the intensity of the fights, the interrogation and what it had revealed. How high up the food chain did this evil go? He wondered if there really was a God who could show the way out of this mess, the kind of God who watches over baby possums and hurting people.

Chapter 37

Paris, France

It had to be an almond cake of some kind. That much was certain. There would be almonds in abundance decorating it. It would have almond slices for light colors. Whole almonds would be used for darker objects. Pure and potent almond extract would be used to flavor it.

Chanti began by sketching out the ideas that had formed in her head. Then she began sorting through the various molds and forms which would be used to shape and sculpt the cake into what she envisioned. Finally, she began mixing the ingredients and pouring the base and inlays into the large pans she would use.

Measure. Mix. Pour. Over and over she repeated these steps. All the while, her mind envisioned the end result her cake would bring about. When she began to learn to bake, it was at the direction of her saviors. When she became an adult, it would provide her with a way to support herself in a modest, if not consistent, manner. "People are always celebrating something," was their reasoning. But her insight into the character and inner secrets of people opened the doors for bigger things.

It was during her intermediate courses, after she had been taught the mechanics of tools and the techniques of whirls and flowers and composition of icing, that she was given the leeway to create her first cake with no definite assignment. The teacher had simply said, "Be creative. Surprise me!" Chanti had done that. She had created a cake designed as a schoolgirl holding a single stem in one hand and a petal in the other. In extremely thin icing, letters formed the words, "He loves me not."

When the teacher saw her cake, her face had dropped, and she actually turned her head away. She quickly moved to examine the work of another student. Later, she asked Chanti if someone among the other professors had let slip a confidence. Chanti had answered in the negative.

When the teacher asked her to explain why she had chosen that theme, Chanti simply said, "I just know things."

The teacher gave her a searching, long look and then replied, "If what you say is true, then your gift will take you very far."

She realized that not only could this ability give her access to a more exclusive clientele with much larger purses, but also it could potentially help her find the people who were hidden and protected by layers upon layers of security. Her rise had been more rapid than she herself had expected. Now she was at the precipice gazing down into the abyss as she squeezed each drop of almond flavoring.

Her mind wandered into the past. Whenever she dropped off her cake for the church's fundraiser auction, she would indulge herself in an hour or two of conversation. Part confession, part counseling, she sought the insight and stability she had gained from the people who had been willing to pull her out of the ugliest of pits and to provide her with a hope and a different future. These private times were always in their home: what had, for a brief time, been her home. Only here could she let down her guard and be transparent.

After she began her career, she received numerous overt as well as subtle offers for dalliances and one-night stands from those who had purchased her cakes. More than once, she was pressured with multiple offers from these people once they had seen her work. While it did not completely surprise her, she still questioned why they seemed so determined to know her intimately. On one of her visits, she asked her saviors for their thoughts.

While they both had intuitive insight into human nature, it was the wife who spoke. "Everyone craves a spiritual experience. Even a pig knows that there is a Creator, but the pig can only gratify its desires as a pig. These men and women long to have intimate contact with the spiritual realm. They sense that you have a doorway into that realm. But because they live as pigs, and not as children of God, they can only seek to fulfill that longing by giving way to their primal urges. They confuse what is primal with what is spiritual. Because of that, they are always hungry and never satisfied."

"So it's not just about power?" asked Chanti.

The husband answered. "Yes and no. For those who wish to know God, they seek intimacy with Him because they acknowledge that He is God alone. These other people, they do not seek to know God, but they want to be 'as gods' themselves. They know that there is a spiritual realm. But they acknowledge it only because they believe they can control it. They will always seek to have intercourse with those who are holy or innocent in order to try and lay hold of holiness or innocence. They do not gain either. They only steal innocence from those they target, as you certainly know."

"Yes. As I do certainly know," Chanti repeated.

"But this is not why you asked the question," said the wife. "There's more going on in your mind than that."

"Yes," said Chanti. "I want to know what I should do. I have this gift, this power. But what should I use it for?"

"It depends," said the wife, "on whether you are a child of God…or a pig. Your actions will flow from your being."

Those words echoed in her mind as she worked today. This day, like so many others, she felt more like a pig. Long ago, in anticipation of a moment such as this, she had purchased the cyanide with cash from a chemist's shop using as many layers of disguise as possible and using a fake ID. It wouldn't matter. Once they ate the cake, the police would know where the cake came from—at least, they would very likely trace it back to her, assuming the Baron kept records of any kind. It depended on how many actually ate it. The almonds had been soaked in cyanide. The extract used in the icing was mixed with it. The almonds and almond flavoring would mask the natural scent of bitter almonds in the poison.

The cake itself began to take shape. It was a sheet cake comprised of several sections placed together and was larger than the first she had made for the Baron. The sheet was then iced with an off-white to beige layer. Chanti used a wave technique that would create the perception of depth once the other objects were added. She then began the process of designing the main figure on the cake using various forms and then the icing, plenty of icing. The almonds and almond slices were used to create the outline and main features of the body.

Slowly, methodically, she worked. If this were to be her last piece, it would be the crowning masterpiece using all of her skills. Every flourish, every detail had to be exact. She worked until she was exhausted and then fell into bed, asleep before she could slip under the covers. She would finish the piece tomorrow.

After another full day of work, the cake was ready. Chanti wiped her brow with a cloth and then washed her hands thoroughly. Only then after a brief respite did she step back to look at what she had made. Her eyes pored over the complete cake and then began to focus in on the details as she imagined the Baron would when he saw it for the first time.

The main pattern was a large sheet cake with off-white icing. Dominating the design was the figure of a young boy apparently of non-Caucasian background. His skin was light brown although not African. He was clad only in a loincloth. His left hand was down by his side. The right hand was decorated so as to appear that he was beckoning with that hand. The outstretched hand covered just the right eye and a small portion of the face. The left eye had an almond, cut round, as its pupil.

The outline of the body had been formed with almonds placed on their sides. Shading and depth had been achieved with sliced and whole almonds dotted around the rest of the body along with the icing that had been used for the skin tone. The look on the child's face was one of wide-eyed terror.

As the wave pattern receded into the distance, there were thin etches in the icing that had been inlaid with a slightly darker icing: not enough to draw immediate attention but enough to differentiate once noticed. These formed the ghostly outline of other children. Each of them had an outstretched arm. Each hand covered the portion of the face containing the right eye. At the bottom, written in blood-red script, were the words, "This is my body. Take and eat."

Knowing what she did about the Baron and his likely guests, Chanti knew that the sight of the cake alone would be compelling. The words would invoke an even greater reaction to the sight. She hoped every guest had at least three pieces, although one should be enough.

154

Slowly and carefully, she placed the cake in her oversized cooler. It was due to be delivered in three days. She knew what would happen afterwards, and there were details to take care of. And she needed to have at least one more conversation—tomorrow.

Chapter 38

Chanti showed up at the house in another district of Paris unannounced. She arrived at lunchtime and knocked her special knock. She knew they would be there. They made time to eat together. It had always been a priority. Their marriage came first, their church work second.

The wife, a petite woman named Nellie McPheil who had a light complexion and ginger hair, answered the door. Her face registered pleasant surprise as she welcomed Chanti inside and shouted back into the house, "Alistair, we have a special visitor!" A burly, dark-haired man with a beard came out of the dining area, saw Chanti, and opened his arms. Chanti embraced him in a warm hug.

An extra place setting was added to the table, where the meal had just begun. They ate. She listened as they talked of what had been going on in their lives. This was the only true home she could ever remember.

When they were finished, the kettle was filled with water and placed on the stove. While they were waiting, Chanti walked to the back garden and took what she supposed would be her last look at the swing, the plants, and the flowers, which had been the nexus of so much of her emotional recovery. She took extra time to smell and touch the flora. Then she asked Nellie, who had joined her, if they could have their coffee in the garden. That having been settled, she sat down on the swing and began to push with her feet rhythmically as her eyes continued to soak in the myriad of tiny details.

Nellie sat down beside her while Alistair prepared their beverages.

"You have much on your mind, Marin. Would you like to tell me about it?"

"I've made a cake for a client."

"You've made many cakes. What is troubling you about this one?"

"It's not the cake. Well, it is, partially. Mainly, it's the client." She paused and exhaled a deep sigh. "It's for the man from my nightmares,

156

Baron Klaus Maginon."

Nellie sat still and listened.

"I've waited for this moment for years. I always knew that I would see him again. I made one cake for him a few weeks ago and passed his test. Now I've prepared another one for him, for the twenty-first—the equinox!"

She looked at Nellie as she spoke the last words. Nellie remained patiently silent.

Chanti got up from the swing, her hands clasped tightly in front of her. She turned and looked at Nellie. "I've spent my lifetime not knowing who I really am. They stole me from my family and stole my family from me. They stole my childhood. They stole my virginity and my innocence. They stole my dreams and gave me only nightmares. They even planned to steal my life! If anything defines me, I want it to be that I took something back from them!"

After a few moments, Nellie said, "So you mean to have your revenge on the Baron. Is that it?"

"I won't say anything more about my plans. I don't want you to be involved in my failures."

"Marin," said Nellie. "We love you. We always have and always will, no matter what you do. You know that."

Chanti's eye moistened with tears. "Yes. I know that."

"I want you to listen to me very carefully. I don't know what you are planning to do. I could guess, but I won't. Do you remember the story of Jesus in the Garden of Gethsemane?"

Chanti nodded.

"When Judas came to betray his master, he brought soldiers with him. Do you remember what Peter did?"

Chanti nodded again. "He took out his sword and cut off the high priest's servant's ear."

"And why did he do that? Do you remember what Papa used to say?"

"It was because he was in a panic and was a very bad aim."

"That's right. He meant to kill the servant. In that story, Jesus picked up the man's ear and placed it back on his head and healed him instantly. He stopped the blood. I wonder sometimes if he even had a scar there.

"I think that the reason why He did that was that He knew Peter was going to pull through all of the future tests. Whenever Jesus arose and left this earth, He didn't want Peter to have to stand trial for one foolish action. If anyone accused Peter of cutting off a man's ear, what proof would they have? 'Show me this man,' the judge would say. 'Why does he have two ears? Why is there no scar? Case dismissed!' he would say.

"I will pray for you, my child, that Jesus will erase your bad decision and give you the same chance He gave to Peter: a future without regret."

"Maybe an ear is an easy thing to repair," said Chanti.

"I believe He would have put the man's head back on if Peter had been a trained soldier instead of a fisherman," answered Nellie.

Alistair came out with the beverages on a tray. He surveyed the somber scene as he approached and simply offered each their cup.

"May we sit silently like we used to?" asked Chanti.

"Only if I may hum," Alistair answered.

Chanti's eyes flickered with a memory. "You may," she replied.

They spent an hour sitting in the tranquil garden. The women were swinging gently. The birds and insects visited the plants. The man hummed the ancient hymns, the same ones he had hummed by Chanti's bedside to get her back to sleep after her night terrors had torn her from slumber. The wife prayed inwardly for the troubled soul she had helped to nurture. Chanti locked the sights and sounds and feelings into her mind so that she could remember them when she was sentenced to prison.

Chapter 39

Sand Mountain, Alabama

The next day after their argument, Janine felt an urge to check the message board she had posted to after their first attackers had come. Once she logged into it with her password, she received a notification that she had a private message awaiting her. When she clicked on it, she read the following:

```
I am writing to you concerning the message
you posted regarding DangleDrop.

I represent a group of online researchers who
have been trying to verify its existence and
authenticity for years. We work independently
of law enforcement, but we are willing to
share our research with them if and when the
need arises.

We are not interested in your identity unless
you choose to reveal it. Our team would
like to study the video if you have a copy
and do our best to authenticate it so that
the parties involved in illegal and immoral
activities will be held accountable.

If you choose to allow us to do so, please
upload the video to any file-sharing site of
your choice using any means at your disposal
to protect your identity. I suggest that you
use an ambiguous filename. Then send me a link
to the file. I will confirm its receipt.
```

As a point of reference, we are comprised of the same group that deciphered the code of the Vatican's statues.

Serious

Janine read it through twice. Then she showed it to Buddy.

"What do you think?" she asked.

"I don't know," he said. "What are the upsides? What are the downsides?"

Janine thought a bit and then answered. "If they're really who they say they are, then they're a really smart group of people. I remember reading about the Vatican statues when all that was in the news. They could probably get more out of the video than anyone else. If they can prove that it's authentic, then it might help with finally bringing some of these people to justice."

"And if they're not?"

"I don't know. They could be the people hunting us. But if they get a copy of the video, how does that help them?"

"Well, what do you want to do?"

Janine rubbed her face with her hands and sighed. "I want to go talk to Sherry. I've got a lot on my mind. Maybe she'll help me sort it out just a little bit."

"Do you want me to drop you off?"

"No. I'll drive. I haven't been much anywhere in a while. It'll be good to get out, I think."

"Okay. I'm going to be working Jack Willoughby's fields today. I'll have my phone. Just call if you need me."

They hugged, and then Buddy left in his truck and trailer while Janine called Sherry.

"Good morning, Janine. How are things your way?"

"Fair to middling, I reckon. I was wondering if I could come over for just a while and talk to you."

"Sure, you can. But wear some work clothes. I'm picking apples this morning. Bring you some buckets or baskets, and you can have as many as you like."

"I will. Thanks. Will you be in the house or down in the orchards?"

"I'll meet you at the barn. I've got to take some baskets back up. I'll go ahead and wash some apples while I wait for you. Are you leaving right now?"

"Just have to get my buckets and put my shoes on. Can I bring Midnight with me?"

"By all means! I love that dog. And Janine, wear long sleeves. The mosquitoes are bad over here right now."

"They don't usually bother me. Buddy says I must have sour blood. I'll see you in a few minutes."

Chapter 40

Twenty minutes or so later, Janine pulled into the Blanton driveway. She loved their property. The tree-lined driveway led down to a green lawn and an older, but still attractive, farmhouse. Unlike a lot of transplant pastors, Pastor Derek and Sherry had both grown up in the county. Derek lived on the family farm, which was comprised of a number of apple orchards. He derived a good portion of his living from the work of his hands and spent much of the rest of his time devoted to the work of his heart.

Janine pulled down to the barn and began unloading her buckets. She could hear a speaker playing worship music inside. Sherry came out wiping her hands on a towel and gave her a big hug. Then she knelt down and petted Midnight, who was busy sniffing everything, including Gabriel, Derek and Sherry's golden retriever.

"Let's get you a ladder, and we'll go on down," said Sherry. After retrieving the ladder, Sherry strapped it to the four-wheeler. She pointed to the other one and told Janine to secure her buckets on the rear rack and drive it with her. They headed across the grassy field into the orchards with Midnight trotting beside them, his tongue lolling as he went. Gabriel was running ahead.

"Do you and Buddy like Honeycrisp?" asked Sherry.

"Love 'em," said Janine.

"Good. That's right where I was working."

She pulled her four-wheeler to a stop by a big tree with a ladder under it. She got Janine's ladder off and set it up near hers. They both set an empty bucket on the ladder's paint tray and climbed up.

"Wow! This tree is loaded with apples," exclaimed Janine.

"They all are. God really blessed us with a great harvest this year," said

Sherry. She began reaching for apples and placing them carefully into the bucket to avoid bruising them.

As they worked, they caught up on life and what was going on in the church and the community. Midnight explored the surrounding area, helped himself to one or two trees for marking and then was generally content to lie on the ground near Gabriel, both dogs panting as they watched the two ladies work. Their arms were in constant motion: reaching, picking, placing. Buckets were filled. Ladders were descended, moved to a new location, and ascended again. Sherry swatted mosquitoes. Janine hardly noticed they were there. In the distance, a goat gave out its plaintive cry as it explored the fence line seeking the sweetest thistles.

After an hour, all the buckets were filled. Sherry suggested they go back to the barn to wash them and then to the house for some lunch. When they had unloaded the apples into the wash basins to soak, Sherry put down a separate dish for Midnight near Gabriel's bowl and gave them both a scoop of dog food before heading into the house.

"How does egg salad sandwiches with fresh apples sound?" Sherry asked.

"Wonderful," said Janine. "I'll slice the apples if you like."

Over lunch, Janine said, "Buddy and I had a big fight last night."

"Oh? What was it about?"

Janine told her the story of what had happened, how she had broken down and how Buddy had acted like everything was her fault. "That hurt me a lot. But you know what hurt me the most out of everything he said?"

"What?"

"He said that I didn't really act like God was real. He said that it seemed like I prayed and talked a big talk about God protecting me only when it was easy but that I didn't really seem to believe it." Her eyes grew moist, and she put down her sandwich and stared at her plate with her elbows on the table and her face in her hands. Sherry waited for her to continue, but she just sat there.

"Tell me how you've been handling it the past few weeks," she said.

"I ain't been sleeping well. I'm jumpy. I don't leave the house unless I have to." She dabbed her eye with her napkin. "I can't concentrate on much. The positive side is the house is clean as a whistle because I've got to keep my mind busy, or I'll go crazy." She looked at Sherry sheepishly. "I've even washed the ceilings."

"Land o' Goshen!" said Sherry. "You must be desperate to do that."

"I feel like I'm about to have a nervous breakdown," said Janine. "It's just that I guess I've always been afraid that they would find me. For years I've been afraid. Almost every night I've gone to bed with that thought in the back of my mind."

"So, is Buddy right?" asked Sherry. "Do you think you're really trusting God for protection?"

"I don't know!" said Janine as she sucked in her breath to hold back her tears. "I want to! I really want to! But how do I do that with people trying to kill me?" She looked at Sherry imploringly, her lower lip trembling.

Sherry sighed and said, "Janine, I want to tell you something that happened to me. Back when Derek and I first got married, not long after, there was a fellow who started stalking me. He claimed that God had told him I was supposed to be his wife and that I was supposed to leave Derek. He said all kind of crazy things because he was really messed up in the head. We ignored him for a while, but he got more aggressive until one time he came to the house when Derek was gone. He started beating on the door telling me to come out or that he was coming in to get his bride. I was terrified. I called Derek and 911 and then got a gun and hid in the bathroom. He actually broke into the house and was starting to look for me when Derek and the officers showed up about the same time. He ran out of the house and down into the orchard. They looked but couldn't find him.

"I was so scared I couldn't think straight. When the police left and we finally sat down, Derek asked me what good my fear and worry were doing me. That made me so mad. I thought he didn't care about how I felt. But he asked me again. He said, 'Sherry, if the worst thing you

164

can imagine were to happen, how is worrying about it going to change it? And if the worst thing doesn't happen, how is worrying about it going to change it?'

"Well, Janine, that really made me stop and think. I could either sit around and worry that that lunatic was going to break into my house and rape me and maybe kill me, or I could choose to think that God was big enough to keep that from happening to me. I couldn't control his choices any more than I could control any other person's choices. All I could control was my own mind.

"So, from that day on, I made a decision that I was going to choose to have faith."

"How do you do that, though?" asked Janine.

"Janine, honey, one thing I learned during that time is that faith is simply acting like the Word of God is true. Do you get that? By our little, daily actions, we show whether or not we really believe God's Word is true. First thing I done, I started putting up Scripture verses around the house. The Bible says to put them on the doorposts of your house. That's why we have that sign by our door. Every door has a Scripture verse beside it." She pointed to the refrigerator, the window above the sink, and then other places around the kitchen and dining room.

"Every room in this house has Scripture verses. They remind me of God's promises. Most of them are just little three-by-five index cards I wrote down with my own hand. Some of them I bought from the Christian bookstore over in Chattanooga or ordered online.

"Then I started acting like those verses were true. If the Bible says, 'No weapon formed against me shall prosper,' and 'He shall give His angels charge over thee to keep thee in all thy ways,' then I needed to act like that was true. I started memorizing those verses like never before, and any time that fear rose up, I would quote them out loud."

"Did it really help, though?" asked Janine.

"Yes—eventually. I won't say that it worked immediately. I had to fight that fear for weeks—months, really. But every time I quoted the Word of God, it was like I chipped away at a big mountain in front of me. I realized that I had some deep-seated fears of being attacked and molested. Those fears had kept me from trusting God with my safety and well-being since I was young. And really, if I couldn't trust God with my whole life, I had to ask if He was really the Lord of my whole life. Believe me, Janine, those were some soul-searching months for me. I was a pastor's wife having to ask if I really believed that God was real."

"What happened?" Janine asked. "Did they ever catch him or lock him up?"

Sherry shook her head. "No. They never did. The last time I saw him was several years later at the farmers' market: two years ago, to be exact."

"Were you afraid?"

"No. That was the strangest thing. He was real thin, looked like he had been on meth. He still looked crazy as ever. His eyes were shining, and he started to smile his creepy old smile. But then he stopped and got a look of fear in his eyes. It was like he saw one of them angels that are around me. He ran off, and I've never seen him since."

Janine took a deep breath and exhaled. "I want that more than anything. I want to be free of this fear."

"The first thing you got to do is repent and tell God you're sorry."

"Repent? For what?"

"Well, for me, I had to realize that my fear was a sin. I was making a bigger idol of that man and my fear than I was God. I told Him that I was sorry that I couldn't trust Him in spite of all that He had done. I asked Him to forgive me and to help me through my weakness. I felt like the man whose son was demon-possessed that the disciples couldn't help. He said to Jesus, 'I believe. Help my unbelief.' I just was honest with God and said that I needed help to believe Him more and that I wanted to. And He did help me as I acted day by day on what His Word said." She looked at Janine and said, "Do you think you can start there?"

Janine nodded.

"Then why don't you pray?"

Janine closed her eyes and began to speak. "God, I've been afraid for a long time. I don't want to be afraid anymore. I want to believe you better. I know you've already protected me and Buddy twice now. Please, God, help me to learn how to trust you every day. I'm sorry that I've not trusted you like I should. Please set me free from this fear." She began to cry.

Sherry spoke, "Father God, I know what Janine feels like. And I know how much you helped me. I rebuke this spirit of fear in Jesus' name. In its place, I ask you to please send your sweet Holy Spirit, the Spirit of power, love, and a sound mind. Amen."

"Now," Sherry said to Janine, "let's say our ten-fingered prayer."

Janine smiled. They held up two fists and opened each finger in turn as they repeated together, "I can do all things through Christ who strengthens me."

"Now," Sherry said, "Let's use these hands to wash some apples, okay?"

"Okay," said Janine.

They spent the next couple of hours washing apples and then waxing them with beeswax and polishing some of them for sale and long-term storage. When Janine left, she had traded a load of worry for a load of fresh apples. Little did she know what awaited her when she would arrive home.

Chapter 41

When she arrived back at the farm, Buddy's truck was already parked near the barn. He was home early. When she got out of her vehicle, she sniffed the air. Buddy was not only home but also had been there long enough to fire up his smoker.

Midnight trotted to the back of the house where the aroma was originating while Janine got out two of the buckets of apples and carried them to the porch. She set them down and then went to retrieve more. As she was walking back to the porch, the front door opened, and Buddy walked out with his apron on. He looked at Janine carrying the buckets and began to walk toward her.

"I've got these," Janine said. "You can get the two on the porch there. Just set them in the kitchen for now."

"All right," said Buddy. "You have anything else to carry?"

"This is it." She followed him into the house. "Something smells good," she said as she gave him a peck on the cheek and a hug. "You've trimmed your mustache. What are you cooking?"

"Big, fat, juicy burgers. Using some of that cherry wood from the tree that fell last year."

"Mmm. I'll cut up some potatoes and make some fren..." The words stopped in her mouth as she walked through the living room and looked at the kitchen table. There sat the biggest bouquet of flowers she had ever seen short of a funeral. She stared at them with her head cocked sideways. Then she turned and looked at Buddy, who was grinning ear to ear. He had seen the expression on her face.

"Are these...for me?" she asked with wide eyes.

"No," Buddy said. "I got 'em for Midnight. He's been such a fine dog..."

She reached over and punched him on the bicep. "Don't you ruin my moment!" she said.

"Of course they're for you."

"But why? It ain't our anniversary."

"I just wanted to let you know that I really am sorry for what I said last night. And I do love you. I hope you know that."

Janine wrapped her arms around him and gave him a big kiss. Then she leaned against him as she looked at the flowers. "Yep. I do. Thank you, Buddy." She let go and went to look closer at them and to smell them. The arrangement had two dozen roses, all red, and a mixture of colorful filler flowers. "This must have cost a fortune!" she said.

"I had 'em delivered from Ann-Other down in Trenton, and I paid cash. So don't ask," he said.

She looked into the kitchen. There was a bowl filled with potatoes already washed and sliced for French fries. On one of her charcuterie boards, Buddy had neatly stacked all the condiments. In a bucket off to the side filled with ice was a bottle of her favorite "fizzy grape juice," as she liked to call it.

"Well, you went all out, didn't you?" she said. "You have any more surprises?"

"Maybe," he said with a wink.

"What do you want me to do?" she asked. "Looks like you've got everything taken care of."

"Nothing. Burgers will be done in twenty minutes."

"In that case, I think I'll take a shower. I probably smell pretty gamey after picking apples."

With that, she left for their bedroom. Buddy finished setting the table and busied himself with the last few details of the meat before pulling the hamburgers from the smoker. He had just placed them on the table when Janine returned. She was wearing one of his favorite outfits and had added a light scent of the perfume he liked the best. She had also added the necklace he had bought for their first anniversary.

Buddy pulled her chair out for her and sat down across from her. He waited for her to give thanks, and then they began their meal. Their conversation was light-hearted, covering topics from the apple picking to hay baling to whether or not to plant savoy cabbage for the winter. Janine looked at her empty plate and exhaled.

"That was delicious! I feel so special, Buddy. Thank you."

"We ain't done just yet," said Buddy. "Close your eyes."

Janine complied and listened to him walk to the pantry. Then she heard the clatter of a couple of dishes and the rattle of a utensil drawer. Then the freezer door was opened and shut. Buddy walked back to the table, placed several things on it, and then said, "Okay. Open your eyes."

When she did, she saw what looked like a freshly made pie with a container of vanilla ice cream sitting in front of her.

"Is that an apple pie?" she asked.

"Blackberry cobbler."

"Cobbler? Where did you get that?"

"Old Mrs. Willoughby had made two today and offered me one after I finished over there this morning."

"Sister Willoughby made it? Oh, I love her cobblers. She always makes them for homecoming at church. She freezes gobs of the berries every year."

They heated the servings of cobbler, topped the plates with ice cream, and then, at Janine's suggestion, took the dessert out onto the back porch to enjoy. Janine sat in her rocker while Buddy sat in his cast iron chair.

After she finished the last bite, Janine said, "Buddy?"

"Yeah, babe?"

"I wanted to tell you something." She paused for Buddy to acknowledge her with his nod. "I had a really good talk with Sherry today. She helped me to realize that what you said last night was true. I really haven't been trusting God much at all, not just the past few weeks but for years."

"Janine, you don't have to…" Buddy started.

She cut him off. "Let me finish. I told God that I was sorry for saying that I believed Him for protection but was acting like He isn't real. Sherry gave me some good ideas to help me. She had a really hard time with something, too, and she knows how I've been feeling. She said it might take time to break out of old habits. But I told God that's what I want. I just wanted to tell you. I guess I haven't been a good example of a Christian."

Buddy looked at her impassively for a few moments. Then his mustache wriggled, and his countenance softened. "You're about the best Christian I've ever known." he said. "I respect what you just said, and I won't ride you hard none if you do have any problems in the future. I just want you to tell me if you are. Deal?"

"Deal," she said. "I don't want there to be any walls between us. I do feel closer to you now knowing that you know what I've been afraid of."

She got up out of her rocker and curled up in his lap. Buddy wrapped his arms around her.

"You smell good," he said, burying his nose in her hair.

"You smell like a really good burger," she said.

He laughed and held her closer. For Buddy, this was as good as life could get. He wasn't really sure about Janine's religion, but if it made her this kind of woman, he wasn't going to be against it. As he held her, a movement out of the corner of his eye caught his attention at the edge of the tree line. He shifted his head slightly to identify it. It was a baby possum waddling along at the edge of the grass. It paused and lifted its head to sniff the air. Buddy could have sworn it looked straight at him.

§ § §

Later that night, before retiring to bed, Janine logged onto her computer. She had already told Buddy her thoughts, and he had seen no reason to disagree. They seemed to have precious few concrete steps to take which were clear. The offer to study and research the video by the anonymous group of Internet users was one of the few options they had.

Janine picked a popular and heavily used file-sharing site in Asia. She stuck an old thumb drive into the laptop and selected two files, one significantly smaller than the other, and began the upload process. She had chosen the names "video1" and "video2" to be anonymous. It took a while for the larger one to complete. Once she was sure that they were both uploaded, she marked them as private files and added a password to them. Then she copied the URLs into a text document. She logged into the message board and sent a note to the user who had contacted her. In it, she wrote:

```
I don't know if you are who you say you are.
But I'm trusting you.  I've uploaded the file
you asked about.  I also added a second file
most people don't know exists.  If you are
able to do anything good with them, you have
my permission.  After all these years, my
biggest prayer is that the people who done
this would be punished.

I think most of the people who saw the original
video are dead.
```

She put the URLs and the password at the bottom, reread the message, and then hit the Send button. Then she disconnected everything, shut down the laptop, and went to bed. When she laid her head on the pillow, she whispered, "Lord, help me to really trust you." She drifted off with her mind replaying the events of the day. For the first time in years, she slept peacefully all night long.

Chapter 42

Cyberspace

The user known as Serious was awake and online. After reading the terse message, the URLs were clicked, the files were downloaded, and the review was begun. Serious was surprised to realize that the smaller of the two files was more of an intro video by a man named Daniel Robertson. Apparently, the person who had sent the files had saved everything related to the event. Serious froze the frame that showed the man's face, opened a folder named DangleDrop, and clicked on a recently saved image. Serious didn't need a biometric software comparison of the faces. The man in the video was the same person whose lifeless eyes stared into eternity from the photo that had been posted with the threatening warning not that long ago. That was a data point which had to be noted.

Using a pen and paper, Serious made notes as the short video was played, replayed, and then played a third time. Then Serious opened the larger file. After years of searching, waiting, praying, and digging, this seemed to be the real deal instead of yet another troll sending cat videos or weird porn. Serious determined to watch the video straight through in order to get an overall sense of its authenticity. In spite of the lore which surrounded the video, the researcher side demanded that it be approached with the same degree of skepticism as any other data posted to the Internet. Serious pressed play.

Some time later, Serious looked at the screen. The video player had stopped at the end of the file. Serious asked the same questions that were applied to every research project, and the first one was always, "Do I sense in my spirit that this is genuine and not a fraud?" If that could not be answered satisfactorily, Serious rarely spent additional time on a research project. Time was too precious to waste on the multitude of wild goose chases. In this case, the answer to that was a simple "yes."

The next question was who should be involved in dissecting the videos. Because of the sensitive nature of the project, Serious decided that the current team of six would probably be sufficient. If they required additional help, there were others who would be willing.

Serious sent out several emails with instructions on where to download the files and some thoughts on what the files contained. Most of the team members were either night owls or in different time zones. They would be involved and in their private chat room within an hour or two. They had their work cut out for them.

Less than four hours later, everyone on the team was in the chat room and had watched both videos at least once, some twice. When examining videos, the team had a web tool that was similar to a wiki-style notation system. They used hyperlinks for names of people (if known), nicknames for unknowns, places, facts, and other data points. Each person could edit entries and add to them. With each entry, there was a timestamp for the video section as well as a particular frame number within each second of video if necessary. They often used screen captures to easily illustrate what was being noted or researched.

The page was a hive of activity as each member made notes. They used voice chat as well as direct messages to communicate what each person was seeing and working on. Serious had parceled out responsibilities based on the skillsets the group members possessed. Within eight to ten hours, they had been able to make significant progress.

One person reviewed satellite imagery to locate the rocky outcropping where Daniel had waited based on topography, height, angles, and cardinal location relative to the estate. The video had clearly shown where the sun was setting and where the estate's direction was.

Another person used satellite imagery of the estate and vector-based software to measure and compare the walls and courtyard with anything readily visible in the video. This provided more data points which validated that Daniel was where he said he was and not outside some other estate on the planet.

The time and date stamps on the video and Daniel's commentary were used to compare the sunset data on record for that day.

The fence was located in the satellite imagery.

Daniel Robertson was identified and confirmed to be the same person as the one in the photo in the threatening message which been posted online by unknown persons. The photo of him on the message board was not taken from any video frames from his camera.

Daniel Robertson's existence was confirmed via birth record and death announcement in an Inverness paper.

The French politician was positively identified based on facial recognition and comparison software.

The software billionaire was positively identified using the same.

Thirteen unique groups of two were delineated from the video.

Thirteen children were visible.

There was one person in a white robe who was distinct from the second figure in the black robe.

If the gates were not automatic, then at least two attendants were involved in the opening of the gates, one on each side.

The estate itself likely had a support staff of some number based on size.

The two men in khakis and black shirts who appeared with the dogs were dressed differently from those in the robes. One face had been possibly identified as belonging to a former Belgian military member.

The faint screams on video were isolated and compared with audio samples. There was a 75% chance of their belonging to adolescents or children based on pitch.

The dagger in the video appeared to have a ruby on the hilt. The blade appeared to be 10"–12" long. The blade's appearance indicated that it was possibly made of stone. It definitely did not shine like metal. If accurate, such a knife would be custom-made. If each hunting party had one, this was another significant detail.

When Daniel wrote out his note for the girl, one researcher commented that on the video, it was evident that he also wore khakis. Whether a sheer bit of luck or otherwise, he was dressed in the same or similar clothing to the other "support staff" at the estate who appeared at the end. This match in clothing likely aided him in his ability to rescue the girl.

The girl was not located, but multiple still images were extracted from the video which would make an ID feasible should a body ever be recovered or should she still be alive.

These and other types of factual data were accumulated and cataloged. They would aid in the proofs of authenticity for the video whenever it was released to the authorities, the public, or both.

The death record had listed a mother who was now deceased. It also listed a stepsister, Nellie McPheil neè MacArthur, lately of Paris. Social media searches listed a Nellie McPheil, wife of Alistair McPheil, who was the bishop of a Faith Mission church in Paris. The couple had no children according to their profile on the church page.

Serious pondered that bit of data. If one were in Daniel Robertson's place, where would Serious send a young teenager for help? An institution? Close friends? Or family? And if Daniel sent the girl to family, would they advertise it or keep it a close secret? If the child actually had survived and made it to the family, she would be in her early twenties now.

After poring over all the related social media posts and news articles that could be found and translated relating to either the couple or the church, one item of interest stood out to Serious and the two members working on that trail. The church had an annual fundraiser. Among the hodge-podge of items which were auctioned off such as furniture, an occasional secondhand automobile or appliances, the noteworthy item was a cake. The cakes always seemed to bring the highest auction price of anything else. While the cakes were not authenticated, they were rumored to be the creations of one "Chanti," one of the most exclusive designers in Europe.

This created a discussion among the group. Why would she design and donate a cake to such a small church? The donation was either a random charitable selection, or it was based on a relationship of some kind with the church or its leadership or, less likely, a parishioner.

The frustrating thing was that Chanti was apparently a modern-day recluse. She had no active social media account that could be located. There were no glamorous photos of her with her clients unveiling her creations. That she had been wildly successful "for one so young," as one current events article had commented, was the closest thing to a lead that they had. They all agreed that Chanti would likely be twenty-five or younger for such a comment to be made about her, with twenty-five itself being the upper age range.

Serious made the decision to explore the angle with the potential family members further. Using a burner social media account on the same platform, Serious sent a message to Nellie McPheil that stated:

```
From: Serious
To: Nellie McPheil
Subject: Your stepbrother Daniel

I am writing to make inquiry as to your
willingness to receive information concerning
your late stepbrother Daniel Robertson,
formerly of Inverness.

This information concerns the night of his
death and may prove useful in seeing some
measure of justice served on those responsible.

Should you wish to continue this conversation,
please reply to this account in the affirmative.
If the matter is of no interest to you or you
desire to be left alone, please let me know.
Either way, the research is ongoing and will
ultimately be turned over to the appropriate
authorities.
```

Serious reviewed the message and then hit send. There were enough details that, if Nellie knew anything about her stepbrother's death, she would know the message was legitimate.

The next message was an email to Alex Ingram, the journalist who had been helpful in the Vatican statue affair.

```
From: Serious
To: Alex Ingram
Subject: Newsworthy

Alex,
We are in possession of video evidence of a
likely murder, child trafficking and crimes
against children, ancillary evidence of other
murders, and a significant amount of data
analysis related to the same.

The crimes involve at least one European
politician and one European former military
member as well as at least one US national. I
would like you to review the same, and I will
be ready to answer any questions you may have
in preparation for US media coverage of the
likely near-future release of the information
into the public domain.
```

Serious included the links to the material for Alex to begin processing from the journalistic side.

The third email was sent to several contacts involved with law enforcement in the European theatre. They were openly carbon copied so that each could see that others were receiving the information. Serious had learned in the past that the chance of corruption always existed, but the mere fact of knowing that other people would be privy to an investigation sometimes spurred the fence-straddlers into action.

```
This message is being sent to the above parties
listed in the address field.

Our research group is making available to
your collective law enforcement organizations
```

evidence pertaining to a crime within your jurisdiction. The crime involves the disappearance and "presumed missing and dead report" of Daniel Robertson of Inverness, Scotland, in the area of Belgium known as the Sonian Forest, more specifically at Chateau Sauvageon, the estate of Klaus Maginon.

The evidence we are making available to you is a firsthand video recording by Daniel Robertson in his own words of child trafficking and crimes against children which occurred on the estate just over eight years ago on June 21.

Our group has analyzed the videos (there are two) and have deemed them to be authentic. In the links I have provided, you will be able to download and view the unedited videos as well as the notes our group has made with supporting documentation and links.

While we understand that you may prefer privacy in this matter for investigative purposes, we believe that full disclosure to the public is warranted due to the nature of the crimes, the public stature of the persons involved, the proclivity of law enforcement in the past to shield such persons from scrutiny or hold them to account, and the overall notoriety of this particular incident. To that end, we intend to go fully public with a release of all of the information you are receiving at some undetermined point in the future based on our continuing research, any new revelations, any significant events relative to the parties involved, and the response we receive back from the law enforcement entities and individuals copied in this email.

You may contact us using the email addresses listed below or by posting an encrypted message addressed "TO 1329" using the public key at the bottom of this email in one of the various message forums listed below.

1329

Then Serious included the various addresses and URLs to the files, supporting documentation, email addresses, and message forum links. The wheels were in motion. They would continue to research more about the principals (not that they had been absent from their radar previously) and watch as the events played out.

Devon Hannah was endowed with a brilliant mind and had chosen to cultivate a wicked character based on everything they had found previously. His lineage included people who had experimented on others and had been involved in global infamy. After he had emerged as a tech tycoon, it had been rumored that his proclivities for entertainment were not wholesome or normal. Jacques Decantes was a corrupt French politician. That summed him up in a nutshell. And then there was Baron Klaus Maginon. He was well known as a member of one of the old-blood ruling families that always seemed to have their hand in everything that was the polar opposite of the good, beautiful, and true.

Serious looked at the calendar again. If these people kept to the rituals and festivals that they had seemed to follow in the past, the autumn equinox was the next likely event. Serious pondered this for a moment and then sent a message to the group in the chat room.

What are the chances we can get a drone to put into the air near the estate in three days?

Chapter 43

Paris, France

Nellie had just finished a women's Bible study at one of the member's houses and was headed home to spend the rest of the evening with Alistair. Out of habit, she pulled her phone out of her purse to check for any messages that might be important while she walked to the car where Alistair was waiting to pick her up. After reading a couple of texts, she opened the messages from her social media app. Her heart seemed to stop, and she almost fell to the sidewalk as she read the subject line "Your stepbrother Daniel." She hurried to the car, gave Alistair a quick peck on the cheek, and then strapped on her seat belt.

"Is anything the matter, love?" Alistair asked her.

"Just drive. I'll let you know in a wee moment," Nellie said.

She read the message, reread it, and then read it a third time.

"Jesus, give me your grace," she said under her breath.

"What's wrong?" Alistair asked again.

In response, Nellie read him the message in its entirety.

"Well, that's a bit of a showstopper, isn't it?" said Alistair.

"It certainly is," said Nellie in a stunned voice.

"Do you think it's on the level?"

"I don't know what to think. I've never had closure about Daniel's disappearance. I always presumed that he was dead based on what Marin told us when she came to us. But never knowing for certain has always just left a hole there. Now I'm staring at a door not knowing whether I should open it or leave it closed."

They drove for several minutes and made it back to their place. A light rain had started to fall. With the wipers turned off, the yellow glow of the streetlights left mottled patterns on Nellie's face as Alistair looked at her with concern.

"Are you ready to go in?" he asked.

Nellie shook her head. "I need to make a decision about this. Help me, please."

Alistair took a deep breath and then exhaled. "Right. This person who sent the message either has real information or he doesn't. If he—or she, we don't know if it's a man or woman, doesn't really know anything, then why just randomly pick Daniel's disappearance after so long a time? It would seem to be totally odd unless this person is a con artist and is simply trying to get some money from you. If you reply and say you're interested and they ask for money, then you'll know.

"On the other hand, if they really do have information, what could their motives be? You weren't involved, but Marin certainly was there. If their motives are impure, then they could be trying to find out what happened to Marin. So, it could be dangerous for her.

"But they say that it's part of an investigation for the purposes of trying to bring people to justice. That could be true. If they have pure motives, they may simply be trying to help you. After all, if we were in the same boat, we'd want a family member to have closure if we could.

"I don't think there's much danger in replying and seeing what this person has in the way of information. If we keep Marin out of it for now, we can look at it together." He reached across the seat and placed his hand on her hand. "The real question, love, is do you want to open that door and endure whatever pain it may bring to know what really happened to Daniel?"

Nellie looked back down at her phone as if it held the answer. Maybe it did. Maybe this person really knew. She could feel tears coming on.

"Thank you," she said. She opened up the app on her phone. "I'm going to say 'yes' and then trust God to help me through it."

Alistair watched as she replied to the message and hit send. Without another word, he got out of the car, opened up the umbrella, and stepped around to her side of the vehicle. He helped her out, put his arm around her, and walked her to the front door.

A quarter of an hour later, her phone dinged with a message on the social media app. They sat together on the sofa and read the contents:

The links below contain two videos your stepbrother made the night of his death. The first is short but informative. The second one is longer and more detailed. WARNING: It contains images which are very disturbing. There is also a link to a document that contains a summary and some detailed notes which, based on research, confirms the authenticity of the videos.

I am sending this information to you for several reasons. The first is, I hope that it provides some closure to you as Daniel's remaining family member.

The second reason is that the child captured in the video has, to my knowledge, never been located or identified. Your stepbrother gave instructions to the child and sent her to someone or some place. My own suspicions are that he may have sent her to you, and there is some evidence to support that theory.

If you know of the whereabouts of this girl— she would be a young lady now—it may be in her best interests to alert her to the existence of these videos, the research, and the fact that the material has been handed over to the appropriate law enforcement authorities with jurisdiction over this matter.

I am not asking that you either confirm or

deny her existence or your involvement, if
any. I just do not want her to be caught
unawares by what may be a very painful or
public disclosure.

With regards to what information I have given,
if you do have anything else to share which you
believe would be of use in the establishment
of a case against the people you will see,
you may send it to me, and I will pass it
along. Or, if you wish to reach the same law
enforcement authorities we have alerted to
this matter, I will be happy to send their
contact information to you.

After reading the message, Nellie took a deep breath and clicked on the first video link. A few moments later, she gave an audible gasp as she saw her stepbrother's face and heard his voice saying, "Hello! It's me, Daniel Robertson." He looked just like she remembered him the last time she had seen him alive, except he looked concerned or worried. After the short video was finished, she clicked on the second one. When she reached the spot where Daniel intruded upon the scene in the woods, she gave a gasp when she recognized Marin.

"It's Jacques Decantes," whispered Alistair, recognizing the politician. "The man's a monster."

By the time they reached the part of the video at the fence where Daniel sent Marin away, Nellie was fully in tears. Then, when the search party found him and ended his life, she broke down in quiet sobs. Alistair sat beside her and held her. He was also weeping.

"I'm so sorry you saw that," Alistair said after several minutes.

"No," said Nellie as she wiped her face with tissues. "I can say with certainty that Daniel is dead, and he died a brave man, just as brave as a soldier in battle. But poor Marin. I never dreamed how bad what she had gone through really was."

"No wonder she was always so frightened," said Alistair. "What a bogeyman, his face in the paper and on TV. And the other bloke with his computer company. It's a miracle she got away at all."

"Alistair, Marin has made a cake for the man who owns that property. I'm not sure what she has planned, but I fear that she's taking matters into her own hands. She wouldn't tell me any details, but she was angry when she spoke of it yesterday."

"What did you say to her?"

"I told her that I would pray that God would give her a second chance like he did for Peter after he cut off the servant's ear."

Alistair looked at the clock. "It's late, but do you think we should give her a phone call?"

"Aye. Maybe the two of us could ask her to come talk to us. If we told her it's urgent, she might."

She reached for her phone and dialed Marin's number. It immediately went to voicemail.

"Her phone's been switched off."

"Send her a text then."

Nellie sent two words to Marin's phone: "Please call."

When she was done, Alistair looked at his wife and said, "The only thing we can do for her now is to pray, to really pray."

They spent the next hour doing just that. Alistair sat on the sofa looking up to the heavens. Nellie knelt beside him with her face in her hands. They implored the God of heaven to save their beloved child from danger and bad choices.

Chapter 44

Chanti awoke at 5:00 a.m. The Baron had requested a 9:00 a.m. delivery if at all possible due to scheduling constraints for his party. The unspoken part was clear: I want you in and out before the guests arrive.

After dressing and preparing a light breakfast, Chanti spent a few minutes looking out the window for some glimpse of light. It was two hours before sunrise proper. Would she ever be free of the dark?

The limousine showed up at 6:00 a.m. sharp. Chanti loaded the cake with help from Frederic, this time in the boot due to its size. The cart went into the passenger compartment to avoid any potential mishaps. As they pulled out into the early-morning Paris commuter traffic and began the trip, Chanti settled back into the plush leather and thought back to her own journey.

Her earliest memory was probably when she was three or four years old. A social worker with horrid breath and coarse features was slapping her face and shouting at her that she would do exactly as she was told. It was sad. Her earliest memory was of abuse and pain. She knew that she had had a family. There was a sense that she had been taken. She remembered something about a home, but she had no images of it. She could hear a mother's voice singing a lullaby to her, but there was no face.

As kilometer after kilometer sped by her window, she replayed the events in her mind. She was moved multiple times from one facility to the next. It was as if the people running the child protection services were playing one big shell game. "Is the child in this home? No, she's here. Now where is she?" Later on, she had realized that the frequent moves had been for the purpose of "losing" children who could be sold off to the ready buyers.

Eventually, she had left the Spanish-speaking region and been moved around to other parts of Europe. Some of the facilities were nothing more than brothels in disguise. Those who ran them spent their time arranging liaisons between adults, many of them rich and famous. Chanti had often wondered why they weren't afraid of being discovered or called out publicly for their actions. Only after she was sent to the Baron's chateau did she realize that they never meant for any of the children to survive long enough to make those accusations public.

She opened her bag and looked at her phone. She had silenced it the evening before out of habit. There was one message from Nellie. "Please call." Something stirred within her to make the call right now, but she resisted it. The die was cast. She placed the phone back into her bag, closed her eyes, and pressed her head against the plush seat. It was almost mid-morning, but the darkness was closing in upon her so heavily.

A few minutes later, they arrived at Chateau Sauvageon. Once again, the limousine pulled to the area near the kitchen. This time, there were no dogs to be seen. Frederic shut down the engine, opened her door, and then waited while she unfolded the cart. Together, they lifted the cake onto the rolling cart, and then Chanti carefully guided it up the ramp to the entrance.

She stood and waited while her arrival was announced. Ten minutes later, the Baron himself was in the kitchen. He greeted her as warmly as his cold blood would allow, which was to say that he effused praise upon her while he kissed her hand.

"Thank you so much for making room in your schedule for this party. I cannot tell you how important it is to me—and to my guests. I would not be surprised if you received many, many new customers after tonight's event is complete."

Chanti wanted to say that she would be surprised if she received any new customers, but instead she replied by stating, "You are too kind for considering me for such an important occasion. Now, I insist that you inspect this cake personally before your guests arrive. I want to see your reaction for myself."

The Baron gave a nod of his head and a smug, wide smile. "If you insist."

"Please close your eyes while I remove the cover."

The Baron stood with his hands beside him and his eyes closed. Chanti removed the cover to the cake, set it aside on a counter, and then said, "Open your eyes."

Chanti watched as his eyes opened. They first looked at the dominant figure. They traveled down and up and then down again. Then they drifted to the smaller children in the background. Finally, the eyes settled onto the words at the bottom. During the whole process, the Baron's eyes had gone from icy blue to something wolfish and predatory. After reading the words, Chanti had to use all of her strength to stifle an involuntary shiver. His eyes almost seemed to change shape to something serpentine. Or had they actually done so momentarily?

"Are you pleased?" she asked in her professional voice.

"Beyond pleased," he said as his eyes continued to absorb, or rather, feast upon, the details. Looking at her directly, he said, "I don't know how you do it, but your capacity to anticipate your clients' wishes is, shall I say, supernatural." His eyes continued to search her face.

"My inspirations come to me in dreams or trances. I simply create what I see. If I have to think about ideas for a client, I cannot create anything."

"Yes, well, you have certainly earned your fee and," he paused to remove a wallet from his inner coat pocket, "deserved a bonus." He withdrew five thousand euro in cash along with the check which had been made out for her.

"Thank you, Baron. You are very generous. You will let me know what your guests think of the cake?"

"Most assuredly. And now I must return to the preparations for my guests. Please excuse me."

"Of course. I will put the cake into the cooler to keep the icing chilled at the proper temperature, and then I will return home."

They parted in the kitchen. Chanti finished her work and then exited the house, where she found Frederic sitting on a bench smoking a cigarette and waiting for her. She folded her cart, placed it into the boot of the car, and then settled herself in for the three-hour drive back to Paris. Mentally, she began to prepare herself for what she would tell the police when they inevitably came for her.

Chapter 45

Sonian Forest, Near Waterloo, Belgium

They had located a high-end drone from a source on the dark web. While there was no problem flying drones in Europe, they simply didn't want anyone to be able to trace the transaction. One of the members of Serious' team lived in Europe and was willing to make the trek. Because of the capabilities of this particular unit (it could travel five miles from the operator with a video feed link of between two and three miles, depending on terrain), the volunteer and the group agreed that the personal risk was likely to be far lower than what Daniel Robertson had encountered.

Coincidentally, they located a cellular tower site a little over two miles from the property. Such a location would have an access road, would generally be devoid of people, and would ensure an excellent signal for the live stream. One of the members noted that it could also provide plausible cover if someone noticed the drone and attempted to triangulate the signal. They had purchased numerous extra batteries. The downside would be that they would have to return the drone to its temporary base, swap batteries, and then launch it again. The downtime was minimal, but they would have no eyes on the property during that time.

Arriving around noon on the planned day, the twenty-first of September, the team member who went by the screen name "Obigrotto" unpacked the drone and the batteries. Then he set up a solar charger and hooked up a new burner cell phone that had been purchased over 100 kilometers away. The cell picked up a signal immediately. He installed and configured VPN software and a couple of other apps to use for connecting to the chat room and servicing the video stream from the drone. Everything had been pretested with another phone elsewhere, so this was mainly an exercise in following the checklist.

After verifying that all connections were working, he sent a message to the chat room indicating that he was about to stream a video from the drone while on the ground. After confirming that worked, the drone was launched for further tests, all of which worked as well.

Serious, who was monitoring the progress, agreed that running some flights to scope out the perimeter should be safe enough if they stayed well clear of the estate's driveway and buildings. These flights revealed the fence they already knew existed. What they hadn't been able to tell from satellite photos but now discovered was that, at least for special occasions such as today, there was a random patrol of an armed two-man team on a four-wheeler with what appeared to be a decent-sized canine companion. The ATV would appear out of paths from underneath the canopy, drive along the fence line for a few moments, and then disappear back into the trees.

They also noted a steady stream of limousines and other luxury vehicles which were turning into the long drive to the estate and then eventually returning. The participants for this event apparently would have none of their usual retinue and support staff with them. Invitation-only meant just that.

Serious would have liked to have gotten much closer to try and identify the occupants as they disembarked their vehicles during daylight hours, but that would have risked exposure to the drone and jeopardized the whole mission. As it was, they were able to eke out about a ninety-minute flight for each of the batteries. The flight back to the tower site and relaunch with a new battery was taking an average of about twelve to fifteen minutes. They were flying above the legal altitude for drones in Europe, but their resident geek who studied flight paths for planes had already stated that no airlines flew anywhere near that area. Personal safety trumped rigorous attention to the rules in cases such as these. The flights would continue as long as they had batteries or until something definitive happened.

Chapter 46

Paris, France

After arriving back at her apartment, Chanti dialed Nellie's number. She answered on the first ring.

"Thank you for calling me back. I really need to speak with you in person about something very important." Nellie did not call her Marin over the phone due to their long-held agreement to maintain her privacy.

Chanti paused and then said, "I'm afraid I won't be able to do that. It wouldn't be best for me to visit you until…everything has been finalized."

Nellie let out a sigh. How much could she say over the phone? "Someone contacted me out of the blue about my stepbrother."

Chanti's blood ran cold. Her thoughts ran in different directions. Had the Baron done more research on her? Had he discovered who she really was? No, he had shown no sign that he knew anything. If he had wanted to, he could have held her at his estate. The police? Would they be pursuing leads on a cold case? Who could it be?

"For your own safety," Chanti said, "I think it best that I stay away— for now. Please try to understand. It will make more sense in a day or two."

On the other end, Nellie bit her lip. How could she reach her? A thought occurred to her.

"At sunset this evening, I'm going to your favorite place at night. Alistair will be with me, I'm sure. Please come."

Another pause, and then came her response. "I will."

Chapter 47

Sonian Forest, Belgium, and Cyberspace

Eight years and three months after Daniel Robertson's efforts to document a crime and his valorous decision to save the life of one child, another group of people gathered in a chat room to watch the events of the evening unfold. The sun had just set. The drone had been sent out with a new battery. The technology was better. The operator, they hoped, was safer. The video feed was clearer and closer due to the eye in the sky with its zoom lens and night vision capabilities.

There was little need for commentary since the operator was seeing exactly the same thing as the rest of the group. As the device closed in on the main building of the estate, the camera picked up the flare of torches. This was a variation on the ritual they had seen. Instead of a circle in the courtyard, there were two lines of participants about three meters apart, all wearing robes or cloaks. Each had a torch which was carried in the hand adjacent to the open aisle between the columns. The lines were in slow procession out of the courtyard following one figure dressed in dark clothing from head to toe.

As the drone drew nearer and lined up behind the two columns, the middle of the procession could be seen clearly. There were three children, each wearing a white robe that covered most of their body and arms and legs, none of which were bound. The group walked out of the courtyard and made a right turn, heading toward a grove of trees that was set apart from the larger surrounding forest. About fifteen minutes later, the group began to enter the grove. Obigrotto attempted to navigate the drone above the grove at various angles, but the canopy was thick enough that attempts to surveil from above were futile.

"Should I fly lower and into the trees?" he asked.

"No. The risk of discovery is too great," said Serious. "Keep the drone high enough to make sure they do not leave without us knowing it."

The image changed as the drone swooped upward until it could see across the entire grove. One of the team members estimated it to be about fifty meters wide. Using the night vision mode, the treetops were distinct. Underneath, an occasional glare emerged as the group made its way to the center. Once there, the lights seemed to be forming into a circle.

"What do we do now?" someone asked.

"We wait," said Serious.

Chapter 48

Paris, France

Paris is called the City of Light, a reputation that began during the reign of Louis XIV as an attempt to discourage thieves, burglars, and lawbreakers from being able to operate in the shadows and darkness of the night. Today, with hundreds of illuminated structures, the city is a visual feast for those who enjoy seeing various architecture from a different perspective.

Sitting on the south (or left) bank of the Seine some few minutes' walk from the Eiffel tower is an imposing and, according to the locals, ugly edifice. The Montparnasse Tower is a massive structure that seems out of place with the skyline. However, those who are aware of its placement also understand its significance. Simply put, it is one of the best locations to view the beauty of the lights of Paris at night—without having to see the Montparnasse Tower.

When the darkness closed in upon Chanti at night, Alistair and Nellie would often take her to the top and let her enjoy the brilliance of Paris. They would talk to one another on the roof while she simply gazed at the lights. Sometimes they would have a hot drink in the restaurant on the top floor if the weather was contrary. Tonight, after exiting the metro and purchasing a ticket, Chanti was whisked fifty-six stories high to the observation level. From there, she ascended the stairs to the roof, which offers a 360-degree view of the city. The sun was disappearing, and the manmade replacements were just beginning to rule the dusk. She walked to the western side and leaned against the railing underneath the awnings.

"I'm here," she said.

Nellie turned from the view and embraced her. "Thank you for coming, dear. Alistair is downstairs holding a table for us in case you want to sit rather than stand."

"I really just want to know what's going on. Who has contacted you? What did they want?"

The roof was not particularly full, so Nellie related the story of the messages she had received and the videos she and Alistair had watched. "I watched a famous man end Daniel's life. But I finally understood just a bit more about the horror you went through."

Chanti was absorbed in her own thoughts. Finally, she spoke. "What does this person want?"

"They have asked for nothing. There have been no threats to me. Everything so far says that they just want to help. They've mentioned that they have turned over the material to law enforcement and that they may release the materials publicly. Other than that, I really can't say."

Chanti thought a bit more and then said, "Well, after tomorrow, it won't matter."

"What do you mean?"

Chanti looked Nellie in the eyes and said, "I won't tell you, but you'll know soon enough. The whole world will know."

Nellie studied her face. It was awash with emotion. Rather than press her for any more details, she placed an arm around her waist and drew her close. "Let's enjoy the lights one more time, shall we?"

Chanti leaned her head against Nellie's shoulder. They stayed there for the better part of an hour. Inky blackness filled the sky as night tried to claim ownership of the land. All over the city, the lights shone brightly as vigilant sentinels who refused to yield to the darkness.

Chapter 49

Sonian Forest, Belgium

Almost thirty minutes after the group had entered the grove of trees, the lights began to move again. Obigrotto lowered the drone's altitude and tracked slightly ahead of the torches so that when the participants emerged from the tree line, the drone was able to capture something close to a forty-five-degree angle or lower as the field of view. The chat room was silent as they watched two, four, six people emerge in the two columns. Then they saw the sixth pair walk out of the woods carrying something. Without prompting, the operator zoomed in on the sight. They were carrying the limp form of a child. One person had the arms, the other the legs. The head lolled limply toward the ground. In the greenish glow, the white tunic appeared to be stained black across the chest.

The procession continued. The camera zoomed out again. Two more people were now visible carrying a body. Then the third child's body entered the field of view. There were two columns of sixteen robed men and women trailed by the figure in dark.

"Get as many faces as you can," Serious said.

Obigrotto lowered the drone just a bit and zoomed the lens at the head of one of the columns. The torches helped provide distinction to the facial features, and the recording taking place on machines around the world was in as high of a definition as the technology allowed. Facial recognition software would make identification matches credible. If those involved were careless enough to have brought their phones with them, location matches would provide more than probable cause for a warrant with a judge or in a court of law. The drone finished the left column and then zipped ahead in order to capture the right column. When that was complete, Serious instructed the operator to do his best to get any part of the face of the figure who appeared to be the leader. The hood worn by the figure obstructed the face entirely from the sides.

"I'll have to lower the drone quite a bit. They might be able to hear it."

"Just track with them. Maybe he'll remove his hood back at the property."

"We'll have about ten to fifteen minutes of battery by the time they get back."

"Maybe that's all we'll need," said Serious. "I'd like to start running those faces right now. Who can do that?"

Two of the members volunteered. They took their video stream and saved what had already been received in order to play it and begin cropping still images from the frames. Then they uploaded the best of the still images into facial recognition search engines and began cataloging the results.

At the estate, Obigrotto had again raised the altitude of the drone as the group neared the entrance in order to avoid hitting any buildings or chance being detected in the lights. As they filed in, those holding the bodies placed them side by side and then joined the rest who had formed a circle around them in the courtyard.

"We've got five, maybe ten minutes of battery left, and I still need to fly it home," he said.

"Zoom in on the leader," said Serious.

Obigrotto did so. The leader had entered the circle and was gesticulating toward the bodies. He also made various motions toward members of the group. Then, suddenly, he reached up and pulled back his hood and began shouting with both arms outstretched to the sky. The image was unmistakably that of Baron Klaus Maginon.

"We've got him," said Serious. "Zoom out slowly and get the whole group. Then zoom in on the bodies again. Then raise the altitude and zoom out so that the chateau's buildings are clearly identifiable."

Obigrotto did that and then said, "Battery indicator is in the red."

"Bring it home," said Serious. "If you feel safe enough, would you consider staying longer to see if the police do respond?"

"Yes," replied Obigrotto.

The drone slipped away into the night and barely made it back to the cell tower site. Obigrotto had already loaded up the vehicle he was using with all the other gear in preparation for a quick departure. Instead of doing that, he replaced the dead battery with a fresh one and connected the dead one to the charger. There were enough batteries for about four to six more hours of flights. He decided to wait an hour or two before launching the drone again. He leaned the driver's seat back and closed his eyes to rest them and set an alarm on the phone in case he drifted off to sleep.

"Do you think we can get any law enforcement to respond immediately to this while they're all still together?" asked one of the members.

"All we can do is try," said Serious.

"We run the risk of alerting them if we pick someone who is paid off by the Baron," someone else noted.

"That's true," said Serious. "But if we pick the right person or persons, they won't get any more evidence later than if they act right now. And if we pick the wrong person, they won't get rid of any more evidence now than they would if we waited days or weeks for someone else to follow up."

The discussion continued for several minutes. Ultimately, the group decided that they would contact both the local police as well as the Belgian Federal Police with a copy of the pertinent section of the video stream, still images, and proof of location. To add a bit of extra pressure, they would include a promise that the data would be made public within 24 hours if no action from authorities had transpired.

While one member began clipping the video and uploading it to a public file storage site, others were collating the still images with the names of those who had been identified. These were uploaded into a folder with a document with the details they were able to obtain on the persons present. Serious used a voice modulator and a free VOIP phone number to call the local police and the nearest Federal Police offices

With the local police, it took some time before the person answering was willing to connect Serious with someone higher up. In both instances, stating that this was an anonymous tip about a multiple homicide in progress and crimes against children helped.

After receiving an email address from an officer at both locations to send the tip information, the emails were sent. Serious used their normal protocols with privacy keys and ways for the law enforcement to respond by email if they needed anything else. They each were also carbon copied on the email and notified that the other party had been given the exact same information.

Serious concluded the emails by writing:

```
I understand that you may find it hard to
believe the information we are sending, but
it is real, and it is happening this very
moment. If you do not act on this, your names
will be released publicly as the contacts for
each law enforcement entity along with the
data you are being provided. Please do the
right thing.
```

Chapter 50

Waterloo, Belgium

Detective Heidi Rademaker with the local police force hung up the phone and immediately checked her email. Sure enough, there was something new from "1329." Opening the message, she wondered if it was going to be spam, porn, or who knew what else. Anonymous tips were usually a waste of time and resources. While the video was downloading, she opened the folder with the still images and the document detailing names. She almost spilled her coffee. That was Baron Klaus Maginon's name and face. Her interest piqued, she checked the download—still going. Hurriedly, she scanned the rest of the names and images. It was a who's who of politicians, celebrities, and elite from all over.

The video was now downloaded. She opened her video player and watched on a speed setting five times faster than normal, as suggested by the anonymous tipster. She could always stop and replay things on normal speed. About fifteen minutes later, she picked up her phone and called the duty chief. "I need a tactical unit immediately."

She then called the Federal Police offices and requested to speak with Inspector Rolf Hagen, who had received the same tip. He was still in the process of reviewing the video but listened as she described her plan of action.

"Do you want the assistance of the Federal Police?" he asked when she was finished.

"If you are able to join us without delaying our response, I believe that the jurisdiction over what is shown on the video will involve more than we are able to handle," she said.

"When do you anticipate your arrival?" asked Rolf.

"The tactical unit is assembling now. We'll go over the plan and then leave. I would say no more than an hour, probably less."

"Then I will drive to your headquarters and join you there. I'll be there in half an hour."

"Very good. Thank you, and...Inspector?"

"Yes."

"Based on what you have already seen, do you concur that this is indeed credible?"

"I believe it is credible enough that we must follow up on it immediately. If we are wrong, there will be repercussions more than I want to imagine. The Baron is a very powerful man, as I'm sure you are aware from serving in this area."

"Yes. And if this is indeed legitimate, it will be a significant breakthrough."

"We'll know soon enough. See you shortly."

Heidi placed the phone back in its cradle. She had never liked the Baron. Most of the ultra-rich had dark secrets that they could pay enough money to make disappear. While the video could be an elaborately staged production, it would take quite a lot to completely mimic the buildings of the Chateau Sauvageon along with the basic layout of the surrounding woodlands. She could confirm that they seemed to match the maps she had studied routinely during her years on the force.

She collected the materials she needed to begin the briefing of the tactical unit and then walked downstairs to the briefing room, where she faced twenty stony-faced special operations members. After greeting them, she clicked on the wall display, typed something on her laptop, and brought up a map of the estate. "This," she said pointing to the main building, "is our target."

Chapter 51

Chateau Sauvageon, Belgium

In the dining hall of the Chateau Sauvageon is a massive white oak table. If everyone squeezed in tightly for a festive and joyous family Christmas celebration, it could seat fifty people. Stained from centuries of wine, beer, fats of various kinds, and the usual detritus of raucous meals, the dark patina glinted dimly in the single chandelier and side wall sconces. On this less-than-noble occasion, Baron Maginon gathered his guests around the main table, sixteen per side with himself at the head. Lifting a cut crystal wine goblet in his right hand, he addressed the assemblage.

"On this day, we remember and indeed celebrate the return of Persephone to the Underworld to live with her husband Hades for the next six months. We know that one day we will go to live with Hades, where we will rule in his kingdom as his faithful servants, we who have kept his feasts and offered his sacrifices at the appointed times."

The group responded with, "Aye!"

"I draw your attention to the center of the table. You have all seen the cake created by the designer Chanti. What could be a more fitting reminder of why we celebrate than this work of art? We prolong our days with the life of these sacrifices in order to instruct others in the hidden knowledge. Shortly, we will indulge in our feast, and we will each of us enjoy this cake. Now, please rise and lift your glass."

He waited as the group rose and did so. Then he continued.

"In this glass is the fruit of the harvest, aged to perfection, mingled with the elixir of life, also aged to perfection. Drink all of it!"

Then, grasping the glasses with both hands, each member of the group guzzled their glass and tilted it upward until the last drop had been drained.

Chapter 52

Sand Mountain, Alabama

It was late in the afternoon when Buddy's cell phone rang as he was driving home. He saw Sheriff Matt's name and answered it.

"Buddy, I just wanted to tell you that we have some closure on the people who were involved in that last attack."

"Oh? What's the word, Sheriff?"

"Out of the five that Don worked on, three of them were pretty well wiped from databases. I wasn't surprised by that. Probably means they worked for groups with a lot of power. We still got IDs on the two drivers. You'll never guess who they worked for, so I'll just tell you. Both of them were active-duty FBI."

"You gotta be kidding me," said Buddy.

"Nope. Not a bit. After running their prints through AFIS and getting hits, I figured we'd probably get a follow-up inquiry from the Bureau when they didn't show up for work. Sure enough, I got a call from one of the feds over in Atlanta asking if I had any knowledge of their whereabouts."

"What did you tell him?"

"Her: it was a woman. Anyway, I knew if the feds got involved, it would drag things out for months or probably years, and I didn't want to cause you and Janine any more grief than what you've already had to deal with and have to go to court and all. I just laid it all on the line. Without giving her any of the names of who was involved locally, I told her that her two fibbies were part of what appeared to be an extrajudicial mercenary hit squad who targeted and tried to kill some people under my jurisdiction and that said hit squad happened to pick the wrong targets. She was a bit shocked by that and found it hard to believe at first.

"I sent her a highly edited copy of the coroner's report along with photos. I also made sure that she understood the significance of the tattoos that each of them were sporting. She recognized the pedo symbols and was also a bit shocked by that. I guess they don't make agents bare their butts as a matter of course for regular inspection over there.

"She had a few more questions about what happened and prodded me from several angles to try and get more details about who was involved here. Finally, I told her that the way I saw it, we could handle things one of two ways. She could come in with federal warrants and subpoenas and force me to give her that information. If she did that, I was going to have a press conference and invite every media channel I could find from Knoxville, to Nashville, to Chattanooga, to Atlanta, to Birmingham, and everyone else in between.

In that press conference, I would lay out the gory details with a heavy emphasis on the fact that two active-duty FBI agents were involved in a highly illegal rendition and assassination attempt on one or more law-abiding US citizens. This would result in yet another black eye for them on top of all the other shady things the Bureau has been involved in like targeting parents at school board meetings and their false flags they've set up all over the place with patsies. Or, she could just let it ride and tell what family they may have that they died in the line of duty or whatever lies they make up all the time in those federal agencies."

"What'd she say?" asked Buddy.

After she looked at the photos and saw the damage you boys caused and heard enough details to convince her that it really was an attack that was coordinated by someone operating outside the law, she said that those two had been on their radar for a while and that she was happy to close out their files. I told her they needed to keep a closer watch and a tighter rein on what their agents did off the clock, and she assured me that they would do so. Not sure what that's worth, but the long and short of it is there ain't gonna be any drawn-out investigation by anybody."

"Thanks a whole lot, Sheriff," said Buddy. "That's a big relief in itself. And Janine's convinced that something's gonna give today. It would be nice to be shed of this whole thing and just move on with life."

"Yeah, Derek told me what Sherry said. She seems to get the newspaper a few days before everybody else does."

"So, you believe her too?" asked Buddy.

"Buddy, I've been in this business for a while. I've seen a lot, most of it bad. But Sherry has told me things that have resulted in some breakthroughs on some tough cases over the years. How she knows it, I have no idea. But, yeah, I've learned to take stock in what she says. I'll take all the help I can get on this job."

"Hmm. That makes me feel better."

"It should. Well, I'll let you go. Oh, one more thing, Buddy."

"Yeah?"

"I never asked what happened to that other fellow."

"You might say that he succumbed to his injuries," said Buddy.

"Oh, well. That's too bad for him," said Matt. "Well, I hope you didn't have any problem with any random tracking devices like the ones we found on the other five."

"Nah. Wouldn't surprise me if it ended up in a coyote or a wild hog or something," said Buddy.

Sheriff Matt chuckled. He loved the people in his county. "Okay then. We'll call it 'case closed.' You have a good rest of the day, Buddy."

"You do the same, Sheriff," said Buddy.

Chapter 53

Chateau Sauvageon, Belgium

Around midnight, the tactical unit breached the entrance to the estate Chateau Sauvageon. Breached was perhaps too strong a word. The main gate at the end of the long driveway was open. The inner gate was also open.

The units advanced as quickly and quietly as two vans loaded with heavily armed officers plus two other vehicles could. They weren't sure if they would encounter any resistance during their approach, but there were no signs of opposition at all. That struck both Detective Heidi and Inspector Rolf as just a bit odd.

"Do you think they've received a tip-off that we were coming?" asked Rolf.

"Anything's possible," said Heidi. "The Baron is a very wealthy man. Who knows how many people he's bought and paid for?"

Once the vehicles reached the main complex of the house and other buildings, the tactical unit leadership took point. They had identified numerous exits, which they sent teams to cover. Once in position, a team of four officers tested the front door. To their surprise, it was unlocked. Slowly and carefully, they opened it and proceeded inside.

Heidi and Rolf listened to the comms on the short-range radio frequency from inside their vehicle. After two minutes of slowly working their way room by room, the team leader spoke in a terse voice. "Detective Rademaker, you're going to need to see this before we proceed any further."

Curious, the two officers approached the entrance together. Once inside, the leader of the team met them inside the entrance hall.

"This way, Detective, Inspector," he said.

He led them down the hallway to an intersection, took a left turn, and then walked down another hallway to a large set of wooden doors. One of them was already open.

When Heidi walked through the door, she realized she was in the dining hall. The inspector walked in behind her. They both looked at the scene in front of them, slowly and methodically taking in the entire room.

"We're going to need the entire homicide division," said Heidi to the team leader. "And everyone who works forensics. Immediately."

The radio interrupted again. One of the two-man units broke in and said, "Captain, you're going to need to come to the kitchen."

The captain led Heidi and Rolf through another set of doors and then down a short passage to a brightly lit room. Once they entered, the officer pointed to a large stainless steel counter against one wall. Heidi gasped, and Rolf swore loudly and repeatedly as they walked slowly toward the counter.

"I'm going to call for more of the Federal Police to help with this," Rolf said coldly. "This is worse than we expected."

In spite of years of doing police work, Heidi's eyes were brimming with tears. "Yes," she said. "This is more than we can handle locally. We're going to have to use every resource we possibly can." Turning to the captain, she said, "Continue a thorough room-by-room search. Don't touch anything, but call in everything you find. Once the house is secure, I want a man at each entrance. Call in K-9 units and more officers to begin searching the outbuildings and then the grounds. Wake up whoever you have to. Have them bring plenty of portable lights. We may need them."

After he departed, Heidi turned to Rolf and said, "Where do we even begin?"

"Let's start outside and see if we can find that grove we saw in the video. We can't do much in the dining room until CSI arrives and we get some type of toxicology test results. And if I stay here in the kitchen much longer, I'm going to have nightmares."

They passed back through the house to the entrance and got their bearings. Once they agreed on the general direction, they began walking toward the grove. Part of the way there, Rolf said, "Hold on a moment. Look here." Shining his light close to the ground, they could pick out a blood trail.

Heidi let out a deep sigh. "It's going to be a very long night."

High above them, a low whir emanated from the drone that had been watching their every move.

Chapter 54

Inspector Hagen had been on the Federal Police force long enough to expect the media to show up sooner than later. He was a bit surprised at just how quickly not just one but three different reporters had already made their way down the driveway and were waiting in the courtyard by the front door when he and Heidi returned from the grove. He growled at the officer on duty in the courtyard.

"How did they get in here so fast?"

"Sorry, Inspector. They left their cars on the main road and made it through the woods and slipped through the outer gate on foot."

Turning to the reporters, Rolf said, "Well, I have to admire your ingenuity and tenacity for doing your job. But this is an active crime scene, and I can't have you contaminating it."

"Come on, Inspector," said the reporter from VRT. "You know us well enough to know that we're not going to interfere with your work. But you also know we aren't going anywhere until we get a story."

"There's nothing to say at this point," said Rolf.

"Yeah, right," said the journalist from Le Soir. "Let's see: two local tactical units, an inspector from the Federal Police, more units on the way if the police frequency is accurate—all of you show up in the middle of the night at the estate of one of the wealthiest men in Europe, and you have nothing to say? Do I look like I believe you?"

Heidi turned to Rolf and said, "We have a good idea of what happened and why it happened and who is likely responsible. We won't be able to keep everyone who is involved in the investigation from talking, whether they're your people or mine."

Rolf sighed. "I guess you're right." Turning to the reporters, he said, "Listen carefully. I'm going to give you an early statement, which you can file as a news flash. The three of you will be allowed to accompany only either myself or Detective Rademaker as we permit with no other movement around this property, or so help me, I will clap you in irons faster than you can blink an eye, and you won't be filing any reports. Do I make myself clear?"

"Perfectly," said the reporter from VRT. "And I'm sure I speak for the three of us when I say we all agree to your terms."

The other two nodded their assent.

"Now, for the statement," said Rolf. "An anonymous tip late in the evening led us to search the property of Baron Klaus Maginon."

"What was the tip concerning?" asked the journalist from Le Soir.

"Let me finish," barked Rolf. "The tip concerned possible homicide and crimes against children."

All three reporters' eyes widened.

"Once we searched the property, we found what appears to be a mass homicide of the Baron and his guests by poisoning. We have a strong lead as to how they were poisoned, but we will, of course, have to await toxicology reports before releasing conclusive statements. We also believe that we have a good lead as to who was responsible for the poisoning. Again, we will not release a statement on that until the crime scene investigators have finished their work." He paused and then added, "Further examination of the property revealed that the Baron and his guests were involved in what appears to be ritual human sacrifice."

"Of children?" asked the reporter from Le Soir.

Rolf exhaled deeply. "Yes. Of children."

"When will we be allowed inside to accompany you?" asked Peter Southerland, the third reporter, in a Stoke-on-Trent accent. He was an independent journalist who often filed with BBC, Daily Mail, Bild, and other outlets.

"We need to coordinate with the leadership of the teams who are arriving first. Go ahead and file your reports. It may be thirty minutes or more before we're ready for you."

Over the next half hour, the reporters lit up the wires with their breaking reports. The unlucky reporters who rushed to the scene too late found themselves greeted by rather severe-looking officers with assault weapons who had been charged with preventing anyone else from breaching the perimeter. All they could do was watch as police vehicles continued to stream into the estate, along with numerous coroner vans.

Once the three reporters were allowed to accompany Rolf and Heidi inside, they were given a view of the dining hall. They were allowed to take a limited number of photos from the edges of the room.

"Pretty fast-acting stuff, wouldn't you say, Inspector?" asked Peter Southerland.

"Had to be. They all ingested it pretty much at the same time, and none of them left the room, as you can see."

"She was just on the cover of our paper this week," said the journalist from Le Soir, pointing to a beautiful woman lying on the floor beside an overturned chair. "And he was on the front page today," he said pointing to a man near her.

"Now you know what they did in secret," said Rolf.

"Look at their faces. You'd think the devil himself came for them," said the VRT reporter.

"The devil can have them all," said Heidi.

"Why do you say that?" asked the same reporter.

"Follow me," she said. Leading them to the kitchen, she said, "Put your cameras and phones on this table. There will be no media photos inside this room now or afterwards. Is that understood?"

The reporters complied by putting their devices onto the long side table sitting outside the kitchen.

Heidi spoke again. "I will warn you that what you are about to see cannot be unseen. If you choose to go in, you may wish that you had not done so. The only reason I am allowing you inside is so that if your media outlet chooses to publish the truth of what went on here tonight, the public will realize just how evil and wicked all of those people were whom you just saw in the dining hall. I must ask that each of you place both hands firmly over your mouths to avoid contaminating the crime scene. Are you ready?"

The reporters looked at one another quizzically and then nodded to Heidi and Rolf. They all lifted their hands and pressed them to their mouths. Heidi opened the door and said, "This way." Once inside, she pointed to the stainless steel counter against the far wall.

The reactions were instantaneous. The VRT reporter gagged and ran from the room with his mouth covered trying to avoid heaving inside the room. He made it outside the door and then collapsed, spoiling the carpet as he did. The journalist from Le Soir took one look and turned his head away. He kept one hand pressed to his mouth, and with the other, he covered his eyes and stumbled back out through the door as if trying to wipe the scene from his mind. The independent journalist had been in enough war zones that the immediate shock did not overwhelm him.

"May I get closer?" Peter asked.

"Three meters' distance," said Heidi.

After nearing the counter, Peter surveyed the scene in front of him. Detective Rademaker was correct. He would never be able to forget what he was looking at. Turning back, he spoke softly to Heidi.

"Detective, I'm truly sorry that you had to see that, or any of the other officers. You are correct. The devil may take every last one of them, and if there is a hell, may they rot there forever."

Heidi locked eyes with him for a few moments and then said, "Thank you for your concern. I only ask that you be respectful in your reporting. Please, nothing sensational."

"You have my word," he said. "I will tell the truth about what I saw and do my best to honor their memory."

Heidi and Rolf escorted the three men back outside the building. The VRT reporter would be useless for the next forty-five minutes. Calls to his cell went unanswered while he sat with his back against a wall in the courtyard. The other two men accompanied the two officers as they walked into the grove. Here they permitted a few more photos and then returned to the entrance.

"Now, if you will excuse us, we have more work to do," said Rolf. "You may remain here in the courtyard, or you may leave the premises. If you do leave, you will not be permitted back inside for any reason."

The VRT reporter chose to depart. He wasn't sure how quickly he could find a strong drink or a strong pill, but he would not be able to function until he had one or the other or both. The other two stayed. Throughout the long night, they composed more snippets of news to feed to the wire services and their main outlets. The independent journalist began writing his detailed first impressions of the main story. Any time they could get a passing officer to answer a question, they added what they could to the growing demand for more information.

Peter Southerland's description of what he saw in that kitchen would be the most consummate account to be published when he released it himself two weeks later; true to his word, he published only the facts. They were sensational enough.

Chapter 55

Philadelphia, Pennsylvania

It was after work and in the early evening hours when Alex checked his email. It was from Serious.

```
Happening in Belgium at Chateau Sauvageon right
now. Expect global news soon. Prepare your
stories immediately if you want to maximize
impact. More to come. View material in links
below.
```

Alex dialed the number of the editor and said, "Clear the front page for tomorrow. I'll be in the office in twenty minutes. We're going to need several writers and editors ready to go. Bombshell coming out of Europe. Ties into big names here in the US."

On the way into the office, he called Happy and said, "Happy? Alex here. Can you bring Stefani down to the offices right now? I'll be there in fifteen minutes. It's about her story. I'll explain when you get there. I want her to know what's going on before she reads it in the paper tomorrow morning. Thanks."

A short time later, they arrived. Alex motioned Happy and Stefani to chairs in his office. "I'm going to be brief because I've got a lot of work ahead of me writing stories before tomorrow's early edition. And there will be a lot more stories to come after that."

Turning to Stefani, he said, "I want to publish your story as early as tomorrow or sometime in the next two or three days."

"What's the sudden rush?" asked Stefani. "I thought you wanted to try and corroborate some other leads before publishing my story."

Alex handed her a sheet of paper with a grainy black and white photo. It was a close up of a man wearing a cloak or robe of some kind. The features were unmistakable: it was Senator Dom Acworth.

"What is this? Where is this from?" she asked as she passed it to Happy to look at.

"It seems that the respected Senator was doing more than molesting minors. This photo is from a mass homicide that occurred in Belgium just hours ago. The Senator and a bunch of other famous people were involved in child sacrifice. Now he's dead."

Stefani's eyes got wide, and her mouth dropped open. Happy flinched and looked up from his studying of the photo.

"What did you just say?" he asked.

"You heard me right the first time," said Alex. "There were about three dozen of them that all appear to have been poisoned. Someone on the inside turned the tables on them, from what I'm hearing. Based on material I've gotten previously about the main guy, this has been going on for years, decades, who knows how long."

"Lord, have mercy," said Happy in a sad voice. "Killing innocent children? And the Senator was part of that?"

"Yes, he was. I've actually seen the video this photo was taken from. And there are some others. They're pretty bad. I don't know which ones we'll actually end up printing, although I'm sure many of them will end up on the Internet eventually if not in print."

"How long had he been doing this?" asked Stefani.

"I don't know," said Alex. "Maybe it was his first time and he just got unlucky. Or maybe he had been doing it for a long time. Why do you ask?"

"Just…certain things he would say when he was with me. It scares me now to think of it. I guess I thought he was joking. I don't want to talk about it right now. Maybe later." She looked at Happy with pleading eyes. "I'm really, really scared right now."

"Don't you worry none," said Happy. "Doesn't sound like Senator Acworth is gonna be bothering you or anybody else from now on."

"There's more than him!" Stefani said. "It's way bigger than just him!"

"I know," said Alex. "And exposing them is the way that we fight them. The more we expose them, the less darkness they have to hide in."

"I can't!" said Stefani. "If you put my name out there, they'll come looking for me. They'll kill me, too! I can't believe what he said to me! What they said to me!" Her voice was getting frantic.

"Hold on, Stefani. Wait a minute!" said Alex. "I'm not going to do a thing without your permission. You can trust me on that. Look at me " He looked her in the eyes. "You believe me, don't you? I'm not going to run your story now or ever if you don't give me your permission. I care too much about you to do that."

Stefani's looked at him for a long time. Her breathing went from heaving to deep long breaths. She nodded. "I believe you. I believe you won't do it. Thank you."

"Listen to me, though," Alex continued. "Your story is a powerful one. There are enough details from the current police reports and investigation that incriminate not just the late Senator but many other men and women. Your testimony can throw them off balance, put them on the run. By naming their names, perhaps other victims will be emboldened to come forward and tell their stories, too. Other reporters, other investigators will begin to think that maybe someone will believe their word about what they've seen or heard." He turned to Happy and said, "You know what I mean. What do you think?"

Happy mused for a moment. "The Bible's full of stories of one man or one woman who was willing to do the hard thing because it was the right thing. But I understand Stefani's fear. It's a powerful demotivator. Older and stronger people than her have said no because of fear." Looking at Stefani, he asked Alex, "I do have one question, though. Would it be possible for you to publish her story without putting her real name on it?"

"A pseudonym wouldn't be as forceful, but yes, I believe my editors would agree. We've done it before in certain circumstances."

"Would you consider letting Mister Ingram print your story if he didn't use your real name?" Happy asked Stefani.

"I think so. As long as they didn't know which girl or boy it was."

"What name do you want to use?" Alex asked Stefani.

"How about you just use the name Jael?" said Happy.

"Jael? How do you spell that?" asked Alex.

"J-a-e-l," said Happy.

"What's the significance of that name?" asked Alex.

"I'll let you read about her in the Bible later. I'm going to take Stefani back home now." Turning to her, he said, "I think we'll find time to read about her tonight, if that's okay with you."

Stefani nodded, and they left Alex sorting through documents and writing key facts on a whiteboard as a line of writers began filing in for their assignments. When they arrived back at the Mission, Happy called Sarah down to his study.

"How about you whip us up some of your good hot chocolate and then join us for a Bible study?"

Sarah eyed him and set her mouth. "Is this a cup or a pitcher-long Bible study?"

"Maybe make a bit ol' pot."

"What you planning on studying?"

"Jael," said Happy. "I want Stefani to get a good introduction to who that woman was and what she did."

Sarah turned toward the kitchen. As she walked down the hall, she began belting out the lyrics, "Wellllll, if I had a hammer, I'd hammer in the mawnin'…"

Happy doubled over with laughter, leaving a very confused Stefani wondering just what was going on.

Chapter 56

Paris, France

The next morning in Paris, Chanti awoke to the smell of breakfast being cooked. Nellie had persuaded her to come home with them and spend the night. It hadn't taken much pressure. Chanti knew the hammer would fall soon enough, and she craved what time she could get with these two people who had loved her for the few years they had known her. They ate together mostly in peaceful silence, although Chanti could tell that there was a bit of tension hanging in the air.

Finally, she found her voice and asked, "What is the news this morning?"

Alistair shot a glance at Nellie, who nodded. In reply, he turned on the television with the remote. There was a helicopter view of a large set of buildings. The driveway and yard were filled with police and emergency vehicles. The news ticker at the bottom of the image streamed various text headlines: "Global child sacrifice ring uncovered. Mass poisoning of members. Klaus Maginon dead at 63. Jacques Decantes, French opposition leader, among those discovered in attendance."

Tears began streaming down her face, but no sound came from her. Nellie and Alistair looked at each other. Alistair motioned to Nellie with his eyes.

"Marin, dear, do you want to talk about it now?" Nellie asked.

"I killed them. I killed all of them," she said quietly as the tears ran down freely. "I baked a cake and laced it with poison. I wanted them to die, not just for what they did to me, but what they did to all of the other children who didn't live." She looked at each of their faces and said, "I probably should feel sorry, but I don't. I'm glad they're dead. I'm glad he's dead. Now they can't hurt anyone else. I should probably turn myself in, but I want to stay here with you until the police come for me. Please tell me you will let me stay until they come to take me into custody."

Nellie heaved a deep sigh. "Of course we will, Marin. I'm sorry for everything you've been through."

"I guess your prayer didn't get answered," said Chanti. "Even God couldn't put back on that many ears."

"Our times are in His hand," said Nellie. "I don't believe your story has to end like this."

"I just wanted to be free from him, from all of them. I never want to remember the nightmares of my childhood again."

"Do you want to keep watching the news? Would it help you or not?" asked Alistair.

"No. It's done. I'd like to sit in the garden for a while," she said. "Would you come with me?"

"Yes," he said. "But only if I can hum."

"You may," she said.

Nellie watched them through the kitchen windows as they walked out the back door and sat down in the swing. She pondered as the only real father Marin had ever known put his arm around her as they swang softly. How terrible a journey this child had been forced to endure. What enormous decisions she had made to lead her to do what she had done.

"Father in heaven, save her. Save our Marin somehow," she prayed as her own tears wet her face. "Have mercy on her, I ask in Jesus' name."

Chapter 57

Global

The shock wave began in Europe, but it traveled across the globe. The first few hours saw the initial release of the major headlines that Baron Klaus Maginon was dead. He had died of suspected poisoning in his own palatial home. He had not died alone. Among his guests were the French politician Jacques Decantes.

The next bombshell had been that the billionaire had been involved in some type of dark ritual sacrifice of children. The bodies of three victims had been discovered. There was ample proof already in hand that they had been murdered the same evening that Baron Maginon had died.

Questions ran wild, and the press, as they often do, gave answers beyond the facts. The police were doing their best to keep up with the requests for more details. They were giving a press conference every three hours, but two reporters seemed to have an inside track and were releasing details a bit more often than anyone else.

It was approaching midday in Europe when everyone was stunned by one of the Philadelphia papers which had devoted the main page and almost the entire first section of their morning edition with a fairly comprehensive list of those who were dead. Citing unnamed sources, Alex Ingram had published a story with thirty-three photos and accompanying names and a brief bio of each person. Added to the stunning revelations was the news that Senator Dom Acworth was dead and had been among those involved. The photos were taken while the people were still alive, and for context, there were more photos showing them walking in two columns.

Additional stories by Ingram and other writers detailed that the participants had marched by torchlight into a grove of trees after sunset with three living children. There, they allegedly performed a ritual of some kind in a circle. After about thirty minutes, they had returned with what appeared to be their dead bodies.

Much to the utter chagrin of the Belgian police, there was a separate article detailing the raid. Obigrotto had gotten plenty of footage of the vehicles approaching, the tactical unit taking positions, and then the follow-up with Inspector Hagen and Detective Rademaker as they entered the house and also the grove. Serious had provided the footage to Alex because of their previous relationship. It was news, and Alex was glad to provide a boost to the sales of papers for his employers.

These stories were distributed worldwide across the wire services. As word began to spread, Alex's list, or the "Evil A-list," as someone referred to it, became the source for numerous talking points on television. He made a few spots appearances via video conference to answer questions, where he promised even more details than they had already released.

Those who read and watched began to realize that Hollywood and the global fashion scene would be without a few more of its idols. A prominent footballer would no longer represent his team at striker. Several politicians would no longer be asked for their opinions. Two seats at the tables of two different royal families would be empty at the next family gathering. In short, the estates of some very rich people would be turned over to their lawyers to determine who got the spoils.

Nobody who died was an unknown. That fact alone was one of the hardest pills for the average public to swallow. Their faces had been on television and the covers of magazines or papers, some of them for many years. Men and women alike had lusted after or coveted their bodies, their wealth, or their power. But who were they really? What would lead someone who had it all to do something so repulsive?

The research forums were a hive of activity as people dissected the information that was publicly available. Although this point had not yet made it into the mainstream media, the autists there were quick to point out that this obviously was not the only such group of people in the world. It was not as if out of seven billion people, only thirty-three were involved in such practices.

Serious read the threads in silence and determined that they would release some of the material into these forums for dissection once the time was right. Although their group was quite capable, extra eyes always seemed to help. Plus, material from these forums was disseminated across multiple social media platforms. They had even heard of church small groups using some of the eclectic research as prayer targets, and more than one politician or media celebrity had been caught repeating talking points that showed up on the forums first.

The first order of business for Serious was to send a message to the person who had been willing to share the DangleDrop video which was tied in with all of it.

Chapter 58

Sand Mountain, Alabama

Janine had just begun frying some bacon and eggs while the toast browned when her phone alerted her to a message. She wiped her hands on a towel and eyed the eggs. She had about a minute or two before they had to be removed from the skillet. She turned down the heat to be safe and then quickly opened her computer, connected to her VPN, and then logged in to retrieve her message. Opening it, she read:

> Please turn on a national television news channel and also read the online newspaper at the link below.
>
> No, we were not responsible. We were attempting to monitor the estate, much like Daniel Robertson did, when this occurred.
>
> We believe that the information you provided will be published soon and will lead to further investigations and possibly prosecutions.
>
> Serious

Clicking on the link to one of Alex's articles that Serious had provided, Janine gasped audibly when she read the headline: GLOBAL CHILD SACRIFICE RING EXPOSED. Quickly, she read through the article and then began clicking on the related stories.

"Janine, what's burning?" Buddy asked as he walked into the kitchen.

Janine looked up and remembered breakfast. She ran to the stove, turned the heat off, and quickly scooped up the extra-crispy bacon and equally crispy eggs. She yanked open the oven door and removed the blackened and pungent toast from inside.

Buddy looked at the furious activity and tried to make light of it by saying, "Well, I'll have to tell Derek that you were practicing your burnt offerings this morning." He grinned.

Janine looked at him with pain in her eyes. Buddy stopped grinning.

"What's wrong, Janine?"

"He's dead! They're dead!" she blurted out.

"Who's dead?"

"The man who killed Daniel Robertson, that French politician. And the man behind it all. He's dead, too."

"What are you talking about?" Buddy asked.

"I got a message to go read an article and to turn on the TV. Oh, hold on," she said as she ran to the living room and turned on the television. She quickly selected a news channel. The story was already making headlines.

Buddy stood beside her as they watched the reports. Photos of Klaus Maginon were being displayed at the moment. News of the horrific event was being given full coverage. More images of the estate were being shown.

"That's the man who was behind it all," said Janine. "Somebody poisoned all of them. There were over thirty of them."

For the next hour, they watched the news together. Janine texted Sherry and told her and Derek to tune in. Buddy texted Sheriff Matt along with Elam and Dale Ray. Like wildfire, the word spread in their community. The people who had tried to hurt Buddy and Janine had finally gotten what was coming to them.

Nobody mourned their loss. Morning notwithstanding, Elam popped the lid off a bottle of beer to celebrate. The more they learned, the angrier they felt to learn what had happened to the innocent children. Their reaction matched the global sense of justice served that was being echoed in online comments on news articles everywhere. The ferocity and echo of the anger that was brewing was a caution to those whose names had not yet appeared in print.

Janine slipped into the kitchen and made more breakfast, which she brought in. They ate it sitting on the couch. The dishes and utensils were placed absentmindedly on the coffee table. When it became apparent that all the main news that was to be had at the moment had been exhausted and that the talking heads were mainly repeating themselves, Buddy switched it off.

"Looks like Sherry was right," he said as he continued to stare straight ahead at the black screen.

"Yep. She said something was going to happen the twenty-first, and it did," said Janine.

"How could she know that?" asked Buddy.

"She couldn't," said Janine. "Not unless God showed her."

"You reckon it's really all over? For us, I mean."

Janine thought for a few moments and then said, "It would be really easy for me to fall back into old habits. I've lived with fear of those people for so long. But I told God that I wanted to act like His Word really is true, and that's what I aim to do." Turning to Buddy, she looked him in the eyes. Hers were glistening with tears. Even though her voice choked up, it was full of confidence as she said, "Buddy, it's over!"

Buddy expected her to collapse in a heap, but she reacted differently than he had ever seen. She jumped up off the couch and began leaping up and down, hands raised, shouting as loudly as she could, "It's over! It's over! Thank you, Jesus! It's over! Thank you, heavenly Father! No more fear! No more worrying! It's over!"

She leaped until she was tired and then walked through the whole house saying the same thing. Buddy sat there alone in his thoughts until she returned.

She knelt down in front of him and said, "Buddy, I know it's over. But I want to know if you are going to believe it too or not." Her eyes were searching his face. There was a shine to her eyes that was brighter than he had seen in all their years together.

Buddy thought long and hard about what it all meant. He heard Derek's words in his mind again. He didn't have to stop being a man and husband to Janine. But what did he really think deep inside about it all?

Swallowing deeply, he looked back at her and said, "Janine, I believe."

Janine looked closely at his face. Then she threw herself into his arms and began kissing his face out of sheer joy. They turned off their phones and spent the rest of the day together.

Chapter 59

Paris, France

Chanti had suffered much throughout the day as more and more news unfolded. Nellie had stayed close to her. They watched the news or read it when she wanted to. They turned it off when she could no longer bear it. Alistair canceled most of his pastoral appointments except for a couple which could not be delayed.

Every hour, Chanti expected her phone to ring. She expected the police to locate her and come to arrest her. The shoe dropped that evening when they were watching the news together. The television anchor stated in a terse, business tone:

"Police announce that they have a suspect in custody in the poisoning of the cult run by Baron Maginon. While they have not released any details as to who was responsible, we have been told that that information will be provided at a news conference tomorrow."

"No!" said Chanti. She looked at Nellie and Alistair. "I can't let them do that! Whoever they have arrested is innocent. I'm the one responsible. I'm going to turn myself in right now." She picked up her phone to dial 17 for the police when Alistair stopped her.

"You'll do nothing of the kind just yet," he said firmly.

She looked at him with anger. "You're a Christian pastor! You can't let someone else go to jail for me!"

"No one is suggesting that. But we should at least wait until we hear what the police have to say before assuming anything."

"Alistair's right, Marin," said Nellie. "If you're responsible for their deaths, then we will stand by your side all the way through whatever you have to endure."

"But I poisoned them!" Chanti said.

"Let's at least wait until we hear what they say," said Nellie. "If you're the one who killed them, it won't hurt you to get one more night of rest."

After much persuasion, Chanti agreed to spend one more night with them. She took a couple of sleeping pills to aid her in that quest. Her dreams were filled with the specters of zombie-like creatures gorging themselves on an endless banquet of her cakes.

Chapter 60

The following day, Chanti was in the sitting room showered and dressed in clean clothes. Nellie had gone to her apartment while she slept and retrieved several changes of garments for her. The television was turned to a news channel awaiting the press conference by the police.

After a brief delay, the podium was filled by a man in uniform with a woman officer at his side. Alistair turned up the volume.

"Good afternoon," said the man. "I'm Inspector Rolf Hagen with the Federal Police, and this is Detective Heidi Rademaker with the Waterloo police. I'm going to read a prepared statement in order to provide you with details. Then we will take a few questions."

Opening a folder, he removed a single sheet of paper and began reading.

"As you are aware, two nights ago, we received a tip that led us to uncover the horrible event which has dominated the news for the past twenty-four hours. After receiving the toxicology reports, we can confirm that Baron Klaus Maginon and thirty-two of his guests were poisoned. The cause of death was conclusively identified as respiratory failure induced by cyanide poisoning."

Chanti lowered her face, and her shoulders drooped when he made that announcement.

"Details which have not been released until today are that there were ten other victims. Six of these appear to have been part of a bodyguard or security service employed by Baron Maginon. Their bodies were discovered in and around other parts of the estate. The other four appear to have been staff including at least one chef, a chauffeur or body man for the Baron, and possibly a butler and cleaning staff. Their identities will be released later pending notification of any next of kin.

"Taken into custody at the estate was a forty-two-year-old German male by the name of Dolph Forney."

Chanti slowly raised her head and stared at the screen in confusion.

"Mr. Forney had been in the employ of Klaus Maginon for some time. He has made a full confession and has promised to cooperate with us as our investigation into other crimes committed by the Baron continues. His only request was that we make public his statement. It reads as follows:

I have been employed by Baron Klaus Maginon since my teens. My late father and grandfather were members of the Ninth Circle of Hades, as the group was called. Since the Baron had no male heir, I was being groomed to take over the leadership upon his death. Because of this, I have intimate knowledge of every detail related to the practices of this group.

For over twenty years, I have been a witness to and participant in some of the worst crimes the human mind could imagine. I do not defend my actions or the actions of any of those who were involved in those crimes.

Five years ago, I fathered a child out of wedlock. The Baron did not approve of this and demanded that the child be included in one of the rituals which were held frequently at his estate. Watching my own flesh and blood undergo such pain and suffering caused me to realize that what I had been involved in was terribly wrong.

I make no excuse, but all my life I had been told that those who were raised to be part of our sacrifices were lesser mortals, not quite human, or unworthy of fullness of life. Frequently, they were referred to as cattle or part of the herd.

Since that time, I have grown increasingly burdened with the truth. After I could bear my situation no longer, I chose to act in the way I felt best. I would end the current members of the Ninth Circle of Hades, even though there are many other former members and future recruits who still walk freely among you.

Because of my knowledge of the rituals, I chose to poison the group when they drank together before their meal. I knew that this was the only way to guarantee that all of the participants would ingest the poison at the same time. Regardless, I also took the liberty of poisoning all of the rest of the food, which included some fruits and vegetables as well as a cake. No one else was responsible for these deaths except myself.

I bear no regrets for my actions. If given the opportunity, I would do it again. I wish I had never met the Baron or ever served in his employ."

The rest of the press conference was a blur to Chanti. She sat dazed and completely disoriented. How could this be? She had poisoned them, she was sure. Yet here was a man who claimed to have done it. And she heard the inspector mention that the main group had all died after drinking. She also heard him say, "No other food at the table was touched, but all of it was tested and found to be loaded with lethal doses of poison."

She looked up at Nellie, who was beaming at her. "I didn't kill them. I wanted to, but I didn't. Why couldn't I kill them?"

"Maybe God has something bigger and better for you than you can ever imagine," said Nellie.

"He put the ear back on, didn't he?" said Chanti.

"Yes, dear. He did. Just like I prayed that He would."

"But I failed the test," Chanti said with anguish on her face. "I made a decision to kill the Baron and everyone else I could. I don't deserve to have God to put an ear back on for me."

"Neither did Peter," said Nellie. "In fact, it was after Jesus healed the servant's ear that Peter failed Jesus again by denying Him three times. And Jesus knew that Peter was going to do it before He ever put that servant's ear back on. None of us deserve His mercy. But He is merciful to us nonetheless."

"What do I do now? I've been preparing myself for prison for the rest of my life."

"Well, Marin, it seems that you'll not be going to prison anytime soon. Instead, you need to start thinking about living a long life, a good life, one that is free from the Baron and his cronies. Why don't you move back in with us for just a wee bit? You're going to need some time to work through all of this and think about what kind of life you really want to follow."

"I'd like that," said Chanti. Then, absentmindedly, she murmured again, "He healed the ear for me."

Chapter 61

Philadelphia, Pennsylvania

After three days of news related to the events in Belgium, Alex felt that it was time to move forward with Stefani's story. The headline for the paper that day blared, "SENATOR AND OTHERS TIED TO LOCAL PEDOPHILE RING."

The lead story gave a summary of the local businessman who had been indicted and the ensuing arrests of the owners of the modeling and photography agency that had been a front for luring in victims. Alex updated the readers on the current state of the legal proceedings. For those who thought he was simply creating a sensational headline out of old news, Alex ended the article with the following paragraphs:

The late Senator Dom Acworth, whose name will forever be associated with his infamous death, was a frequent client of this ring. His abuse of children under the age of consent is proof of the danger associated with living in a society which favors the rich and powerful while exercising less scrutiny on every part of our leaders' lives than we should. The Senator was a pedophile, a corrupter of innocent children, a man who abused not only the trust the public placed in him but also the very bodies and memories of children who were just like the ones in our homes, our churches, our neighborhoods.

Today, we begin publishing the first in a series of seven interviews with one of the survivors of this pedophile ring. To protect the identity of the person, we have used the pseudonym Jael. Jael is a real person whom I believe implicitly. She is brave enough to tell her story and has already submitted to a polygraph and other tests to verify the truth of her story. More importantly, she has given recorded

statements under oath to the prosecutor's office.

What we will print is not even half of what the prosecutor's office knows, and we remind both you, the reader, and those who represent the justice system in this country that justice delayed is justice denied. We share these stories not to further darken Senator Acworth's name but to bring to light the names of many others who still prey freely upon those who are voiceless and vulnerable.

The next article immediately following this had the headline, "JAEL'S STORY: FROM SCHOOL GIRL TO CALL GIRL." It began with these lines:

When I answered the advertisement for a free modeling photography session, I never imagined that I would end up far from home, naked in a room with a US Senator and a table filled with illicit drugs. I only wanted to fulfill a dream of being beautiful and famous. Instead, I became a thing, an object that could be used in every way imaginable by the people I was told to look up to and eventually discarded as worthless by those same people.

The response to the story was overwhelming. Social media quotes and mentions of the article peaked higher than even the stories about the Baron. The comments in the online edition included persons who said that the story mirrored theirs or that of someone in their family. Interestingly enough, the paper received no fewer than three cease and desist letters from law firms which were known for representing politicians and celebrities.

As Alex said to his editor when he heard about it, "How do they know what we're going to print unless their clients know that it's true and that their names are going to be in it?"

The decision was made to continue with the stories until all seven had been printed.

§ § §

That Wednesday, Alex had his usual supper at the Mission. Over a meal (which Stefani had cooked all by herself) of chicken and dumplings, steamed vegetables, and a light salad with chocolate zucchini bread for dessert, Alex pointed his fork at her and said, "You've created quite a stir with your stories, young lady."

"Really?" Stefani asked offhandedly as she offered Happy second helpings of the dumplings.

"Are you not aware of what's going on?" he asked her.

"No. I just knew that you were printing them this week."

Alex stopped chewing and looked at her. "I just knew..." he repeated. "Well, first of all, we've gotten more social media engagement on your articles than anything else we've printed in a long, long time. The company hosting our website said that their servers had something called a denial of service attack trying to take them offline. That lasted for hours, but they had measures in place so that the site kept running. We've heard now from six different lawyers' offices threatening us with everything from defamation of character lawsuits to utter annihilation if we print their clients' names—which they won't even reveal to us. I find that one particularly amusing. Then there are the confidential messages I've been getting personally. Probably twenty to thirty per day have been coming in from people who say they've been victims of similar circumstances as yours." He pointed at her again and said, "They all say that they found courage to contact me because you were willing to speak up."

Stefani looked down at her plate for a few moments and then looked up. "I had no idea my story would affect so many other people."

Sarah smiled at her and said, "You're taking that hammer and giving the bad guys a splitting headache."

Happy laughed at the reference. Looking at Stefani, he said, "One of the biggest steps to overcoming your past is being willing to face it honestly. I think you're doing that with these articles Alex is publishing."

"I guess I am," said Stefani. "I wish none of it had ever happened the way it did. But if I can help other people find a way out, like you and Sarah have been doing for me, I want to help them any way that I can."

Happy caught Alex's eye before he spoke. He knew what Alex was thinking. To the group, Happy said, "I'm sure that opportunity will present itself when the time is right." He said the last part looking directly at Alex.

"I'm sure it will," said Alex, locking eyes with Happy. "Now, how about some more of those dumplings? I have a spot that isn't quite filled up yet."

Chapter 62

Europe

Two weeks after the main story had broken, Peter Southerland, the independent journalist who had promised to write an article about the victims, released his story without sensation. Despite his stellar record and long relationships with numerous outlets, none of them would print it. Part of that was due to the nature of the content. It was considered too severe for even the most senior of editors. Part of it was due to the police, who refused to verify the details. To be fair, they cited ongoing investigations as their cover. But the memories of what the officers had seen were still too real, too fresh, and too painful to want to relive them.

Working with Detective Rademaker, mostly off the record, he had been able to match the identities of two of the victims. The third was completely unknown as far as being able to trace dental records, fingerprints, or any other standard methods of victim identification. She simply did not exist. They had names, which he would not include for the sake of their privacy and the sheer chance that some family still existed who might be traumatized by the knowledge of what had happened to their loved ones.

The two they had identified, a boy of twelve and a girl of nine, had passed through foster homes and a mixture of child protective services institutions. When he asked for a comment on the whereabouts of children who were supposed to be in their care, no one at the various facilities seemed to remember them or were willing to talk if they did. Their movements from one place to the next seemed to be designed to confuse anyone who ever would look for them. The third child, a girl of approximately eleven or twelve years of age, likely came from the same system.

With a follower count numbering close to half a million subscribers, he posted a link on his own social media account to the article on his personal website. Both the post and the website contained numerous warnings and disclaimers that reading the story could result in strong emotions, nightmares, and more. Still, the story went viral and spiked to over a million views in just the first week. That didn't include the reposting by other websites or mentions of the content in countless other places.

After taking the readers through the horrors of what he had witnessed personally by describing in plain and simple detail what had been done to the three bodies in the kitchen, he concluded with several summary points and a call to action. This is what he wrote:

> First, there should be no leniency for those who are involved in this sort of crime. While I have written strongly against the death penalty in the past, I would fully support its reinstitution in every place where such a crime exists. After leaving the kitchen, I passed once again through the dining hall, where I looked upon the contorted face of the monster who had been called Baron, a title of prominence and even respect. I felt no pity for him and indeed found myself thinking that if ever there was a man who had gotten his just punishment, he was such a one. Nor did I feel any pangs of anguish for the model who lay in her own vomit or the athlete near her or the movie actor whose films I can no longer bear to watch.

> Second, this crime happened in part because our society provided a convenient and risk-free way for children to be sold or swapped as items of commerce. How is it that children can be lost in institutions charged with their safekeeping and care? How can dozens, hundreds or even thousands of orphans never be reunited with family members or, at the very least, be given the opportunity for a new life when there is an endless line of parents who are willing to adopt them and love them?

> Third, evil such as this cannot operate on so lurid and grand a scale without an even larger network

of enablers. Who are these people? Are they the doctors who refuse to document abuse? Are they lawyers and judges who make backroom deals which keep children in the system? Maybe they are the former military members who have no moral compass and are willing to provide their services to the highest bidder. All of these people need to be exposed for the part they played in what transpired.

There are more questions than answers for me. What I do know with certainty is that I can never go back. What I saw that night has scarred me, but in a healthy way. As long as the weakest are prey for the powerful, I must hurt with them. From this moment on, I will no longer assume a posture of ignorance in my reporting or my interactions with those I cover. I am educating myself to be able to easily recognize the signs of pedophiles and child abusers. When I find you, I will expose you. I urge every person who reads this account to do the same. Hunt down the pedophiles in your communities, your schools, your churches, your synagogues, your public offices or in your entertainment choices. Do not let them operate in the shadows any longer.

Below is a list of resources that have been helpful to me in getting started.

After the story had spread, one result he did not expect was to receive a phone call from an American number. Answering, he listened as a man on the other end said, "Peter Southerland? My name is Alex Ingram with the Philadelphia Black and White. I'm not sure if you realize how big of a hornet's nest you've just kicked. As someone who has done it before, if you've got some time, I'd like to tell you my story."

Chapter 63

Philadelphia, Pennsylvania and Other Locations

As the days went by, the fallout from the events at Chateau Sauvageon continued to materialize, many of them producing further repercussions of their own. At the paper, Alex published a story with the headline "Questions for Devon Hannah." In it, he detailed the story of Daniel Robertson as recorded in the video. He confirmed that he had received a copy of the recording, had reviewed it, made notes, and had the newspaper's legal counsel review it with him. He also stated that the material had been turned over to "more than one" law enforcement agency for investigation.

He gave a detailed walkthrough of the video and included several of the conversations which occurred. Photos of the estate, grainy though they were, provided a tie-in to the recent occurrence at the late Baron's residence. There were also photos of Devon Hannah holding a knife, Devon Hannah threatening a child (whose face was obscured), and finally, Devon Hannah standing over Daniel Robertson and thrusting his blade downward.

Alex did his best to convey the sheer courage that Daniel Robertson had exhibited that night. He confessed that he had no idea what had happened to the child and whether she was still alive or not, but she had at least survived her encounter with Devon Hannah thanks to the sacrifice of one valiant man. He included the relevant facts that Daniel's body had never been found and that his disappearance was listed as a missing person report that had never been solved.

The real questions which needed to be asked according to Alex were why was Devon Hannah involved with a homicidal cult, how many victims had he personally killed, what other crimes had he committed both at home and abroad, and how soon would he be taken into custody and charged for his crimes?

Once the word DangleDrop appeared in print and online, the autists and denizens of the research forums went wild. They had believed in its existence in spite of it's being only a legend or a myth to most people. Now here it was being confirmed by someone who had a track record of legitimacy. In the middle of the excitement, Serious made the decision to post a copy of both videos with the face of the child digitally blurred. If she happened to be alive, and Nellie MacPheil had neither confirmed nor denied that to Serious, she didn't need the infamy of being known as the girl who was about to be murdered by Jacques Decantes and Devon Hannah.

The researchers tore apart every detail they could find. Most of them had been noted by Serious and the group. Some items the autists caught were new. None of them changed the fact that Baron Maginon, Jacques Decantes, and a host of other predators were dead and buried. But the amplification of the message continued to bring Devon Hannah's name before the public.

To the surprise of most, Devon Hannah made a statement on his social media accounts that such claims were libelous and that he was contacting his attorneys to sue both Alex Ingram and his publisher for the story. Perhaps it was a combination of hubris and sheer ignorance of the magnanimity of the effect the story was having on the public. Whatever the cause, he continued his daily routines until a cadre of federal marshals showed up at his door with a warrant for his arrest. An honest prosecutor with jurisdiction had swiftly convened a grand jury in secret, presented evidence, obtained an indictment, gotten a judge to agree to a warrant, and then acted on the evidence.

Despite the best efforts of his lawyers to have bail set at any amount, the judge refused it after deeming him to be a significant flight risk with the resources at his disposal to do so. He was remanded to the custody of law enforcement and was placed in a high-security wing pending trial.

§ § §

In Europe, the Federal Police were having a rather difficult time keeping their mass murderer alive. On the way to the first court appearance where Dolph Forney was to be formally charged, a motorcycle with two riders attempted to attach an explosive device to the side of the van carrying him. The chase vehicle happened to be manned by an observant team. They had noted the approach of the motorcycle and had alerted the van driver to a possible problem. When the passenger pulled out the device and was about to place it on the side of the vehicle, presumably using magnets, the van driver swerved hard into the adjacent lane, slammed on his brakes, and ended up behind the chase car and motorcycle. It departed at a high rate of speed. The stolen bike was found, but the riders were never located.

The second incident occurred in the detention facility itself. Whether it was a sixth sense or premonition of some kind, the prisoner decided to not eat one of his meals and offered it to his cellmate. The cellmate ate half of the food on the tray before going into convulsions. In horror, Forney called the guards. Ironically, the man who had poisoned over forty people survived an attempt to kill him the same way. Realizing that he was likely not long for this world given his confined location, Forney informed his attorney that he wished to speak with investigators of both the Federal Police and Interpol—as soon as possible.

§ § §

At the estate itself, detailed searching of the property had revealed several disturbing features. One whole hidden and secure room, which was uncovered thanks to Forney, seemed to have been devoted to preserving mementos of the Baron's cult's victims. Among these were the partial remains of a middle-aged adult male. Dental records confirmed that they belonged to Daniel Robertson. As for the rest, forensics investigators identified just a handful of children. The names of most would continue to be a mystery, although their details would be entered into a database. Maybe someone somewhere would search for them and find the answers they sought.

One curious, but macabre, detail the forensics team noted was that none of the child victims' remains included a pinky finger on either the left or right hand. This was never publicized, but it was noted and included with the rest of the investigation. It would prove to be useful information in the future.

Chapter 64

Sand Mountain Vicinity, Alabama

In mid-October on a Sunday afternoon, while the weather was still "fair to middling," a group of about eighty people stood on the banks of a creek. The worship leader of Faith Friendship Baptist Church had just finished leading the group through an old hymn. A boy was being reprimanded by his father for attempting to skip a stone during the singing. On the surface of the water, bright yellow-and-red leaves floated casually down this section of the creek which deepened and broadened into a natural basin. It was perfect for baptisms—or the occasional skinny-dipping by the local youngsters.

Pastor Derek, wearing his hip waders, was already standing waist deep. He motioned with his hand. From the front of the crowd, Buddy walked down into the waters wearing a pair of khakis and a thick cotton t-shirt. He waded out to where Derek was standing and then turned to face the group on the bank. Janine was there, wearing a new dress she had bought for the occasion. Sitting attentively at her feet was Midnight. "Might as well bring the whole family," Janine had said.

"Buddy, you and have talked quite a bit the past couple of weeks about this decision," Derek said loudly in his preacher voice. "I'm going to ask you publicly today what we have discussed together."

Buddy nodded an affirmation.

"Buddy Akers, do you today publicly declare that you have accepted Jesus Christ as your Lord and Savior, that you believe that He died and rose again for your sins, and that you are willing to follow Him until He calls you home?"

Buddy's eyes scanned the entire crowd slowly. Derek had encouraged him to do so in order to embrace the significance of his decision. He saw Dale Ray and Elam in the back standing apart from the rest of the people. They had come at his invitation and insistence. His eyes then rested on Janine and locked with hers.

"Yes, I do."

"Then in obedience to our Lord's command, I now baptize you in the name of the Father, and of the Son, and of the Holy Ghost."

With that, Pastor Derek leaned Buddy's stout frame into the water and then brought him up again. To a scattering of "Hallelujah!" and "Praise the Lord!" from the congregants on the bank, Buddy stood there wiping his eyes as his body streamed a flood of droplets back down into the pool.

Derek addressed him again loudly. "It is my privilege to publicly welcome you into the family of God." He held out his arms, and the two embraced for a few moments while standing in the water. "Brother Buddy," said Pastor Derek to him privately. "I'm so glad that you made this decision. You and Janine have been through a lot together recently. But now you are able to walk together in a new way. You're going to have to learn what it means to be a man of God. That will take some time, but with God's help, nothing is impossible."

"Thank you, Derek…Pastor," said Buddy.

"Just Derek is fine."

"I know something has changed inside me. I've never felt alive in this way."

Derek summed it up by saying, "Buddy, you have truly been born again."

"I guess you're right."

The two of them waded back out. The children rushed to find rocks to throw into the pool or sticks to cast in and imagine as boats while the others bombarded them with their stones. Many of the men gave Buddy a handshake or a hug, as did several of the ladies. When he was finished with the fellowship, Buddy walked to Janine and Midnight. Her face was beaming up at him.

"I love you, Buddy," she said as she drew close and put her arms around him. She sniffed his shirt a couple of times and then said, "You smell like a catfish."

Buddy laughed out loud. "I love you, too, Janine. More than I ever thought I could."

She let go, and they walked back to the truck with Midnight beside them. After they got in and were headed home, Janine asked him, "Buddy, I just want to know, why did you change your mind? What made you really choose to accept Jesus?"

Buddy kept driving for a bit as he thought about it. Then he said, "I guess part of me kind of always believed that there was a God up there somewhere. I just didn't think He really cared about me or knew what was going on in my life. Watching your life since we've been married, I've seen that God is real to you."

"Buddy, I don't want you believing in my God; I want Him to be your God."

"Let me finish," said Buddy. "There have been a lot of things you've prayed about that really happened just the way you prayed they would. Little things, big things. They kept adding up. I was getting to the point that I couldn't deny it. Then this whole summer with everything that happened the way it did, God kept you and me both safe in spite of it all. Just like you prayed. Sherry having that vision or whatever about the twenty-first and it happening just like she said." He turned to her and said, "But really, you've loved me. In spite of everything, you've been the kind of wife I never thought really existed. I realized that God had to be real for you to be able to love me like you have."

Janine wiped her eyes quickly and said, "Watch the road, or you'll get us killed."

Buddy continued to drive with one hand. He reached over with the other and placed it on her shoulder. Janine leaned her face against it. As they drove the rest of the way in peaceful silence, her thoughts were flooded with memories.

She didn't think of herself as a particularly good Christian. She had struggled with fear and nightmares for years until recently. But something a visiting evangelist had said many years ago came back to her mind.

"The Bible says," he had thundered, "that when Jesus was in the house, He could not be hid! That's the way it is in your life. If He's really in there, people will know it!"

Epilogue

Inverness, Scotland

On a cold and gray winter afternoon in Inverness, three people stood by a gravesite. There was no local minister present. The undertaker had arranged for the remains of Daniel Robertson to be transported to his native Scotland in coordination with the Belgium police. They were placed in the ground next to his mother's grave. At the family's request, the workers had been instructed to leave the area for the space of half an hour. After they had departed, Alistair, Nellie, and Chanti huddled close together as they looked upon the box in the ground.

"I'm glad that we were able to lay him to rest," said Nellie. "Next to Mum. I used to wish Mum had died without wondering what happened to her son. Now I'm glad that she never knew."

The sounds of the city were a mixed cacophony in the background as she spoke again.

"Oh, Daniel! You were such a good brother to me. You never treated me like anything but your own sister." She began to cry.

They stood there in the bitter cold absorbed in their own thoughts of the impact of one man's life.

"I'm glad he did what he did," said Chanti. She was wrapped up in a thick parka with the fuzzy hood drawn tightly around her face. "If he hadn't, I'm sure I would be dead now. I still have never really understood why he was willing to give his life for me. He didn't even know me."

"That's just the kind of man he was," said Nellie as she dabbed her eyes with a tissue. "Even as a boy, he was kind and gentle. He cared about people because God's love was alive in him."

"He knew," said Chanti. "He knew that if he tried to run with me that they would catch us straight away. When he let me escape, he knew that he would probably be killed."

"Yes," said Nellie. "But he faced his fate without fear of death."

Alistair spoke up. "When you think about it, it's incredible how such a random group of people, like Daniel, all had a part in what happened that night. No doubt some of them might have chosen differently if they had known how it would all turn out."

"Not Daniel," said Nellie. "He would do the same thing all over again."

"Aye," said Alistair. "That he would."

Nellie picked up a handful of dirt. The other two followed suit. Throwing it onto the box below, she said, "Goodbye, Daniel. Until we meet in heaven."

After they departed, the workers filled the grave. Later that week, the granite headstone was set in place. On it was written:

Here lies Daniel Robertson,
Beloved son and brother.
He died to save a child.

Acknowledgments

First, I would like to thank my wife and family for their patience as I spent time researching and writing the manuscript.

My editor, David Thompson, has continued to make me a better writer by his corrections and suggestions. Any remaining errors are my own. As his schedule has gotten busier, he still made time to accept my manuscript into his workflow.

In the past year, more has come to light about the corruption at all levels of government across the globe. If you have not come unplugged from mainstream media, you should. Begin to research online more yourself. Question the narrative. Connect with people who do the same.

If you found some parts of the story depressing or disturbing, consider what the honest people in law enforcement have to deal with. Think of what the honest pastors and counselors listen to from those who have been abused—or the few perpetrators who do repent. Pray for them. Pray for those who know way more than this book divulged and who are trying to fight the evil that has persisted for generations.

Ultimate thanks is due to my Creator and best friend, Jesus Christ. As in Colossus, some of the spiritual experiences related in this book come from things I've seen personally or heard about from people I know. If you want to know God more because of this book, let Him know that. He's listening to you.

Comments

Did you enjoy this book? If so, we would really enjoy hearing from you. To share a comment on this book or a story about how it helped you, send us a note at:

books@walkwithgod.com

Please visit us on the Internet at https://thompsonpublishers.com, where you can find other good books and resources.

You may also find the author on Gab:

https://gab.com/craigthompson

Follow that account for updates and information about new books.

Errata

A list of corrected errata is maintained at:

https://www.thompsonpublishers.com/

The publisher requests that any additional errata be sent via the form on that site.

If you enjoyed reading Animus, you may also like Colossus. In this story, a gifted sculptor is asked to create statues for less-than-noble purposes. But does the sculptor harbor secrets from his own past? You will also be introduced to the backstory of Alex Ingram and the Reverend Happy Lewis along with a host of other characters.

www.ingramcontent.com/pod-product-compliance
Lightning Source LLC
Chambersburg PA
CBHW020616110726
47899CB00002B/523